Getting into Death

Getting into Death

and other stories

by Thomas M. Disch

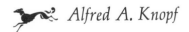 Alfred A. Knopf   New York   1976

THIS IS A BORZOI BOOK
PUBLISHED BY ALFRED A. KNOPF, INC.

Copyright © 1967, 1968, 1969, 1970, 1971, 1973, 1974,
1975, 1976 by Thomas M. Disch

Some of these stories were originally published in the following: *Orbit 6, New Worlds, Penthouse, Antaeus, Paris Review, Fantastic,* and *The Ruins of the Earth.*

Library of Congress Cataloging in Publication Data

Disch, Thomas M
Getting into death and other stories.

CONTENTS: Apollo.—The Asian shore.—The birds.
[etc.]
I. Title.
PZ4.D615CG5   [PS3554.I8]   813'.5'4
ISBN 0–394–49803–8   75-30998

Manufactured in the United States of America

FIRST EDITION

For Michael Moorcock

✍ Contents

Getting into Death

◄ *Apollo*

With special thanks to Robert Graves

I. *Apollo and Daphne*

Everyone knows about Apollo and Daphne—how he pursued her, how she resisted, how at the last possible moment she was changed into the lovely Lever House, which we can see to this day on the corner of 53rd Street and Park Avenue. Not as many people are familiar with the story of Leucippus (the son of Oenomaus), who was Apollo's ill-fated rival for Daphne's love.

Daphne, at that time, was a sophomore at Sarah Lawrence. Those were the days before admissions policies had been relaxed to allow boys to attend girls' colleges. Leucippus, being passionately in love with Daphne, and just as passionately jealous, even of her female acquaintances, contrived to enter Sarah Lawrence under the assumed name of Lucille Parsons. Lucille and Daphne became the closest friends, taking all the same classes, sharing each other's books and clothing, and joining the college's volleyball team, which they led, together, to a series of dazzling victories.

Apollo, inspecting some entrails, learned of his rival's deceit and wrote to the unsuspecting Daphne, who was the captain of the volleyball team, advising her to have all the players shower together naked after their next game, thereby making sure that they were all women. Leucippus, who, as Lucille, had heretofore escaped discovery by claiming to be morbidly shy, was exposed as a man. The offending difference was at once removed by the incensed players. Shortly after Leucippus' dismemberment, Daphne was metamorphosed, and the Sarah Lawrence volleyball team, lacking its best two players, lost the next twelve games in a row.

II. Apollo and Marsyas

In general Apollo didn't care for the Village, but gods, like politicians, have to make a showing in every part of town. Tonight that meant taxiing downtown for a dinner at Remembrance, a new feminist restaurant on West 10th, just off Bleecker. The main courses were rather too fussy, little bits and pieces of things in cream sauce on beds of rice, but the desserts were dynamite.

Then—after Remembrance? Who knows what the Fates held in store? Last week it had been the gentle Thalia; the week before, the nymph Phthia of the bouncing bosoms; before that, the charming and compliant Hyacinthus. (Apollo was the first of the gods to try bisexual chic.)

As it turned out, the Fates had something altogether less appealing in mind. Just as Apollo took his first bite of Remembrance's voluptuous chocolate-chestnut cake (actually, a kind of purée), a drunk back in the shadowy nether regions of the place started in on the piano. Chorus after vain chorus declared, in a diffident, soft-throated tenor, that he'd done it *his* way, he'd done it *his* way, he'd done it *his* way.

Intolerable! And Apollo, as a god, did not have to tolerate it. Setting aside his scarcely tasted cake, Apollo strode over to the piano and glowered at the drunk satyr, who was doing a medley from *Carousel*, filling in nonsense syllables for the forgotten words.

"Off!" Apollo commanded.

Marsyas, cringing before the terrible beauty of the god, obeyed.

To his own exquisite accompaniment Apollo sang Schubert's *"An die Leier," "Freiwilliges Versinken,"* and the pathetic *"Fahrt zum Hades."*

By the time he was done, all the customers, except the sulky Marsyas, had fled from the restaurant, foreseeing something awful. The Muses, who actually owned and managed Remembrance, were gathered round the piano, weeping for joy at the sublimity of Apollo's interpretations, which surpassed even the high standard set by Fischer-Dieskau. Marsyas wasn't even in the running.

Even with the Muses helping to hold Marsyas down, it took Apollo most of that evening to peel off his skin. He worked carefully so it would come off in a single piece. When he was done, he insisted on having the anguished satyr sing "I Left My Heart in San Francisco." Then he and the Muses polished off sixteen pieces of their chocolate-chestnut cake. Gods can eat anything they like without ever getting full.

III. *Apollo and Hyacinthus*

Apollo was the inventor of the Frisbee, and therefore the patron deity of Frisbee players. That is how he met Hyacinthus and how he compelled that young man's love. It ought to be emphasized right at the start that Hyacinthus had never been and, but for Apollo, never would have become gay. He loved one thing and one thing only—his championship Frisbee. He had been the first Frisbee thrower to break the hundred-yard limit, and it is certain that he would have led the American Frisbee team to the 1980 Olympics in Russia if it hadn't been for Apollo.

This is what happened. The West Wind also loved the dynamic young Frisbee hurler, but Hyacinthus, despite every delicate attention and flattering caress, adamantly refused to notice anyone but Apollo. Apollo in his linen and polyester suit. Apollo in his faded-denim jacket, on the back of which the muse Thalia had embroidered his two favorite mottoes—"Know thyself!" and "Nothing in excess!"—using her own silvery hair for threads. Apollo in his lizard shoes leaping high to catch the Frisbee soaring toward him. Apollo drowsy in silk pajamas. Apollo glorious in corduroy, the toast of Washington Square.

The West Wind, desperate to be seen, to be felt, to be recognized as a living being, whirled madly about the Square, bowling through Stanford White's elegant marble arch (unheeded), scattering the fountain's jet of water into rainbows (unnoticed), breaking branches from the trees (unremarked), until at last, wild with the pain of unrequited love, he took the Frisbee that the infatuated Hyacinthus had hurled toward his adored god and dashed it back, with incredible violence, against his head. The blood from the concussion spattered a Good Humor cart standing in the Square; Apollo, foreseeing the fatal blow, had turned his back.

Another of Apollo's favorite mottoes was, "There's no use crying over spilled milk."

IV. Apollo and Dryope

Apollo, looking terrific and dressed to the nines, was going to a party at George Plimpton's, when he noticed a funny shift in the light. Turning round, he recognized Dryope, out with a bunch of Hamadryads, looking aimless and a little wistful.

She smiled. They started talking. The Hamadryads, saying that they had to get to the Paris, where the new Buñuel film was showing, excused themselves, and that left just them, the god and his old girl friend.

"How's Amphissus?" Apollo asked.

Amphissus was their son. Apollo had never seen him.

"He says he's fine," Dryope answered. "Now that he's off at boarding school, I only see him at holidays. How are you?"

"As ever. Great."

He raised the handle of his Lucite cane to his mouth and gave it a nip with those dazzling teeth. When Apollo smiled in a certain way there was no resisting the power of his suggestions; but even while Dryope felt her old deep-sworn resentment melt away like the cream on top of an Irish coffee, a new resentment began forming in the void the first had left: How easy it is for the Apollos of this world! How hard, correspondingly, for its Dryopes.

It wasn't that she wasn't beautiful herself. By almost any standard but his she was a knockout. Witness his smile. Having him smile at you that way was as good as winning the Miss Universe contest. But it was just that—her being beautiful and knowing the exact degree of it relative to anyone else's beauty—that made her, in the face of his perfections, such a helpless dishrag.

Four years! Four endless years since he had up and gone, without a word of parting or excuse, with never a birthday card for his little bastard or so much as a phone call when she'd gone to St. Vincent's after her little attempt. How could she *not* resent such treatment? Yet here she was, with her spine overcharging like some interstate power line during August's most intensive days, and nothing remained to be decided but whether they'd go to his place or to hers.

Look at him. Who could resent those thighs swelling beneath impeccable orange gabardine? The branching veins just visible on the backs of his perfect hands? The golden hair? The honeyed voice? As well try to resist a painting by Matisse or Frankenthaler! As well argue against the immortal delight of Château d'Yquem!

She agreed that her place, being closer by, would suit them better, but then, as they were going past Battaglia's windows, Apollo spotted a pair of spectator shoes, and he swore that he had to have them. He'd been looking for just these shoes for months without any success.

"This must be your lucky day," Dryope said bitterly.

With not a hint of sarcasm he said he thought it really must. Would she wait? It would only take a minute.

Even after he'd gone inside and she was freed from the compulsion of his presence, there was nothing she could do. She stayed rooted to the square of cement on which he'd left her and wished that he were dead, which was impossible, since gods don't die, then wished he were back beside her, touching her, embracing her, ravishing her once again, but this was just as impossible, since he was inside Battaglia's buying shoes. It was intolerable. She closed her eyes and willed Time to a stop, but Time went on in its slow, accustomed way, and the shoppers passing on the sidewalk bumped into her and stared and scoffed in an endless procession of pocked and mortal faces. She couldn't bear it. She prayed to her father, a river-god in Westchester, and—altogether to her chagrin—he answered her prayer.

When Apollo came out of Battaglia's with his new spectator shoes under his arm, there was no sign of Dryope. In the place where she had stood, right there in the middle of the sidewalk, was a little traffic light that blinked when he looked at it from green to red, and then, without a beat, back to green. Red, green, red, green—all night long and ever since. Such was the nature of poor Dryope, and such is the fate of all mortals luckless enough to love a god.

The Asian Shore

I.

There were voices on the cobbled street, and the sounds of motors. Footsteps, slamming doors, whistles, footsteps. He lived on the ground floor, so there was no way to avoid these evidences of the city's too abundant life. They accumulated in the room like so much dust, like the heaps of unanswered correspondence on the mottled tablecloth.

Every night he would drag a chair into the unfurnished back room—the guest room, as he liked to think of it—and look out over the tiled roofs and across the black waters of the Bosphorus at the lights of Üsküdar. But the sounds penetrated this room too. He would sit there, in the darkness, drinking wine, waiting for her knock on the back door.

Or he might try to read: histories, books of travel, the long dull biography of Atatürk. A kind of sedation. Sometimes he would even begin a letter to his wife:

"Dear Janice,

"No doubt you've been wondering what's become of me these last few months. . . ."

But the trouble was that once that part had been written, the frail courtesies, the perfunctory reportage, he could not bring himself to say what *had* become of him.

Voices. . . .

It was just as well that he couldn't speak the language. For a while he had studied it, taxiing three times a week to Robert College in Bebek, but the grammar, based on assumptions wholly alien to any other language he knew, with its wavering boundaries between verbs and nouns, nouns and adjectives, withstood every assault of his incorrigibly Aristotelian mind. He sat at the back of the classroom, behind the rows of American teen-agers, as sullen as convicts, as comically out of context as the machineries melting in a Dali landscape—sat there and parroted innocuous dialogues after the teacher, taking both roles in turn, first the trustful, inquisitive John, forever wandering alone and lost in the streets of Istanbul and Ankara, then the helpful, knowing Ahmet Bey. Neither of these interlocutors would admit what had become increasingly evident with each faltering word that John spoke—that he would wander these same streets for years, inarticulate, cheated, and despised.

But these lessons, while they lasted, had one great advantage. They provided an illusion of activity, an obelisk upon which the eye might focus amid the desert of each new day, something to move toward and then something to leave behind.

After the first month it had rained a great deal, and this provided him with a good excuse for staying in. He had mopped up the major attractions of the city in one week, and he persisted at sightseeing long afterward, even in doubtful weather, until at last he had checked off every mosque and ruin, every museum and cistern cited in boldface in the pages of his Hachette. He visited the cemetery of Eyüp, and he devoted an entire Sunday to the land walls, carefully searching for, though he could not read Greek, the inscriptions of the various Byzantine emperors. But more and more often on these excursions he would see the woman or the child or the woman and the child together, until he came almost to dread the sight of any woman or any child in the city. It was not an unreasonable dread.

And always, at nine o'clock, or ten at the very latest, she would come knocking at the door of the apartment. Or, if the outer door of the building had not been left ajar by the people upstairs, at the window of the front room. She knocked patiently, in little clusters of three or four raps spaced several seconds apart, never very loud. Sometimes, but only if she were in the hall, she would accompany her knocking with a few words in Turkish, usually *Yavuz! Yavuz!* He had asked the clerk at the mail desk of the consulate what this meant, for he couldn't find it in his dictionary. It was a common Turkish name, a man's name.

His name was John. John Benedict Harris. He was an American.

She seldom stayed out there for more than half an hour any one night, knocking and calling to him, or to this imaginary Yavuz, and he would remain all that while in the chair in the unfurnished room, drinking Kavak and watching the ferries move back and forth on the dark water between Kabatas and Usküdar, the European and the Asian shore.

He had seen her first outside the fortress of Rumeli Hisar. It was the day, shortly after he'd arrived in the city, that he had come out to register at Robert College. After paying his fees and inspecting the library, he had come down the hill by the wrong path, and there it had stood, mammoth and majestically improbable, a gift. He did not know its name, and his Hachette was at the hotel. There was just the raw fact of the fortress, a mass of gray stone, its towers and crenelations, the gray Bosphorus below. He angled for a photograph, but even that far away it was too big—one could not frame the whole of it in a single shot.

He left the road, taking a path through dry brush that promised to circle the fortress. As he approached, the walls reared higher and higher. Before such walls there could be no question of an assault.

He saw her when she was about fifty feet away. She came toward him on the footpath, carrying a large bundle wrapped in newspaper and bound with twine. Her clothes were the usual motley of washed-out cotton prints that all the poorer women of the city went about in, but she did not, like most other women of her kind, attempt to pull her shawl across her face when she noticed him.

But perhaps it was only that her bundle would have made

this conventional gesture of modesty awkward, for after that first glance she did at least lower her eyes to the path. No, it was hard to discover any clear portent in this first encounter.

As they passed each other he stepped off the path, and she did mumble some word in Turkish. Thank you, he supposed. He watched her until she reached the road, wondering whether she would look back, and she didn't.

He followed the walls of the fortress down the steep crumbling hillside to the shore road without finding an entrance. It amused him to think that there might not be one. Between the water and the barbicans there was only a narrow strip of highway.

An absolute daunting structure.

The entrance, which did exist, was just to the side of the central tower. He paid five lire admission and another two and a half lire to bring in his camera.

Of the three principal towers, visitors were allowed to climb only the one at the center of the eastern wall that ran along the Bosphorus. He was out of condition and mounted the enclosed spiral staircase slowly. The stone steps had evidently been pirated from other buildings. Every so often he recognized a fragment of a classic entablature or a wholly inappropriate intaglio design—a Greek cross or some crude Byzantine eagle. Each footfall became a symbolic conquest: one could not ascend these stairs without becoming implicated in the fall of Constantinople.

This staircase opened out onto a kind of wooden catwalk clinging to the inner wall of the tower at a height of about sixty feet. The silolike space was resonant with the coo and flutter of invisible pigeons, and somewhere the wind was playing with a metal door, creaking it open, banging it shut. Here, if he so wished, he might discover portents.

He crept along the wooden platform, both hands grasping the iron rail stapled to the stone wall, feeling just an agreeable amount of terror, sweating nicely. It occurred to him how much this would have pleased Janice, whose enthusiasm for heights had equaled his. He wondered when, if ever, he would see her again, and what she would be like. By now undoubtedly she had begun divorce proceedings. Perhaps she was already no longer his wife.

The platform led to another stone staircase, shorter than the first, which ascended to the creaking metal door. He pushed it open and stepped out amid a flurry of pigeons into the full dazzle of the noon, the wide splendor of the elevation, sunlight above and the bright bow of water beneath—and, beyond the water, the surreal green of the Asian hills, hundred-breasted Cybele. It seemed, all of this, to demand some kind of affirmation, a yell. But he didn't feel up to yelling, or large gestures. He could only admire, at this distance, the illusion of tactility, hills as flesh, an illusion that could be heightened if he laid his hands, still sweaty from his passage along the catwalk, on the rough warm stone of the balustrade.

Looking down the side of the tower at the empty road he saw her again, standing at the very edge of the water. She was looking up at him. When he noticed her she lifted both hands above her head, as though signaling, and shouted something that, even if he could have heard it properly, he would surely not have understood. He supposed that she was asking to have her picture taken, so he turned the setting ring to the fastest speed to compensate for the glare from the water. She stood directly below the tower, and there seemed no way to frame an interesting composition. He released the shutter. Woman, water, asphalt road: it would be a snapshot, not a photograph, and he didn't believe in taking snapshots.

The woman continued to call up to him, arms raised in that same hieratic gesture. It made no sense. He waved to her and smiled uncertainly. It was something of a nuisance, really. He would have preferred to have this scene to himself. One climbed towers, after all, in order to be alone.

Altin, the man who had found his apartment for him, worked as a commission agent for carpet and jewelry shops in the Grand Bazaar. He would strike up conversations with English and American tourists and advise them what to buy, and where, and how much to pay. They spent one day looking and settled on an apartment building near Taksim, the commemorative traffic circle that served the European quarter of the city as a kind of Broadway. The several banks of Istanbul demonstrated their modern character here with neon signs, and in the center of the traffic circle, life-size, Atatürk led a small but representative group of his countrymen toward their bright, Western destiny.

The apartment was thought (by Altin) to partake of this same advanced spirit: it had central heating, a sit-down toilet, a bathtub, and a defunct but prestigious refrigerator. The rent was six hundred lire a month, which came to sixty-six dollars at the official rate but only fifty dollars at the rate Altin gave. He was anxious to move out of the hotel, so he agreed to a six-month lease.

He hated it from the day he moved in. Except for the shreds of a lousy sofa in the guest room, which he obliged the landlord to remove, he left everything as he found it. Even the blurry pin-ups from a Turkish girlie magazine remained where they were to cover the cracks in the new plaster. He was determined to make no accommodations: he might have to live in this city; it was not required that he *enjoy* it.

Every day he picked up his mail at the consulate. He sampled a variety of restaurants. He saw the sights and made notes for his book.

On Thursdays he visited a *hamam* to sweat out the accumulated poisons of the week and to be kneaded and stomped by a masseur.

He supervised the growth of his young mustache.

He rotted, like a jar of preserves left open and forgotten on the top shelf of a cupboard.

He learned that there was a special Turkish word for the rolls of dirt that are scraped off the skin after a steambath, and another that imitated the sound of boiling water: *fuker, fuker, fuker*. Boiling water signified, to the Turkish mind, the first stages of sexual arousal. It was roughly equivalent to the stateside notion of "electricity."

Occasionally, as he began to construct his own internal map of the unpromising alleyways and ruinous staircase streets of his neighborhood, he fancied that he saw her, that same woman. It was hard to be certain. She would always be some distance away, or he might catch just a glimpse out of the corner of his eye. If it were the same woman, nothing at this stage suggested that she was pursuing him. It was, at most, a coincidence.

In any case, he could not be certain. Her face had not been unusual, and he did not have the photograph to consult, for he had spoiled the entire roll of film removing it from the camera.

Sometimes after one of these failed encounters he would feel a slight uneasiness. It amounted to no more than that.

He met the boy in Üsküdar. It was during the first severe cold spell, in mid-November. His first trip across the Bosphorus, and when he stepped off the ferry onto the very soil (or, anyhow, the very asphalt) of this new continent, the largest of all, he could feel the great mass of it beckoning him toward its vast eastward vortex, tugging at him, sucking at his soul.

It had been his first intention, back in New York, to stop two months at most in Istanbul, learn the language; then into Asia. How often he had mesmerized himself with the litany of its marvels: the grand mosques of Kayseri and Sivas, of Beysehir and Afyon Karahisar; the isolate grandeur of Ararat and then, still moving east, the shores of the Caspian; Meshed, Kabul, the Himalayas. It was all these that reached out to him now, singing, stretching forth their siren arms, inviting him to their whirlpool.

And he? He refused. Though he could feel the charm of the invitation, he refused. Though he might have wished very much to unite with them, he still refused. For he had tied himself to the mast, where he was proof against their call. He had his apartment in that city which stood just outside their reach, and he would stay there until it was time to return. In the spring he was going back to the States.

But he did allow the sirens this much—that he would abandon the rational mosque-to-mosque itinerary laid down by his Hachette and entrust the rest of the day to serendipity. While the sun still shone that afternoon they might lead him where they would.

Asphalt gave way to cobbles, and cobbles to packed dirt. The squalor here was on a much less majestic scale than in Stambul, where even the most decrepit hovels had been squeezed by the pressure of population to heights of three and four stories. In Üsküdar the same wretched buildings sprawled across the hills like beggars whose crutches had been kicked out from under them, supine; through their rags of unpainted wood one could see the scabbed flesh of mud-and-wattle. As he threaded his way from one dirt street to the next and found each of them sustaining this one unvarying tone, without color, without counterpoint, he began to conceive a new Asia, not of mountains and vast plains, but this same slum rolling on perpetually across grassless hills, a continuum of drabness, of sheer dumb extent.

Because he was short and because he would not dress the part of an American, he could go through these streets without calling attention to himself. The mustache too, probably, helped. Only his conscious, observing eyes (the camera had spoiled a second roll of film and was being repaired) would have betrayed him as a tourist today. Indeed, Altin had assured him (intending, no doubt, a compliment) that as soon as he learned to speak the language he would pass for a Turk.

It grew steadily colder throughout the afternoon. The wind moved a thick veil of mist over the sun and left it there. As the mists thinned and thickened, as the flat disc of sun, sinking westward, would fade and brighten, the vagaries of light whispered conflicting rumors about these houses and their dwellers. But he did not wish to stop and listen. He already knew more concerning these things than he wanted to. He set off at a quicker pace in the supposed direction of the landing stage.

The boy stood crying beside a public fountain, a water faucet projecting from a crude block of concrete, at the intersection of two narrow streets. Five years old, perhaps six. He was carrying a large plastic bucket of water in each hand, one bright red, the other turquoise. The water had splashed over his thin trousers and bare feet.

At first he supposed the boy cried only because of the cold. The damp ground must be near to freezing. To walk on it in bare wet feet. . . .

Then he saw the slippers. They were what he would have called shower slippers, small die-stamped ovals of blue plastic with single thongs that had to be grasped between the first and second toes.

The boy would stoop over and force the thongs between his stiff, cold-reddened toes, but after only a step or two the slippers would again fall off his numb feet. With each frustrated progress more water would slop over the sides of the buckets. He could not keep the slippers on his feet, and he would not walk off without them.

With this understanding came a kind of horror, a horror of his own helplessness. He could not go up to the boy and ask him where he lived, lift him and carry him—he was so small—to his home. Nor could he scold the child's parents for having sent him out on this errand without proper shoes or winter clothes. He could not even take up the buckets and have the child lead him to his home. For each of these possibilities demanded that he be able to *speak* to the boy, and this he could not do.

What *could* he do? Offer money? As well offer him, at such a moment, a pamphlet from the U.S. Information Agency!

There was, in fact, nothing, *nothing* he could do.

The boy had become aware of him. Now that he had a sympathetic audience he let himself cry in earnest. Lowering the two buckets to the ground and pointing at these and at the slippers, he spoke pleadingly to this grown-up stranger, to this rescuer, words in Turkish.

He took a step backward, a second step, and the boy shouted at him, what message of pain or uncomprehending indignation he would never know. He turned away and ran back along the street that had brought him to this crossway. It was another hour before he found the landing stage. It had begun to snow.

As he took his seat inside the ferry he found himself glancing at the other passengers, as though expecting to find her there among them.

The next day he came down with a cold. The fever rose through the night. He woke several times, and it was always their two faces that he carried with him from the dreams, like souvenirs whose origin and purpose have been forgotten; the woman at Rumeli Hisar, the child in Usküdar: some part of his mind had already begun to draw the equation between them.

II.

It was the thesis of his first book that the quiddity of architecture, its chief claim to an esthetic interest, was its arbitrariness. Once the lintels were lying on the posts, once some kind of roof had been spread across the hollow space, then anything else that might be done was gratuitous. Even the lintel and the post, the roof, the space below, these were gratuitous as well. Stated thus it was a mild enough notion; the difficulty was in training the eye to see the whole world of usual forms—patterns of brick, painted plaster, carved and carpentered wood—not as "buildings" and "streets" but as an infinite series of free and arbitrary choices. There was no place in such a scheme for orders, styles, sophistication, taste. Every artifact of the city was anomalous, unique, but living there in the midst of it all you could not allow yourself too fine a sense of this fact. If you did. . . .

It had been his task, these last three or four years, to re-educate his eye and mind to just this condition, of innocence. His was the very reverse of the Romantics' aims, for he did not expect to find himself, when this ideal state of "raw" perception was reached (it never would be, of course, for innocence, like justice, is an absolute; it may be approached but never attained), any closer to nature. Nature, as such, did not concern him. What he sought, on the contrary, was a sense of the great artifice of things, of structures, of the immense interminable wall that has been built just to exclude nature.

The attention that his first book had received showed that he had been at least partially successful, but he knew (and who better?) how far short his aim had fallen, how many clauses of the perceptual social contract he had never even thought to question.

So, since it was now a matter of ridding himself of the sense of the familiar, he had had to find some better laboratory for this purpose than New York, somewhere that he could be, more naturally, an alien. This much seemed obvious to him.

It had not seemed so obvious to his wife.

He did not insist. He was willing to be reasonable. He would talk about it. He talked about it whenever they were together—at dinner, at her friends' parties (his friends didn't seem to give parties), in bed—and it came down to this, that Janice objected not so much to the projected trip as to his entire program, the thesis itself.

No doubt her reasons were sound. The sense of the arbitrary did not stop at architecture; it embraced—or it would, if he let it —all phenomena. If there were no fixed laws that governed the furbelows and arabesques out of which a city is composed, there were equally no laws (or only arbitrary laws, which is the same as none at all) to define the relationships woven into the lattice of that city, relationships between man and man, man and woman, John and Janice.

And indeed this had already occurred to him, though he had not spoken of it to her before. He had often had to stop, in the midst of some quotidian ritual like dining out, and take his bearings. As the thesis developed, as he continued to sift away layer after layer of preconception, he found himself more and more astonished at the size of the demesne that recognized the sovereignty of convention. At times he even thought he could trace in his wife's slightest gesture or in her aptest phrase or in a kiss some hint of the Palladian rule book from which it had been derived. Perhaps with practice one would be able to document the entire history of her styles—here an echo of the Gothic Revival, there an imitation of Mies.

When his application for a Guggenheim was rejected, he decided he would make the trip by himself, using the bit of money that was still left from the book. Though he saw no necessity for it, he had agreed to Janice's request for a divorce. They parted on the best of terms. She had even seen him to the boat.

The wet snow would fall for a day, two days, forming knee-deep drifts in the open spaces of the city, in paved courtyards, on vacant lots. Cold winds polished the slush of streets and sidewalks to dull-gleaming lumpy ice. The steeper hills became impassable. The snow and the ice would linger a few days and then a sudden thaw would send it all pouring down the cobbled hillside in a single afternoon, brief alpine cataracts of refuse and brown water.

A patch of tolerable weather might follow this flood, and then another blizzard. Altin assured him that this was an unusually fierce winter, unprecedented.

A spiral diminishing.

A tightness.

And each day the light fell more obliquely across the white hills and was more quickly spent.

Cne night, returning from a movie, he slipped on the iced cobbles just outside the door of his building, tearing both knees of his trousers beyond any possibility of repair. It was the only winter suit he had brought. Altin gave him the name of a tailor who could make another suit quickly and for less money than he would have had to pay for a readymade. Altin did all the bargaining with the tailor and even selected the fabric, a heavy wool-rayon blend of a sickly and slightly iridescent blue, the muted, imprecise color of the more unhappy breeds of pigeons. He understood nothing of the fine points of tailoring, and so he could not decide what it was about this suit—whether the shape of the lapels, the length of the back vent, the width of the pantlegs—that made it seem so different from other suits he had worn, so much . . . smaller. And yet it fitted his figure with the exactness one expects of a tailored suit. If he looked smaller now, and thicker, perhaps that was how he *ought* to look and his previous suits had been telling lies about him all these years. The color too performed some nuance of metamorphosis: his skin, balanced against this blue-gray sheen, seemed less "tan" than sallow. When he wore it he became, to all appearances, a Turk.

Not that he wanted to look like a Turk. Turks were, by and large, a homely lot. He only wished to avoid the other Americans who abounded here even at this nadir of the off-season. As their numbers decreased, their gregariousness grew more implacable. The smallest sign—a copy of *Newsweek* or the *Herald-Tribune*, a word of English, an airmail letter with its telltale canceled stamp —could bring them down at once in the full fury of their good-fellowship. It was convenient to have some kind of camouflage, just as it was necessary to learn their haunts in order to avoid them: Divan Yolu and Cumhuriyet Cadessi, the American Library and the consulate, as well as some eight or ten of the principal well-touristed restaurants.

Once the winter had firmly established itself he also put a stop to his sightseeing. Two months of Ottoman mosques and Byzantine rubble had brought his sense of the arbitrary to so fine a pitch that he no longer required the stimulus of the monumental. His own rooms—a rickety table, the flowered drapes, the blurry lurid pinups, the intersecting planes of walls and ceilings— could present as great a plentitude of "problems" as the grand mosques of Suleiman or Sultan Ahmet with all their mihrabs and minbers, their stalactite niches and faienced walls.

Too great a plentitude actually. Day and night the rooms nagged at him. They diverted his attention from anything else he might try to do. He knew them with the enforced intimacy with which a prisoner knows his cell—every defect of construction, every failed grace, the precise incidence of the light at each hour of the day. Had he taken the trouble to rearrange the furniture, to put up his own prints and maps, to clean the windows and scrub the floors, to fashion some kind of bookcase (all his books remained in their two shipping cases), he might have been able to blot out these alien presences by the sheer strength of self-assertion, as one can mask bad odors with incense or the smell of flowers. But this would have been admitting defeat. It would have shown how unequal he was to his own thesis.

As a compromise he began to spend his afternoons in a café a short distance down the street on which he lived. There he would sit, at the table nearest the front window, contemplating the spirals of steam that rose from the small corolla of his tea glass. At the back of the long room, beneath the tarnished brass tea urn, there were always two old men playing backgammon. The other patrons sat by themselves and gave no indication that their thoughts were in any way different from his. Even when no one was smoking, the air was pungent with the charcoal fires of nargilehs. Conversation of any kind was rare. The nargilehs bubbled, the tiny die rattled in its leather cup, a newspaper rustled, a glass chinked against its saucer.

His red notebook always lay ready at hand on the table, and

on the notebook his ballpoint pen. Once he had placed them there, he never touched them again till it was time to leave.

Though less and less in the habit of analyzing sensation and motive, he was aware that the special virtue of this café was as a bastion, the securest he possessed, against the now omnipresent influence of the arbitrary. If he sat here peacefully, observing the requirements of the ritual, a decorum as simple as the rules of backgammon, gradually the elements in the space about him would cohere. Things settled, unproblematically, into their own contours. Taking the flower-shaped glass as its center, this glass that was now only and exactly a glass of tea, his perceptions slowly spread out through the room, like the concentric ripples passing across the surface of an ornamental pond, embracing all its objects at last in a firm, noumenal grasp. Just so. The room was just what a room should be. It contained him.

He did not take notice of the first rapping on the café window, though he was aware, by some small cold contraction of his thoughts, of an infringement of the rules. The second time he looked up.

They were together. The woman and the child.

He had seen them each on several occasions since his trip to Üsküdar three weeks before. The boy once on the torn-up sidewalk outside the consulate, and another time sitting on the railing of the Karaköy bridge. Once, riding in a *dolmus* to Taksim, he had passed within a scant few feet of the woman and they had exchanged a glance of unambiguous recognition. But he had never seen them together before.

But could he be certain, now, that it *was* those two? He saw a woman and a child, and the woman was rapping with one bony knuckle on the window for someone's attention. For his? If he could have seen her face. . . .

He looked at the other occupants of the café. The backgammon players. A fat unshaven man reading a newspaper. A dark-skinned man with spectacles and a flaring mustache. The two old men, on opposite sides of the room, puffing on nargilehs. None of them paid any attention to the woman's rapping.

He stared resolutely at his glass of tea, no longer a paradigm of its own necessity. It had become a foreign object, an artifact picked up out of the rubble of a buried city, a shard.

The woman continued to rap at the window. At last the owner of the café went outside and spoke a few sharp words to her. She left without making a reply.

He sat with his cold tea another fifteen minutes. Then he went out into the street. There was no sign of them. He returned the hundred yards to his apartment as calmly as he could. Once inside he fastened the chain lock. He never went back to the café.

When the woman came that night, knocking at his door, it was not a surprise.

And every night, at nine or, at the very latest, ten o'clock.

Yavuz! Yavuz! Calling to him.

He stared at the black water, the lights of the other shore. He wondered, often, when he would give in, when he would open the door.

But it was surely a mistake. Some accidental *resemblance*. He was not Yavuz.

John Benedict Harris. An American.

If there had ever been one, if there had ever been a Yavuz.

The man who had tacked the pinups on the walls?

Two women, they might have been twins, in heavy eye make-up, garter belts, mounted on the same white horse. Lewdly smiling.

A bouffant hairdo, puffy lips. Drooping breasts with large brown nipples. A couch.

A beachball. Her skin dark. Bikini. Laughing. Sand. The water unnaturally blue.

Snapshots.

Had these ever been *his* fantasies? If not, why could he not bring himself to take them off the walls? He had prints by Piranesi. A blowup of Sagrada Familia in Barcelona. The Tchernikov sketch. He could have covered the walls.

He found himself trying to imagine of this Yavuz . . . what he must be like.

III.

Three days after Christmas he received a card from his wife, postmarked Nevada. Janice, he knew, did not believe in Christmas cards. It showed an immense stretch of white desert—a salt-flat, he supposed—with purple mountains in the distance, and above the purple mountains, a heavily retouched sunset. Pink. There were no figures in this landscape, or any sign of vegetation. Inside she had written:

"Merry Christmas! Janice."

The same day he received a manila envelope with a copy of *Art News*. A noncommittal note from his friend Raymond was paperclipped to the cover: "Thought you might like to see this. R."

In the back pages of the magazine there was a long and unsympathetic review of his book by F. R. Robertson. Robertson was known as an authority on Hegel's esthetics. He maintained that *Homo Arbitrans* was nothing but a compendium of truisms and —without seeming to recognize any contradiction in this—a hopelessly muddled reworking of Hegel.

Years ago he had dropped out of a course taught by Robertson after attending the first two lectures. He wondered if Robertson could have remembered this.

The review contained several errors of fact, one misquotation, and failed to mention his central argument, which was not, admittedly, dialectical. He decided he should write a reply and laid the magazine beside his typewriter to remind himself. The same evening he spilled the better part of a bottle of wine on it, so he tore out the review and threw the magazine into the garbage with his wife's card.

The necessity for a movie had compelled him into the streets and kept him in the streets, wandering from marquee to marquee, long after the drizzle of the afternoon had thickened to rain. In New York when this mood came over him he would take in a double bill of science-fiction films or Westerns on 42nd Street, but here, though cinemas abounded in the absence of television, only the glossiest Hollywood kitsch was presented with the original sound-track. B-movies were invariably dubbed in Turkish.

So obsessive was this need that he almost passed the man in the skeleton suit without noticing him. He trudged back and forth on the sidewalk, a sodden refugee from Halloween, followed by a small Hamelin of excited children. The rain had curled the corners of his poster (it served him now as an umbrella) and caused the inks to run. He could make out:

KIL G

STA   LDA

After Atatürk, the skeleton-suited Kiling was the principal figure of the new Turkish folklore. Every newsstand was heaped with magazines and comics celebrating his adventures, and here he was himself, or his avatar at least, advertising his latest movie. Yes, and there, down the side street, was the theater where it was playing: *Kiling Istanbulda*. Or: *Kiling in Istanbul*. Beneath the colossal letters a skull-masked Kiling threatened to kiss a lovely and obviously reluctant blonde, while on the larger poster across the street he gunned down two well-dressed men. One could not decide, on the evidence of such tableaus as these, whether Kiling was fundamentally good, like Batman, or bad, like Fantomas. So. . . .

He bought a ticket. He would find out. It was the name that intrigued him. It was, distinctly, an English name.

He took a seat four rows from the front just as the feature began, immersing himself gratefully into the familiar urban imagery. Reduced to black and white and framed by darkness, the customary vistas of Istanbul possessed a heightened reality. New American cars drove through the narrow streets at perilous speeds. An old doctor was strangled by an unseen assailant. Then for a long while nothing of interest happened. A tepid romance developed between the blond singer and the young architect, while a number of gangsters, or diplomats, tried to obtain possession of the doctor's black valise. After a confusing sequence in which four of these men were killed in an explosion, the valise fell into the hands of Kiling. But it proved to be empty.

The police chased Kiling over tiled rooftops. But this was a proof only of his agility, not of his guilt: the police can often make mistakes in these matters. Kiling entered, through a window, the bedroom of the blond singer, waking her. Contrary to the advertising posters outside, he made no attempt to kiss her. He addressed her in a hollow bass voice. The editing seemed to suggest that Kiling was actually the young architect whom the singer loved, but as his mask was never removed this too remained in doubt.

He felt a hand on his shoulder.

He was certain it was she and he would not turn around. Had she followed him to the theater? If he rose to leave, would she make a scene? He tried to ignore the pressure of the hand, staring at the screen where the young architect had just received a mysterious telegram. His hands gripped tightly into his thighs. His hands: the hands of John Benedict Harris.

"Mr. Harris, hello!"

A man's voice. He turned around. It was Altin.

"Altin."

Altin smiled. His face flickered. "Yes. Do you think it is anyone?"

"Anyone else?"

"Yes."

"No."

"You are seeing this movie?"

"Yes."

"It is not in English. It is in Turkish."

"I know."

Several people in nearby rows were hissing for them to be quiet. The blond singer had gone down into one of the city's large cisterns. Binbirdirek. He himself had been there. The editing created an illusion that it was larger than it actually was.

"We will come up there," Altin whispered.

He nodded.

Altin sat on his right, and Altin's friend took the seat remaining empty on his left. Altin introduced his friend in a whisper. His name was Yavuz. He did not speak English.

Reluctantly he shook hands with Yavuz.

It was difficult, thereafter, to give his full attention to the film. He kept glancing sideways at Yavuz. He was about his own height and age, but then this seemed to be true of half the men in Istanbul. An unexceptional face, eyes that glistened moistly in the half-light reflected from the screen.

Kiling was climbing up the girders of the building being constructed on a high hillside. In the distance the Bosphorous snaked past misted hills.

There was something so unappealing in almost every Turkish face. He had never been able to pin it down: some weakness of bone structure, the narrow cheekbones; the strong vertical lines that ran down from the hollows of the eyes to the corner of the mouth; the mouth itself, narrow, flat, inflexible. Or some subtler disharmony among all these elements.

Yavuz. A common name, the mail clerk had said.

In the last minutes of the movie there was a fight between two figures dressed in skeleton suits, a true and a false Kiling. One of them was thrown to his death from the steel beams of the unfinished building. The villain, surely—but had it been the true or the false Kiling who died? And come to think of it, which of them had frightened the singer in her bedroom, strangled the old doctor, stolen the valise?

"Do you like it?" Altin asked as they crowded toward the exit.

"Yes, I did."

"And do you understand what the people say?"

"Some of it. Enough."

Altin spoke for a while to Yavuz, who then turned to address his new friend from America in rapid Turkish.

He shook his head apologetically. Altin and Yavuz laughed.

"He says to you that you have the same suit."

"Yes, I noticed that as soon as the lights came on."

"Where do you go now, Mr. Harris?"

"What time is it?"

They were outside the theater. The rain had moderated to a drizzle. Altin looked at his watch. "Seven o'clock. And a half."

"I must go home now."

"We will come with you and buy a bottle of wine. Yes?"

He looked uncertainly at Yavuz. Yavuz smiled.

And when she came tonight, knocking at his door and calling for Yavuz?

"Not tonight, Altin."

"No?"

"I am a little sick."

"Yes?"

"Sick. I have a fever. My head aches." He put his hand, mimetically, to his forehead, and as he did he *could* feel both the fever and the headache. "Some other time perhaps. I'm sorry."

Altin shrugged skeptically.

He shook hands with Altin and then with Yavuz. Clearly, they both felt they had been snubbed.

Returning to his apartment he took an indirect route that avoided the dark side streets. The tone of the movie lingered, like the taste of a liqueur, to enliven the rhythm of cars and crowds, deepen the chiaroscuro of headlights and shop windows. Once, leaving the Eighth Street Cinema after *Jules et Jim*, he had discovered all the streets signs of the Village translated into French; now the same law of magic allowed him to think that he could understand the fragmented conversation of passers-by. The meaning of an isolated phrase registered with the self-evident uninterpreted immediacy of "fact," the nature of the words mingling with the nature of things. Just so. Each knot in the net of language slipped, without any need of explication, into place. Every nuance of glance and inflection fitted, like a tailored suit, the contours of that moment, this street, the light, his conscious mind.

Inebriated by this fictive empathy he turned into his own darker street at last and almost walked past the woman—who fitted like every other element of the scene, so well the corner where she'd taken up her watch—without noticing her.

"You!" he said and stopped.

They stood four feet apart, regarding each other carefully. Perhaps she had been as little prepared for this confrontation as he.

Her thick hair was combed back in stiff waves from a low forehead, falling in massive parentheses to either side of her thin face. Pitted skin, flesh wrinkled in concentration around small pale lips. And tears—yes, tears—just forming in the corners of her staring eyes. With one hand she held a small parcel wrapped in newspaper and string, with the other she clutched the bulky confusion of her skirts. She wore several layers of clothing, rather than a coat, against the cold.

A slight erection stirred and tangled in the flap of his cotton underpants. He blushed. Once, reading a paperback edition of *Krafft-Ebing*, the same embarrassing thing had happened. That time it had been a description of necrophilia.

God, he thought, *if she notices!*

She whispered to him, lowering her gaze. To him, to Yavuz.

To come home with her. . . . Why did he? . . . Yavuz, Yavuz, Yavuz . . . she needed . . . and his son. . . .

"I don't *understand* you," he insisted. "Your words make no sense to me. I am an American. My name is John Benedict Harris, not Yavuz. You're making a mistake—can't you see that?"

She nodded her head. "Yavuz."

"*Not* Yavuz! *Yok! Yok, yok!*"

And a word that meant "love" but not exactly that. Her hand tightened in the folds of her several skirts, raising them to show the thin, black-stockinged ankles.

"No!"

She moaned.

. . . wife . . . his home . . . Yalova . . . his life.

"Damn you, go away!"

Her hand let go her skirts and darted quickly to his shoulder, digging into the cheap cloth. Her other hand shoved the wrapped parcel at him. He pushed her back but she clung fiercely, shrieking his name: *Yavuz!* He struck her face.

She fell on the wet cobbles. He backed away. The greasy parcel was in his left hand. She pushed herself up to her feet. Tears flowed along the vertical channels from eyes to mouth. A Turkish face. Blood dripped slowly out of one nostril. She began to walk away in the direction of Taksim.

"And don't return, do you understand? Stay away from me!" His voice cracked.

When she was out of sight he looked at the parcel in his hands. He knew he ought not to open it, that the wisest course was to throw it into the nearest garbage can. But even as he warned himself, his fingers had snapped the string.

A large lukewarm doughy mass of *borek*. And an orange. The saliva sprouted in his mouth at the acrid smell of the cheese.

No!

He had not had dinner that night. He was hungry. He ate it. Even the orange.

During the month of January he made only two entries in his notebook. The first, undated, was a long extract copied from A. H. Lybyer's book on the Janissaries, the great slave-corps of the sultans, *The Government of the Ottoman Empire in the Time of Suleiman the Magnificent.* The passage read:

Perhaps no more daring experiment has been tried on a large scale upon the face of the earth than that embodied in the Ottoman Ruling Institution. Its nearest ideal analogue is found in the Republic of Plato, its nearest actual parallel in the Mamluk system of Egypt; but it was not restrained within the aristocratic Hellenic limitations of the first, and it subdued and outlived the second. In the United States of America men have risen from the rude work of the backwoods to the presidential chair, but they have done so by their own effort and not through the gradations of a system carefully organized to push them forward. The Roman Catholic Church can still train a peasant to become a pope, but it has never begun by choosing its candidates almost exclusively from families which profess a hostile religion. The Ottoman system deliberately took slaves and made them ministers of state. It took boys from the sheep-run and the plough-tail and made them courtiers and the husbands of princesses; it took young men whose ancestors had borne the Christian name for centuries and made them rulers in the greatest of Muhammadan states, and soldiers and generals in invincible armies whose chief joy it was to beat down the Cross and elevate the Crescent. It never asked its novices "Who was your father?" or "What do you know?" or even "Can you speak our tongue?" but it studied their faces and their frames and said: "You shall be a soldier and, if you show yourself worthy, a general," or "You shall be a scholar and a gentleman and, if the ability lies in you, a governor and a prime minister." Grandly disregarding the fabric of fundamental customs which is called "human nature," and those religious and social prejudices which are thought to be almost as deep as life itself, the Ottoman system took children forever from parents, discouraged family cares among its members through their most active years, allowed them no certain hold on property, gave them no definite promise that their sons and daughters would profit by their success and sacrifice, raised and lowered them with no regard for ancestry or previous distinction, taught them a strange law, ethics, and religion, and ever kept them conscious of a sword raised above their heads which might put an end at any moment to a brilliant career along a matchless path of human glory.

The second and briefer entry was dated the twenty-third of January and read as follows:

"Heavy rains yesterday. I stayed in drinking. She came around at her usual hour. This morning when I put on my brown shoes to go out shopping they were wet through. Two hours to dry them out over the heater. Yesterday I wore only my sheepskin slippers—I did not leave the building once."

IV.

A human face is a construction, an artifact. The mouth is a little door, and the eyes are windows that look at the street, and all the rest of it, the flesh, the bone beneath, is a wall to which any manner of ornament may be affixed, gewgaws of whatever style or period one takes a fancy to—swags hung below the cheeks and chin, lines chiseled or smoothed away, a recession emphasized, a bit of vegetation here and there. Each addition or subtraction, however minor in itself, will affect the entire composition. Thus, the hair that he had trimmed a bit closer to the temples restores hegemony to the vertical elements of a face that is now noticeably *narrower*. Or is this exclusively a matter of proportion and emphasis? For he has lost weight too (one cannot stop eating regularly without some shrinkage), and the loss has been appreciable. A new darkness has given definition to the always incipient pouches below his eyes, a darkness echoed by the new hollowness of his cheeks.

But the chief agent of metamorphosis is the mustache, which has grown full enough now to obscure the modeling of his upper lip. The ends, which had first shown a tendency to droop, have developed, by his nervous habit of twisting them about his fingers, the flaring upward curve of a scimitar (or *pala*, after which in Turkey this style of mustache is named: *pala biyik*). It is this, the baroque mustache, not a face, that he sees when he looks in a mirror.

Then there is the whole question of "expression," its quickness, constancy, the play of intelligence, the characteristic "tone" and the hundreds upon hundreds of possible gradations within the range of that tone, the eyes' habits of irony and candor, the betraying tension or slackness of a lip. Yet it is scarcely necessary to go into this at all, for his face, when he sees it, or when anyone sees it, could not be said to *have* an expression. What was there, after all, for him to express?

The blurring of edges, whole days lost, long hours awake in bed, books scattered about the room like little animal corpses to be nibbled at when he grew hungry, the endless cups of tea, the tasteless cigarettes. Wine, at least, did what it was supposed to do—it took away the sting. Not that he felt the sting these days with any poignance. But perhaps without the wine he *would* have.

He piled the nonreturnable bottles in the bathtub, exercising in this act (if in no other) the old discrimination, the "compulsive tact" he had made so much of in his book.

The drapes were always drawn. The lights were left burning at all hours, even when he slept, even when he was out, three sixty-watt bulbs in a metal chandelier hanging just out of plumb.

Voices from the street impinged. Vendors in the morning, and the metallic screak of children. At night the radio in the apartment below, drunken arguments. Scatterings of words, like illuminated signs glimpsed driving on a thruway, at high speeds, at night.

Two bottles of wine were not enough if he started early in the afternoon, but three could make him sick.

And though the hours crawled, like wounded insects, so slowly across the floor, the days rushed by in a torrent. The sunlight slipped across the Bosphorus so quickly that there was scarcely time to rise and see it.

One morning when he woke there was a balloon on a stick propped in the dusty flower vase atop his dresser. A crude Mickey Mouse was stenciled on the bright red rubber. He left it there, bobbing in the vase, and watched it shrivel day by day, the face turning small and black and wrinkled.

The next time it was ticket stubs, two of them, from the Kabatas-Usküdar ferry.

Till that moment he had told himself it was a matter only of holding out until the spring. He had prepared himself for a seige, believing that an assault was not possible. Now he realized that he would actually have to go out there and fight.

Though it was mid-February the weather accommodated his belated resolution with a series of bright blue days, a wholly unseasonable warmth that even tricked early blossoms from a few unsuspecting trees. He went through Topkapi once again, giving a respectful, indiscriminate and puzzled attention to the celadon ware, to golden snuffboxes, to pearl-embroidered pillows, to the portrait miniatures of the sultans, to the fossil footprint of the Prophet, to Iznik tiles, to the lot. There it was, all spread out before him, heaps and masses of it: beauty. Like a salesclerk tying price tags to items of merchandise, he would attach this favorite word of his, provisionally, to these sundry bibelots, then step back a pace or two to see how well or poorly it "matched." Was *this* beautiful? Was *that?*

Amazingly, none of it was beautiful. The priceless baubles all just sat there on their shelves, behind the thick glass, as unresplendent as the drab furniture back in his own room.

He tried the mosques: Sultan Ahmet, Beyazit, Sehazade, Yeni Camii, Laleli Camii. The old magic, the Vitruvian trinity of "commodity, firmness, and delight," had never failed him so enormously before. Even the shock of scale, the gape-mouthed peasant reverence before thick pillars and high domes, even this deserted him. Go where he would through the city, he could not get out of his room.

Then the land walls, where months before he had felt himself rubbing up against the very garment of the past. He stood at the same spot where he had stood then, at the point where Mehmet the Conqueror had breached the walls. Quincunxes of granite cannonballs decorated the grass; they reminded him of the red balloon.

As a last resort he returned to Eyüp. The false spring had reached a tenuous apogee, and the February light flared with deceiving brilliance from the thousand facets of white stone blanketing the steep hillside. Small flocks of three or four sheep browsed between the graves. The turbaned shafts of marble jutted in every direction but the vertical (which it was given to the cypresses to define) or lay, higgledy-piggledy, one atop another. No walls, no ceilings, scarcely a path through the litter: this was an architecture supremely abstract. It seemed to him to have been piled up here, over the centuries, just to vindicate the thesis of his book.

And it worked. It worked splendidly. His mind and his eye came alive. Ideas and images coalesced. The sharp slanting light of the late afternoon caressed the jumbled marble with a cold careful hand, like a beautician adding the last touches to an elaborate coiffure. Beauty? Here it was. Here it was abundantly!

He returned the next day with his camera, redeemed from the repair shop where it had languished for two months. To be on the safe side he had asked the repairman to load it for him. He composed each picture with mathematical punctilio, fussing over the depth of field, crouching or climbing atop sepulchers for a better angle, checking each shot against the reading on the light meter, deliberately avoiding picturesque solutions and easy effects. Even taking these pains he found that he'd gone through the twenty exposures in under two hours.

He went up to the small café on the top of the hill. Here, his Hachette had noted respectfully, the great Pierre Loti had been wont to come of a summer evening, to drink a glass of tea and look down the sculptured hills and through the pillars of cypress at the Fresh Waters of Europe and the Golden Horn. The café perpetuated the memory of this vanished glory with pictures and mementos. Loti, in a red fez and savage mustachios, glowered at the contemporary patrons from every wall. During the First World War, Loti had remained in Istanbul, taking the part of his friend, the Turkish sultan, against his native France.

He ordered a glass of tea from a waitress who had been got up as a harem girl. Apart from the waitress he had the café to himself. He sat on Pierre Loti's favorite stool. It was delicious. He felt right at home.

He opened his notebook and began to write.

Like an invalid taking his first walk out of doors .after a long convalescence, his renascent energies caused him not only the predictable and welcome euphoria of resurrection but also a pronounced intellectual giddiness, as though by the simple act of rising to his feet he had thrust himself up to some really dangerous height. This dizziness became most acute when, in trying to draft a reply to Robertson's review, he was obliged to return to passages in his own book. Often as not what he found there struck him as incomprehensible. There were entire chapters that might as well have been written in ideograms or futhorc, for all the sense they made to him now. But occasionally, cued by some remark so irrelevant to any issue at hand as to be squeezed into an embarrassed parenthesis, he would sprint off toward the most unforeseen—and undesirable—conclusions. Or rather, each of these tangents led, asymptotically, to a single conclusion: to wit, that his book, or any book he might conceive, was worthless, and worthless not because his thesis was wrong but precisely because it might be right.

There was a realm of judgment and a realm of fact. His book, if only because it was a book, existed within the bounds of the first. There was the trivial fact of its corporeality, but, in this case as in most others, he discounted that. It was a work of criticism, a systematization of judgment, and to the extent that his system was complete, its critical apparatus must be able to measure its own scales of mensuration and judge the justice of its own decrees. But could it? Was not his "system" as arbitrary a construction as any silly pyramid? What was it, after all? A string of words, of more or less agreeable noises, politely assumed to correspond to certain objects and classes of objects, actions and groups of actions, in the realm of fact. And by what subtle magic was this correspondence to be verified? Why, by just the assertion that it was so!

This, admittedly, lacked clarity. It had come to him thick and fast, and it was colored not a little by cheap red wine. To fix its outlines a bit more firmly in his own mind he tried to "get it down" in his letter to *Art News*:

Sirs:

I write to you concerning F. R. Robertson's review of my book, though the few words I have to say bear but slightly upon Mr. Robertson's oracles, as slightly perhaps as these bore upon Homo Arbitrans.

Only this—that, as Gödel has demonstrated in mathematics, Wittgenstein in philosophy, and Duchamp, Cage, and Ashbery in their respective fields, the final statement of any system is a self-denunciation, a demonstration of how its particular little tricks are done—not by magic (as magicians have always known) but by the readiness of the magician's audience to be deceived, which readiness is the very glue of the social contract.

Every system, including my own and Mr. Robertson's, is a system of more or less interesting lies, and if one begins to call these lies into question, then one ought really to begin with the first. That is to say, with the very questionable proposition on the title page: Homo Arbitrans *by John Benedict Harris.*

Now I ask you, Mr. Robertson, what could be more improbable than that? More tentative? More arbitrary?

He sent the letter off, unsigned.

V.

He had been promised his photos by Monday, so Monday morning, before the frost had thawed on the plate-glass window, he was at the shop. The same immodest anxious interest to see his pictures of Eyüp possessed him as once he had felt to see an essay or a review in print. It was as though these items, the pictures, the printed words, had the power to rescind, for a little while, his banishment to the realm of judgment, as though they said to him: "Yes, look, here we are, right in your hand. We're real, and so you must be too."

The old man behind the counter, a German, looked up mournfully to gargle a mournful *ach*. "Ach, Mr. Harris! Your pictures are not aready yet. Come back soon at twelve o'clock."

He walked through the melting streets that were, this side of the Golden Horn, jokebooks of eclecticism. No mail at the consulate, which was only to be expected. Half-past ten.

A pudding at a pudding shop. Two lire. A cigarette. A few more jokes: a bedraggled caryatid, an Egyptian tomb, a Greek temple that had been changed by some Circean wand into a butcher shop. Eleven.

He looked, in the bookshop, at the same shopworn selection of books that he had looked at so often before. Eleven-thirty. Surely, they would be ready by now.

"You are here, Mr. Harris. Very good."

Smiling in anticipation, he opened the envelope, removed the slim warped stack of prints.

No.

"I'm afraid these aren't mine." He handed them back. He didn't want to feel them in his hand.

"What?"

"Those are the wrong pictures. You've made a mistake."

The old man put on a pair of dirty spectacles and shuffled through the prints. He squinted at the name on the envelope. "You are Mr. Harris."

"Yes, that is the name on the envelope. The envelope's all right, the pictures aren't."

"It is not a mistake."

"These are *somebody else's* snapshots. Some family picnic. You can see that."

"I myself took out the roll of film from your camera. Do you remember, Mr. Harris?"

He laughed uneasily. He hated scenes. He considered just walking out of the shop, forgetting all about the pictures. "Yes,

I do remember. But I'm afraid you must have gotten that roll of
film confused with another. I *didn't* take these pictures. I took
pictures at the cemetery in Eyüp. Does that ring a bell?"

Perhaps, he thought, "ring a bell" was not an expression a
German would understand.

As a waiter whose honesty has been called into question
will go over the bill again with exaggerated attention, the old man
frowned and examined each of the pictures in turn. With a
triumphant clearing of his throat he laid one of the snapshots face
up on the counter. "Who is that, Mr. Harris?"

It was the boy.

"Who! I . . . I don't know his name."

The old German laughed theatrically, lifting his eyes to a
witnessing heaven. "It is you, Mr. Harris! It is you!"

He bent over the counter. His fingers still refused to touch
the print. The boy was held up in the arms of a man whose head
was bent forward as though he were examining the close-cropped
scalp for lice. Details were fuzzy, the lens having been mistakenly
set at infinity.

Was it his face? The mustache resembled his mustache, the
crescents under the eyes, the hair falling forward. . . .

But the angle of the head, the lack of focus—there was room
for doubt.

"Twenty-four lire please, Mr. Harris."

"Yes. Of course." He took a fifty-lire note from his billfold.
The old man dug into a lady's plastic coin purse for change.

"Thank you, Mr. Harris."

"Yes. I'm . . . sorry."

The old man replaced the prints in the envelope, handed
them across the counter.

He put the envelope in the pocket of his suit. "It was my
mistake."

"Good-bye."

"Yes, good-bye."

He stood on the street, in the sunlight, exposed. Any moment
either of them might come up to him, lay a hand on his shoulder,
tug at his pantleg. He could not examine the prints here. He returned to the sweetshop and spread them out in four rows on a
marble-topped table.

Twenty photographs. A day's outing, as commonplace as it had been impossible.

Of these twenty, three were so overexposed as to be meaningless and should not have been printed at all. Three others showed what appeared to be islands or different sections of a very irregular coastline. They were unimaginatively composed, with great expanses of bleached-out sky and glaring water. Squeezed between these, the land registered merely as long dark blotches flecked with tiny gray rectangles of buildings. There was also a view up a steep street of wooden houses and naked wintry gardens.

The remaining thirteen pictures showed various people, and groups of people, looking at the camera. A heavyset woman in black, with black teeth, squinting into the sun—standing next to a pine tree in one picture, sitting uncomfortably on a natural stone formation in the second. An old man, dark-skinned, bald, with a flaring mustache and several days' stubble of beard. Then these two together—a very blurred print. Three little girls standing in front of a middle-aged woman, who regarded them with a pleased, proprietorial air. The same three girls grouped around the old man, who seemed to take no notice of them whatever. And a group of five men: the spread-legged shadow of the man taking this picture was roughly stenciled across the pebbled foreground.

And the woman. Alone. The wrinkled sallow flesh abraded to a smooth white mask by the harsh midday light.

Then the boy snuggling beside her on a blanket. Nearby small waves lapped at a narrow shingle.

Then these two still together with the old woman and the three little girls. The contiguity of the two women's faces suggested a family resemblance.

The figure that could be identified as himself appeared in only three of the pictures: once holding the boy in his arms; once with his arm around the woman's shoulders, while the boy stood before them scowling; once in a group of thirteen people, all of whom had appeared in one or another of the previous shots. Only the last of these three was in focus. He was one of the least noticeable figures in this group, but the mustached face smiling so rigidly into the camera was undeniably his own.

He had never seen these people, except, of course, for the woman and the boy. Though he had, hundreds of times, seen people just like them in the streets of Istanbul. Nor did he recognize the plots of grass, the stands of pine, the boulders, the shingle beach, though once again they were of such a generic type that he might well have passed such places a dozen times without taking any notice of them. Was the world of fact really as characterless as *this*? That it *was* the world of fact he never for a moment doubted.

And what had *he* to place in the balance against these evidences? A name? A face?

He scanned the walls of the sweetshop for a mirror. There was none. He lifted the spoon, dripping, from his glass of tea to regard the reflection of his face, blurred and inverted, in the concave surface. As he brought the spoon closer, the image grew less distinct, then rotated through one hundred eighty degrees to present, upright, the mirror image of his staring, dilated eye.

He stood on the open upper deck as the ferry churned, hooting, from the deck. Like a man stepping out of doors on a blustery day, the ferry rounded the peninsular tip of the old city, leaving the quiet of the Horn for the rough wind-whitened waters of the Sea of Marmara. A cold south wind stiffened the scarlet star and cresent on the stern mast.

From this vantage the city showed its noblest silhouette: first the great gray horizontal mass of the Topkapi walls, then the delicate swell of the dome of St. Irena, which had been built (like a friend carefully chosen to demonstrate, by contrast, one's own virtues) just to point up the swaggering impossibility of the neighboring Holy Wisdom, that graceless and abstract issue of the union commemorated on every capital within by the twined monograms of the demon-emperor Justinian and his whore and consort Theodora; then, bringing both the topographic and historic sequence to an end, the proud finality of the Blue Mosque.

The ferry began to roll in the rougher water of the open sea. Clouds moved across the sun at quicker intervals to mass in the north above the dwindling city. It was four-thirty. By five o'clock he would reach Heybeli, the island identified by both Altin and the mail clerk at the consulate as the setting of the photographs.

The airline ticket to New York was in his pocket. His bags, all but the one he would take on the plane, had been packed and shipped off in a single afternoon and morning of headlong drunken fear. Now he was safe. The certain knowledge that tomorrow he would be thousands of miles away had shored up the crumbling walls of confidence like the promise of a prophet who cannot err, Tiresias in balmy weather. Admittedly this was the shameful safety of a rout so complete that the enemy had almost captured his baggage train—but it was safety for all that, as definite as tomorrow. Indeed, this "tomorrow" was more definite, more present to his mind and senses, than the actual limbo of its preparation, just as, when a boy, he had endured the dreadful tedium of Christmas Eve by projecting himself into the morning that would have to follow and which, when it did finally arrive, was never so real, by half, as his anticipations.

Because he was this safe, he dared today confront the enemy (if the enemy would confront *him*) head on. It risked nothing, and there was no telling what it might yield. Though if it were the *frisson* that he was after, then he should have stayed and seen the thing through to its end. No, this last excursion was more a gesture than an act, bravado rather than bravery. The very self-consciousness with which he had set out seemed to ensure that nothing really disastrous could happen. Had it not always been their strategy before to catch him unaware?

Finally, of course, he could not explain to himself why he had gone to the ferry, bought his ticket, embarked, except that each successive act seemed to heighten the delectable sense of his own inexorable advance, a sensation at once of almost insupportable tension and of dreamlike lassitude. He could no more have turned back along this path once he had entered on it than at the coda of a symphony he could have refused to listen. Beauty? Oh yes, intolerably! He had *never* known anything so beautiful as this.

The ferry pulled into the quay of Kinali Ada, the first of the islands. People got on and off. Now the ferry turned directly into the wind, toward Burgaz. Behind them the European coast vanished into the haze.

·　　·　　·

The ferry had left the Burgaz dock and was rounding the tiny islet of Kasik. He watched with fascination as the dark hills of Kasik, Burgaz, and Kinali slipped slowly into perfect alignment with their positions in the photograph. He could almost hear the click of the shutter.

And the other relationships between these simple sliding planes of sea and land—was there not something nearly as *familiar* in each infinitesimal shift of perspective? When he looked at these islands with his eyes, half-closed, attention unfocused, he could almost. . . .

But whenever he tried to take this up, however gently, between the needle-tipped compasses of analysis, it crumbled into dust.

It began to snow just as the ferry approached Heybeli. He stood at the end of the pier. The ferry was moving eastward, into the white air, toward BÜYÜK ADA.

He looked up a steep street of wooden houses and naked wintry gardens. Clusters of snowflakes fell on the wet cobbles and melted. At irregular intervals street lamps glowed yellow in the dusk, but the houses remained dark. Heybeli was a summer resort. Few people lived here in the winter months. He walked halfway up the hill, then turned to the right. Certain details of woodwork, the proportion of a window, a sagging roof caught his attention momentarily, like the flicker of wings in the foliage of a tree twenty, fifty, a hundred yards ahead.

The houses were fewer, spaced farther apart. In the gardens snow covered the leaves of cabbages. The road wound up the hill toward a stone building. It was just possible to make out the flag waving against the gray sky. He turned onto a footpath that skirted the base of the hill. It led into the pines. The thick carpet of fallen needles was more slippery than ice. He rested his cheek against the bark of a tree and heard, again, the camera's click, systole and diastole of his heart.

He heard the water, before he saw it, lapping on the beach. He stopped. He focused. He recognized the rock. He walked toward it. So encompassing was his sense of this scene, so inclusive, that he could feel the footsteps he left behind in the snow, feel the snow slowly covering them again. He stopped.

It was here he had stood with the boy in his arms. The woman had held the camera to her eye with reverent awkwardness. He had bent his head forward to avoid looking directly into the glare of the setting sun. The boy's scalp was covered with the scabs of insect bites.

He was ready to admit that all this had happened, the whole impossible event. He did admit it. He lifted his head proudly and smiled, as though to say: *All right—and then? No matter what you do, I'm safe! Because, really, I'm not here at all. I'm already in New York.*

He laid his hands in a gesture of defiance on the outcropping of rock before him. His fingers brushed the resilient thong of the slipper. Covered with snow, the small oval of blue plastic had completely escaped his attention.

He spun around to face the forest, then round again to stare at the slipper lying there. He reached for it, thinking to throw it into the water, then drew his hand back.

He turned back to the forest. A man was standing just outside the line of the trees, on the path. It was too dark to discern any more of his features than that he had a mustache.

On his left the snowy beach ended in a wall of sandstone. To his right the path swung back into the forest, and behind him the sea dragged the shingle back and forth.

"Yes?"

The man bent his head attentively, but said nothing.

"Well, yes? Say it."

The man walked back into the forest.

The ferry was just pulling in as he stumbled up to the quay. He ran onto it without stopping at the booth to buy a ticket. Inside under the electric light he could see the tear in his trousers and a cut on the palm of his right hand. He had fallen many times, on the pine needles, over rocks in furrowed fields, on cobbles.

He took a seat by the coal stove. When his breath returned

to him, he found that he was shivering violently. A boy came round with a tray of tea. He bought a glass for one lira. He asked the boy, in Turkish, what time it was. It was ten o'clock.

The ferry pulled up to the dock. The sign over the ticket booth said BÜYÜK ADA. The ferry pulled away from the dock.

The ticket taker came for his ticket. He held out a ten-lire note and said, "Istanbul."

The ticket taker nodded his head, which meant no.

"Yok."

"No? How much then? Kaç para?"

"Yok Istanbul—Yalova." He took the money offered him and gave him back in exchange eight lire and a ticket to Yalova on the Asian coast.

He had got onto a ferry going in the wrong direction. He was not returning to Istanbul, but to Yalova.

He explained, first in slow precise English, then in a desperate fragmentary Turkish, that he could not go to Yalova, that it was impossible. He produced his airline ticket, pointed at the eight o'clock departure time, but he could not remember the Turkish word for "tomorrow." Even in his desperation he could see the futility of all this: between BÜYÜK ADA and Yalova there were no more stops, and there would be no ferries returning to Istanbul that night. When he got to Yalova he would have to get off the boat.

A woman and a boy stood at the end of the wooden dock, at the base of a cone of snowy light. The lights were turned off on the middle deck of the ferry. The man who had been standing so long at the railing stepped, stiffly, down to the dock. He walked directly toward the woman and the boy. Scraps of paper eddied about his feet then, caught up in a strong gust, sailed out at a great height over the dark water.

The man nodded sullenly at the woman, who mumbled a few rapid words of Turkish. Then they set off, as they had so many times before, toward their home, the man leading the way, his wife and son following a few paces behind, taking the road along the shore.

⚑ The Birds

"I fail to understand," Daffy said, in a kind of squawk, "how they could have done this."

"People," Curtis commented. It was his explanation for everything.

"But *how?*" She plucked gluey pieces of down from the soft, dead eggs.

"It's not *your* fault, darling. It's that spray they spray things with. Science."

"Hate, I call it."

"Well, well." Curtis dug his beak into his oily brown feathers. These outbursts of his wife's always rather embarrassed him. "You've got to try and look at things from *their* point of view."

"All right, smartass, look at *this* from their point of view." And she dug down savagely into the feeble shell and lifted out a half-formed featherless duckling. "That's what all your damned. . . ." But with the duckling in her beak she couldn't pronounce the word "objectivity."

Curtis, alarmed, spread his wings and rose a few feet into the air, but the oiled feathers did not permit sustained flight. He settled a few yards off on the slicked surface of the pond.

Daffy dropped her lifeless burden back into the nest. She felt a hopelessness more extreme than any sorrow. Everything she'd ever done, every instinct that had ever driven her, every scrap of down she'd ever plucked from her scrawny breast, had issued at last in this . . . futility.

Curtis, while his wife mooned about on the shore, kept diving down to the bottom and rooting about for something edible in the nonbiodegradable debris. He worked with a sullen, steady determination until he discovered a strand of weed not quite two feet long. He waddled up to the shore with it, proud with accomplishment and coated with muck. He laid the weed at his wife's feet.

She gobbled down half its length greedily, then, gagging, spit out the whole black mulch. "It tastes like . . . !" She used an unprintable epithet.

Curtis nibbled at the weed. "I wish it did," he joked, cocking his head to one side. "I wish it tasted *half* that good."

Daffy laughed.

"Try and force yourself to eat it, darling," Curtis urged, resuming his manner of maddening reasonableness. "You must keep up your strength."

"*Why* must I? To what purpose?"

"Do you love me?"

Daffy turned her head away, almost tucking it under her left wing.

"Well? Do you?"

"Yes."

"That's why, then. We've still got each other. As long as we've got each other, the world isn't coming to an end."

Her first impulse was to question even this. Love? Daffy's whole being was instinct with love—but not for Curtis, only for those poor lifeless creatures in the nest. But she couldn't expect her husband to understand this, and really, did she want him to? Stifling her protest, she bent down and forced herself to eat the putrid black weed.

It was autumn. Such leaves as had survived the summer had long since fallen from the trees. The ever-changing multitudes of insects that had sustained Daffy and Curtis through August and September had disappeared as suddenly and unaccountably as they had come. The bottom of the pond was scraped bare of all but its plastic and aluminum.

They knew what must be done. The necessity of flight tingled in the muscles of their wings and breasts like the thrill of sex, and yet a strange reluctance made them linger by the exhausted pond. Some counterinstinct, a kind of hysteria, as strong as the need that drove them upward ever and again, would force them each time to return, baffled, to the water still rippling from their departure.

Curtis proposed a number of theories to account for their aberrant behavior: panic syndrome, genetic alteration, their unaccustomed diet, a shift in the magnetic poles. But reason was no proof against what they *felt* each time they reached a certain altitude, the absolute, invincible terror.

"But we can't stay here," Daffy protested. Her only mode of argument was to repeat some incontestable fact. "I mean, we just can't."

"I know that."

"Something terrible will happen."

"I know that too."

"Well, I *feel* it—a kind of chill."

"Daffy, I'm *trying* to think."

"Think! You've been thinking for weeks, and where has it got us? Look at those trees! Feel this water—it's ice!"

"I know, I know."

"Tomorrow we've just got to. I mean we've *got* to."

"We say that every night, Daffy, and every morning it's the same old story—funk."

"I feel this incredible *urge*. To fly."

"That's it!"

Daffy nodded gloomily. "Of course that's it. So why don't we?"

"Flying: whenever we try to fly from here we always get up to a certain point and then the other thing sets in. Right?"

"But I thought you just said . . . ?" She was confused again.

"We'll walk."

"Walk? All that way?"

"As far as we can get. Maybe it's only right in this area that we can't lift off. Maybe it's the sight of the pond, I don't know."

"But I don't *like* to walk, not for any distance."

Curtis said no more. He tucked his feet up and buried his head and pretended to be asleep. Daffy, who liked to weigh all the pros and cons of any major decision, soliloquized restlessly, swimming around in abstracted circles, but at last she had to admit that Curtis was right.

In the morning they began to waddle south.

The highway stretched before them as far as the eye could see, parched and gray and unproviding, smooth as the calmest water. Gigantic machines hurtled past, so fast they seemed to fall toward the horizon. The two ducks trudged on, ignoring the machines and ignored by them. Daffy would have preferred keeping to the stubble, but Curtis insisted they'd make better time on the road. It wasn't so much that she felt threatened; it was just that the incessant *zoom, zoom, zoom* made any kind of conversation impossible.

They were both unutterably weary, and yet the urge to mount upward persisted as strongly as ever. Once, earlier, saying that she would just ruffle her wings at bit, Daffy had spread herself to the air, and instinct had lifted her body like the updraft of a cyclone. Curtis had caught hold of the little metal band around her foot in the nick of time. For a while it had hung in the balance whether he would rise up with her or she fall back to earth with him. Then her wings had given out and she lay on the ground in an agony of shame and longing.

"I can't walk any more. I *can't*. You've broken my leg."

"Nonsense," Curtis said uncertainly.

"I think I'm dying. I've got to fly."

"If you fly now the same thing is going to happen."

"No, Curtis, I'm over that now. I really think I am."

"You'll get up there and you'll see the pond and just head right back to it. All this effort will have been wasted."

"I'll be careful. I promise."

"I won't argue about it any more, Daffy." And he had set off down the road. She had waited for him to look back, but he didn't, and finally she'd followed him, clenching her wings tightly to her side.

Toward evening the highway curved over to where the sun was sinking into smog. They'd been on the right side of the road, and so there was no way for them to continue south except by crossing it. The traffic, however, was worse than it had been at any point that day.

"If we flew . . ." Daffy ventured.

"We'll wait," Curtis said in a tone that brooked no contradiction.

They waited and waited and waited, but there was never a let-up in both directions at the same time. The cars had turned their headlights on, and Daffy grew dizzy watching her shadow swoop and disappear, swoop and disappear across the concrete. At last they gave up and climbed down into the ditch alongside the road, where by a stroke of luck they found a lovely puddle to sleep in.

The first thing Daffy saw when she awoke was the malevolent glint of a rat's eyes not one yard away. Without thinking she tried to spring up out of the water, but her wings refused to move. She honked hysterically. Curtis woke and saw the rat, yet he too remained strangely immobile. So, for that matter, did the rat.

None of this is real, Daffy thought. I'm having a nightmare.

But Curtis, in his usual unruffled way, had come to a different conclusion. "The puddle froze during the night. That's why we can't move—we're trapped in ice."

"But the rat!"

"The rat is dead, Daffy."

"But look at it—those teeth!"

"*You* look at it. Better than that, smell it. I'd estimate that it's been lying there like that for a week."

Curtis methodically began pecking at the ice in which he was embedded, and in a little while he was able to come over and help Daffy extricate herself. She'd been sleeping in a shallower part of the puddle, and it was much harder work. In her haste she lost a good many feathers.

The whole length of the ditch was covered with rats in various stages of decomposition, as well as two dead weasels and a half-eaten owl. Daffy felt a disturbing mingling of pleasure and fear as she regarded the slain legions of her enemies. On the one hand, the world was certainly better off without predators; she could not as easily define what it was on the other hand, but it was there.

"Daffy, look over here at this cave."

"For goodness sake, Curtis, don't you know better than to—you're not going *in* there, are you? Curtis!" She rushed over to the opening too late to prevent him from entering.

"Look! At the other end. I can see light! This goes right under the highway to the other side."

"Curtis, come back!" She advanced a few steps into the darkness. Curtis was already yards ahead. She could see him silhouetted against the disc of light at the other end of the cave.

"We're going south, Daffy. *South!*" His voice echoed weirdly.

Daffy took another cautious step forward, right onto the furry body of a rat. She screamed and sprang up in terror, only to dash her head against the top of the culvert.

"Don't be afraid, darling. All these rats are dead, just like—"

At that moment the last living rat sprang for Curtis's throat. Curtis struggled to escape, rising again and again, battering his wings against the concrete and against his assailant, who clung with feeble tenacity. However often he was struck, however often Curtis collapsed on top of him, he did not lose his purchase. Their struggle continued until they were both dead.

Daffy flew south. She had flown for days—past great gray lakes and greater, grayer cities, above the writhings of rivers and roads, through stinging clouds and blinding smoke: south. She had forgotten Curtis, it seemed, the moment she'd risen into the air. She became a rhythm of wings. Once or twice she knew an instant of panic, but it was not the old self-betraying urge to return to the nest moldering beside the pond. She simply felt lost, out of formation. In the first migrations of her youth she had been a single mote in a multitude of eight or nine, forming with the rest one entity, one action, one desire. But those panics subsided and were replaced by a growing certainty that the previous unity was somehow about to be restored to her.

She began to talk to herself. "Everything works out in the end," she would say. "You worry and you fret and you think the whole world is falling to pieces, and then lo and behold—the next day it's raining! I'm not saying that this is an *ideal* world. That would be silly. You only have to look around you to see, well, all sorts of things. But if you just keep going along and doing as best you can the thing you've *got* to do, it all works out."

She flew and she flew and in no time at all (though actually she was more tired than she cared to admit) she had come to the ocean. Her spirits soared. It would only be a little way now, another day at the most.

But as her flight took her out over the water, something strange happened. At first she thought it was just a symptom of fatigue. Her wings would reach for the air—and miss. It was as though here above the ocean the nature of the atmosphere were changing. She became confused about her direction and had to veer far to the right and to the left to get back to a clear sense of the south. She seemed to hear thunder out of the cloudless sky, usually faint but sometimes so loud that if she'd closed her eyes she would have believed herself to be in the middle of a storm.

"This is absurd," she quacked irately. If there had been any-thing tangible to be afraid of, she would have been afraid. But there wasn't.

The air cracked and a few seconds were ripped out of the steady southern progression of time. The thunder became mon-strous and then, just when she thought she couldn't bear any more, ceased.

"Well! Let's hope. . . ."

The sky collapsed. As the Concorde passed invisibly above her, Daffy plummeted, lifeless, into the ruined ocean.

⚜ *The Colors*

The walls were orange. The rug, an antique Kashan, was a brilliant red ornamented with blue, ochre, and white. Taken all together, it was rather much.

Raymond poured glass jewels into his hand from a yogurt container. When he rattled them about in his palm, each facet flared with a different color of refracted light.

"I doubt that glass beads have realized such a price since the sale of Manhattan," he said, intending a joke.

"Of course it uses transparencies too," Raymond said. (It was not Raymond's style, any longer, to make jokes.) "The only substantial material expense is the cabinet. The control elements are really quite cheap. Though I don't pretend to understand the programming. It's that, the design, that they pay for."

"Still . . . five hundred dollars?"

"Because it has to be custom-made now. If Boyd can find a manufacturer there's no telling what the price would be cut to."

"*And* if there were a market."

Raymond smiled. "Oh, there's a market."

The blond girl drifted out of the kitchen and lay down, beside Boyd, in the Turkish corner. A moment later Anita brought in the tea.

Catching his look, Raymond said, "Regency. But mismatched."

Good old Raymond seemed to be sweating money these days. On the whole, it was a smell that became him.

"You'll try it then?"

"I'll try anything once," he said.

"Oh, but once you *start*, you know. . . ."

Anita poured the tea into the vulgar, but surely quite expensive, cups. ("Lowestoft blue and white.")

"One lump or two?" Raymond asked, the tongs poised.

"You're pulling my leg."

"One lump, then."

"Aren't you having any?"

"We started early, thank you."

"Yes, I did think Boyd seemed . . . a bit beside himself."

"Boyd is beautiful," Anita said.

"No doubt," he said, and then, *sotto voce*, "Hail, blythe spirit."

Raymond turned on the machine—an outsized television with the screen gone and its guts on view. Tubes twinkled. Colors flowed and faded on the back-projection screen. Prisms revolved, blinking. All distinctly pastel, like the somnolent Boyd.

"And now? . . ."

"Wait," Raymond said. "Ripeness is all."

"Contemplate," Anita said.

(He didn't, he decided, like Anita.)

"How *long*?"

But either they did not reply or he was distracted by a sudden dazzle of yellow, shower of gold, behind the small proscenium of the cabinet, following which (and this surely could not be only an optical phenomenon) the space within the machine seemed to expand or (if not this) to take on a larger, though purely spacial, significance. One could not say that it had become thereby "beautiful" (the colors seemed very nearly as pastel as before), but something, something in no way tangible, had altered, and he was interested in this change.

There was a second, more golden flash attended by what seemed to be violet "echoes" that diminished rhythmically. The screen occupied the entire field of his vision now, or rather the colors were no longer confined to the interior of the machine.

Raymond said something that could not have been very important.

Now it was orange, a Chinese orange that veered toward red

(mandarin?), but lavender was somehow associated with it. One could not quite be certain about this orange. One needed to learn more before coming to a final decision.

It was fascinating. Yes, it was fascinating.

And a machine did this. How? Electrons, synapses, metered impulses, circuitry. But all *inorganic*—that was, somehow, the wonder of it: that these vagaries of light should have such a relevance not only to his retina but to every underlying conscious process, to these not quite articulated thoughts, to. . . .

But no—"identity" did not come into it. "Identity" was, in this connection, quite beside the point.

That was the first thing he had learned, but already he sensed that it was *only* the first thing, that, as the thing developed, it would be dwarfed, its only significance residing in the fact that it *had* been the first.

He felt the hand that was placed on his hand. He expected it would be Raymond, but it was the girl, the blond girl.

"I'm Helen," she said.

He continued to look at her: instead of their being diminished (as he had feared), these new intuitions incorporated her face, reinterpreted it, played with it, just as the shifts of orange light from the machine, as they washed over the pale flesh, made it impossible to know the precise color of her eyes, a problem which, in some other light, might not even have interested him.

"Do you like it?"

"That isn't the point, is it? Whether I like it. Whether I don't."

She smiled, seeming to agree. She laid her head on his shoulder and he looked back into the unfolding spaces—the high ceilings, the daedal corridors, the blossoming walls—of the machine, where everything, still, was orange and still more orange and then oranger.

The delta of these considerations continued to broaden, branch, but only at the cue of color. Thus, if Helen were to become an obsession, it was because her fluorescing flesh could be seen in one sense as a great uncompleted canvas, a Rubens still unglazed, the improbable tincts a little raw, yellows citrine, neon oranges, no modulations of coolness and warmth. She remained a latency.

She stroked his armpit. Like the rest of them, she rarely smiled—that would be one of the harder things to learn.

He did not touch her. It was possible, with this much time, an entire Sunday morning, perhaps the day, to approach the matter of Helen with suitable deliberation, a sense of particularity, rather than (as last night) to plunge in, gasping, to the undistinguished mass of sensation, as into a great bed of pink floss—to come to an awareness of the brushwork by disregarding for the time being the modeling of the limbs, the foreshortening, the "expression" of her lips.

"How are you?" she asked, turning onto her side, slipping out of focus.

"Oh, fine. I'm just fine."

"And I can stay? For a while."

He nodded, glad that she had been the one to ask.

And though all this (these sensations and his examination of these sensations) was surely interesting, he was aware already (had he not, just last night, proved himself a quick student?) of the main problem posed by these new "colors": whether they existed, whether there was, *always*, a direct relation between stimulus and response, the act of seeing and the fact of the seen. Not that he would have loved Helen any the less (Helen representing now not the sensory object but the catalyst) if there were no such relation. But what a difference it would make in other respects! How much more valuable the *world* became if these colors were regarded as innate, not his or hers or theirs, but its very own, inalienable.

Yes, it was interesting—he would hang on to that. Though was there any prospect, really, of that interest soon coming to an end? Hadn't she been the one to ask if she could stay?

"I can do simple things around the apartment," she said. "Little jobs."

"If you like. And there are lots of books."

She looked at the wall of books looming above the bed, laughed.

"Why is that?" he asked.

"Oh, everywhere there is always such a lot of books."

She had the habit, which he was to pick up eventually, of speaking in such absolute terms ("always," "every," "never"), though seldom, despite this, with any precision, just as, much later, when she was gone and he would try to remember the exact contours and colors of her flesh, he could recapture only the gross image, an absolute Helen, the name, as one recalls of some painting one has seen many years ago the name and nothing else. But of these things he had, as yet, no notion.

Time, then, was the sequence of these colors, the oranges less and less in prominence, yellow in the ascendant. Only at work would he be aware of the irksome revolutions of the numbered hours, the tally of days; but even here sometimes he would have a sense of less stable orderings, of unexpected congruencies and omissions, of the intrusion (even here) of the special claim that the "inorganic" now made upon him. The process of change was accelerating, and it made scant difference whether these changes were an interior or an exterior event. Polarities of any kind seemed rather beside the point.

He began to see that Raymond and his set, far from lacking a sense of humor, lived in a perpetual state of hilarity: for them the special occasions of wit were supererogatory. Every artifice in the city's infinite treasury could tell its own small joke but one cannot go about laughing *all* the time.

Twice he returned to the studio, once with Helen and once, when Helen had gone off somewhere, alone. Now that its colors had "run" into the world at large, the machine did not possess the same fascination. With the journey so well advanced one could feel only an affectionate nostalgia for these snapshots of the first ports of call. Instead of baring his mind to the spray blowing down from the brimming lip of light, without even entering the sanctuary, he sat in the kitchen with his host, asking questions about Helen.

"I think she told me she comes from the Bronx," Raymond said.

"The Bronx?"

"Or Yonkers—I'm not sure."

"How did you meet her?"

"At a party, I suppose. I can never keep track of all the people who are in and out of this place. The fellow in the astrakhan, for instance—I haven't the faintest clue to what he's doing here or who brought him. He's been about for two or three days now. Says he writes."

"How old is she?"

"Hey, what is this, a quiz show?"

"I think I'm falling in love with her. Or something like that."

"Well, that's your own lookout."

"You don't think I should?"

"Man, if you're going to fall in love, you'll *fall* in love. Won't you?"

"The funny thing is—she seems to have so little to do with it herself. I mean, it's not love that connects me and her—it's Helen that connects me and love."

Raymond shrugged: it was all philosophy to him.

For a while he watched the coffee percolating on the stove, like a dark brown Nola light, then left without saying good-bye to Raymond, who was helping the boy in the astrakhan be sick in the bathroom.

He decided to walk home rather than go down into the subway. A summer night, green trees, music, the city's munificent life. The sidewalk strewn with portents, *trouvailles*, and the sequence of faces slipping past his that touched, like the knobs on the metal disc of a music box, each, a different chord of perception.

Without Helen none of this would have made sense. She was his link not only to "love" but to the world.

When he arrived home, early in the morning, Helen was still out. He decided not to go to work. He made coffee and a kind of omelette from the food still left in the icebox. Morning lengthened into afternoon: olive-drab, muddied tans and ochres, mahogany and mother-of-pearl. Not dazzling, to be sure, but with their own distinct fascination nevertheless.

Orange:

Yellow:

And then a stage of virescence. The days of her absence had been like the sere March fields before the new grass—with this difference, that love cannot be relied on to recur seasonally: its sere days, when they come, seem to come forever.

Now, at the end of August, it was veritable spring. They spent their weekends (he was at work again) in the park, where alone in that city could be found a sufficiency of green, of grass and veined leaves that took their life, as he did, from the light, arching toward it, turning with it, amorous.

Helen always present, with Helen, touching her.

It was Helen's special grace that she allowed all things to be reduced to their surfaces, and it became his task, as her lover, to read, from a swell of muscle, from the underpainting of her skin (green, as in an early Sienese Madonna) the meanings hidden in her name, to which end he would investigate the slightest clue.

They ate, in the evenings, miraculous salads—when they bothered to eat. Their days were not demarcated by necessities. Seldom had he been so slim, so self-indulgent, so exalted.

This was to be the apogee of his delight, when he looked neither forward nor back, the weightless instant at the crest of the wave. And so it was that when, one Sunday evening, beside the artificial lake on the west side of the park, they ran into Raymond and Anita, it required the most strenuous effort of memory to recall that these two had been so closely implicated in bringing him to this height (where *they* were scarcely visible) of happiness.

He left most of the talking to Helen. The conversation twined and intertwined its allusions, intentions, names, numbers across the trellis of his consciousness in Persian intricacies. Raymond made a joke, and their mingled laughter rose, like a little fountain, into the chilled air. When they finally left he was exhausted.

"Shall we go to the party?" Helen asked.

"What party?"

"At Raymond's. Tonight."

He stared at her closed lips, stained with the chocolate coating from the ice cream, unable to read their expression.

"Do *you* want to? We'll go there if you want to."

"Well, I'd like to go *somewhere*, you know."

He nodded, and dabbed at her lips with a paper napkin.

"Well?" she demanded.

"Yes. Yes, let's go."

He lay back on the abused and tenuous grass, gazed up, resisting the new era.

"What day is it?" he asked.

"Sunday, of course. What did you think?"

"I mean the date."

"I don't know. October something or other. Why?"

"Because the leaves are turning."

"You mean you just noticed that?"

"But the sky is incredibly blue, isn't it?"

Helen looked up at the sky. She shrugged. "I suppose so."

It was only then, with the initiation of the descent, that he knew he was committed: to just this action and no other. Beforehand such an event may seem painful, but he had never bothered to anticipate events. And now? Pain?

No—nor ever again, for it was only now in the dizzying descent that he had been able to find time to appreciate just how far he had come and what rare air he breathed in these altitudes. It was not as though his downward course were to be no more than a recapitulation, a reverie: the sensation of it was wholly new and the motion was downward only in the sense that he could no longer reverse its direction. In fact, there was no "down" or "up" at all, for it had always been downward in that he had never resisted or wished to resist, and always upward in that each successive transformation, each new tonality, brought his mind to a higher and a finer pitch.

And how various each realm! what millesimal gradations from shade to shade! But especially the blues—the blues were like no other color he had known before.

The sky. The sky flattened against the window of his room, a del Piombo, the morning paleness burnished, hour by hour, to the lapis lazuli of noon, a pigment of ground jewels costlier than gold leaf.

Or the azure veins sealing her closed eyes, azure veins lacing her arms. The nameless blue of those eyes opened. The shadows revolving in slow measure about the shabby furniture, the hours.

And, sometimes, clouds—though these were white and dazzling.

The hyacinthine evenings and his body, lax, falling into

night, and the night itself, indigo, and her name, Helen, and her body, the few highlights, the deep shadows, the indelible sense of just that instant in time, futureless, absolute, here, just here, Helen.

Too often, of course, she would not be here. He would be alone, wondering where she was, when she would return.

Once, during such a crisis, Raymond came around.

"I tried to call," Raymond explained, "but you've been cut off."

"Oh, yes," he said. "The telephone."

Raymond put the groceries he had brought into the refrigerator.

"How are you?"

"I'm fine."

"We haven't seen you for some time."

"I'm fine."

"Is Helen still living here?"

"Sometimes." Then, looking away from the window: "Have you seen Helen?"

"Last night she was with a friend of mine. No, Thursday night."

"I'm. . . ." But he forgot.

"Are you sure you're all right? I know a doctor—"

"If you should see Helen, give her my love," he said, without intending irony.

Raymond carried out the garbage when he left, and that same night Helen was there. She'd brought a bottle of wine and they celebrated. When she undressed there were bruises on her legs and arms.

"Don't touch them," she said.

And now? he asked himself. Would there be another color? What could come after violet (which had gone past almost before he'd had a chance to notice)? Black? Black was the only thing left, so far as he could imagine.

Helen was running water into the bath.

"How are you?" he asked above the rear of the tap.

"Me? I'm fine."

.   .   .

Then, prodigious as a comet, unannounced, the brightness fell, dazzling. And her smile, the sun in suspension above Gibeon, dazzling. Between her and this new light that shone through her he did not trouble to distinguish.

He looked into her eyes; they were white.

The fields of vision flooded, and every sense spread back to accept the absolute gift. Pools of dazzling water reflected the retinal skies. Deserts blossoming.

Eyes and fingers reached, like vines, toward that light through endless stretches of white sand, white flowers.

Only the white.

Her body, so blanched now as to be invisible, suspended beneath his, and his, baked and basking in the perpetual light—as though they had been lifted outside the cone of earth's shadow into the unchanging midday of space, into beauty beyond imagining, which still grew and only sometimes (that it might grow again) ebbed.

During the rare intervals, long or brief, he could understand, partially, what had happened and what still remained to happen. A rainbow, revolving, would be white: white, the harmony of all colors, their resolving chord, unprismed light.

She always returned to him, and he knew that she always *would* return to him: here, just here. Touching. Perhaps not even that, perhaps only being near.

Then again the electric arc would leap the gap to consciousness, and then again, and then, more powerfully, again. He would look into the apotheosis of her eyes, and the light would grow behind them until the image was dissolved in its own radiance.

Crystal! Not the facets' partial truths but the immaculate inorganic core of chrysolite. Jewels spilled into his hands, ran through his veins, sprang dazzling into the light, arched higher, turned to beads of spray that hung there, constellations of the noon.

He cried aloud.

Everything—all colors, the filthy walls, the sky falling against the windows, snow, sheets of ice—was white, and he knew there would be no colors after this, the journey's end, and on the sign there, the white crystals of her name (which was all that could be known of her, finally): not Helen now, not with such sure syllables, no; just the white insatiable crystals, the name, the blinding white, the name whispered so incessantly in his veins, the dazzle, the only possible desire.

Death and the Single Girl

At four-thirty of a rainy afternoon late in June Jill Holzman made up her mind that she'd had it. Life was not worth living, and in any case *her* life was not an example of living. She'd come to the same decision once in her college days and taken some pills, but she'd also arranged to be discovered. This time, though, she was sincere.

She pulled a chair over to the bookshelves she'd carpentered herself, stood on it, and got down her copy of *Gestalt Therapy* from the top shelf. Inside on the blank front matter before the title page she'd written down the telephone number of Death. She'd got it from a boy she'd talked to on a bus on her way up to a World Fellowship camp in the Catskills. The boy lived at an ashram near Ashokan and was into everything occult. He gave Jill almost a full address book of organizations to get in touch with—a psychic healer in Mexico City, a Reichean therapist in the Albert Hotel, a radical-left splinter group of Scientologists— and Death.

She dialed Death's number. It was busy.

After a few pages of *Gestalt Therapy* she tried again. This time there was an answer, but it wasn't Death himself, just an answering service. She left her number.

Then, feeling rejected and thoroughly depressed, she went into the closet she called a kitchen and made a double batch of tollhouse cookies. When she'd finished washing the bowls and the tin sheets, she dumped all the warm cookies in a black plastic trash liner, sealed it, and sent it down the chute to the incinerator. Cooking always cheered her up, but the thought of having to eat those cookies was too much. Anyhow, she was trying to lose weight.

Two days later in the middle of an NBC special on drug abuse there was a phone call.

"Hello," she said, hopefully.

"Hello. I'd like to speak to Miss Jill Holzman."

"Speaking."

"Miss Holzman, this is Death. You tried to reach me two days ago, and I wasn't in."

"Oh, yes." Her knees had gone all weak, as though she'd just been elected class president and had to give an extempore speech that moment to an assembly. "Thank you for calling back."

Death said nothing. You couldn't even hear him breathing into the receiver.

"I was wondering," she began haltingly, "if you would like to come over. . . ." The silence stretched on. She took a deep breath. "I live at 35 Barrow Street. Apartment 3-C. If you take the 7th Avenue subway, you get off at Sheridan Square and I'm just around the corner." It occurred to her that he might have wanted her to come to him. "Or if you're too busy . . . ?"

"No," he said, after a pause sufficiently long to make it clear that he meant yes. "I have been busy, of course, or I'd have returned your call much sooner. It's this rain. A long stretch of bad weather is always the busiest time for me."

Jill wondered if that was all that had been depressing her. The rain had gone on now for five days, the tattered edge of a hurricane that had accomplished a hundred million dollars of damage. But no, this was more than a mood. She would have stood by her decision on the sunniest day of the year.

"It is awful," Jill agreed, meaning not just the weather but existence in general.

"You still haven't mentioned, Miss Holzman, what it is, exactly, that you want."

"Oh." She tried to keep from sounding annoyed. "Do I have to come right out and say it?" Death said nothing. "What I want is to be dead."

"Fine. How's tomorrow morning? Say, ten o'clock?"

"We couldn't make it in the afternoon? Usually I don't get *up* till eleven, and I'm not wholly *conscious* till after lunch." She was about to launch into the whole sorry story of careers, of job after job lost because she couldn't wake up and go to it. Then she thought better of it. Other people just aren't interested.

"I'm afraid tomorrow afternoon is already filled. Would Thursday do?"

Jill looked at the engagement calendar on her desk. Thursday was a page away, next to a Brancusi pencil drawing. She couldn't imagine watching Lucille Ball and "The Flintstones" till then.

She gave in. "Make it tomorrow morning. I'll get up early." When he made no reply to this she panicked. I've offended him, she thought, and now he'll never come. "Really," she pleaded, "tomorrow morning would be *wonderful*. Did you say ten?"

"Yes, I'm just noting it down. Thirty-five Barrow Street?"

"Apartment 3-C."

"Ten o'clock. Very good. *À tout à l'heure.*" Which he mispronounced.

She wondered if she were making a mistake.

She woke at six A.M. with an intense realization that her apartment was squalid and unpresentable. The record cabinet was covered with stacks of dusty records out of their sleeves. The sheets were dirty, the prayer plant was languishing, a tray of butts and ashes had spilled across the bathroom tiles. Months of cooking grease filmed the mirror inside the closet, and the sight of herself in the mirror, clouded as it was, was the most discouraging datum of all.

She worked frantically, and by the time Death arrived, punctually at ten, the most obvious disorders had been disguised.

He looked down at his dripping umbrella. "Where can I put this?"

"Let me take it." She spread it open, scattering raindrops, and set it to dry in the tub, which was speckled with cleanser. Rather than let him see inside the closet, she hung his coat in the bathroom too. A London Fog.

"Well," he said, settling creakily in the painted bamboo chair.

Jill sat on the edge of the bed, her legs spread slightly apart and her hands forming a relaxed cup expressive of an open, trustful attitude. "Here we are."

For the last two years Jill had worked, when she'd worked at all, as an office temporary. It occurred to her, looking at Death, that she might well have filled in at his office sometime. She had had so many employers, and their faces had all melted together into one averagely good-looking, averagely used-up, middle-aged face that was exactly the face smiling at her now.

"You have a very attractive apartment," Death commented.

"Thank you. Actually I'm afraid I've rather let things get out of control. The view, of course, that's its best feature." No sooner were the words out of her mouth than she realized that there wasn't any view. The rain had blotted out all but the nearest rooftops. The World Trade Center had disappeared.

Or was this, she wondered, the first prefiguring of her death? Would the city shrink around her till there was nothing left but this room, this bed, her own body, and finally a single blue eye, closing?

Death spread his suitcoat and unzipped his fly. "Shall we get down to business?" he asked. He wriggled a finger inside his Jockey shorts to flip out his cock, which was limp and wrinkly and the uncertain undulant pastel of an A&P chicken.

Involuntarily Jill looked away—at Death's trouser cuffs, at the perforations in his wing-tip shoes, at his bland, self-effacing smile. "What am I supposed to do?" she asked.

"Whatever feels most natural for you, Jill."

Tentatively she took the flaccid organ in her hand and squeezed. The glans became a brighter shade of salmon. Death edged forward on the chair. The bamboo creaked.

"Perhaps," he suggested, "if you kissed it. . . ."

"You mean you want a blow job?"

Death winced. His cock shriveled with embarrassment. "If you'd rather not go on with this," he said huffily, "I can leave now."

Mentally squaring her shoulders, Jill recollected her despair, her weariness, her anomie, and all the other reasons she had for dying. It wasn't as though she were a virgin, after all, or even invincibly squeamish about the act in question, as an episode with her most recent boyfriend (Lenny Rice—he'd left for California eight months ago) had borne witness to. If Death had only been a little less perfunctory, had shown the slightest tenderness or respect for her as an individual. . . .

"No!" she protested, getting on her knees and gathering her wits. "Don't go. I was just a bit . . . taken aback. I'll do whatever you want."

"Only if *you* want to, too," Death insisted.

"Oh, I do, I do."

And, resolutely, for fifteen minutes, she did, but to no avail. Once or twice it seemed that Death might be getting it up, and Jill, responsively, would increase her efforts. However in proportion as she exerted herself, his energy diminished. It was self-defeating, a labor of Sisyphus. She began to wonder if he were impotent.

Death disengaged himself and wiped his cock dry with a Kleenex. "I suppose you're wondering if I'm impotent."

"No. No, it's my own fault."

"Well, I'm not. Usually it's a simple matter of one, two, three. It's just that, as I explained, I've been so busy. There's a limit to what one person can do."

"I'll keep trying," Jill promised wanly.

"I have another appointment at eleven-thirty on East Seventy-fourth. I'll be late as it is."

"You're not leaving! But what about me? Aren't you going to . . . to. . . ." She looked out the window. There seemed to be even fewer rooftops visible than when Death had arrived. "Or am I dead already?"

Death snorted derisively. "If you were dead, my dear girl, you wouldn't know it. It's tit for tat—I come, and you go."

Jill folded her arms. "That doesn't seem fair."

"I'll tell you what. I'll return this evening—on my own time. How's that?"

What could she say but yes?

True to his word, Death returned at eight-thirty. The bottle of Almaden burgundy he'd bought at the liquor store on Christopher Street went nicely with Jill's beef bourguignon. For dessert there were parfaits of chilled vodka over pistachio ice cream. Jill wore a canvas raindress from Lord & Taylor with the bottom three buttons undone. She had debated her more provocative macramé shift but decided that the circumstances called for an appearance of compliance rather than zest.

The phonograph repeated the same six Strauss waltzes over and over and over. "Artists' Life." "The Blue Danube." "Dynamation." "Tales of the Vienna Woods." "Vienna Blood." "The Emperor Waltz." And then, returning to band one, "Artists' Life." "The Blue Danube." And so on.

Death so far relaxed as to allow her to take off his suitcoat and loosen his tie, but then, anxious to make up for that morning's failure, he took the initiative himself.

At first Jill had some hope. Initially, at least, Death evinced a larger promise of success, and they were, this time, on the bed instead of wobbling about on the bamboo chair. But this hope soon faded. At last, her make-up smudged, an eyelash lost in his pubic hair, she gave up.

"Damn," said Death.

Jill was too tired to care even that much.

"I don't know what to tell you."

"It's all right," she assured him.

"Another time?"

"Maybe I should come round to your office," she suggested.

"Good idea." He would have agreed to a tryst anywhere at that moment—a church, a graveyard, the Statue of Liberty.

After sharing a dribble of Kahlúa, the last remnant of a Twelfth Night party of two years ago, he left. Jill went over to the phonograph and lifted the needle from "Vienna Blood."

She didn't even rinse the sauce off the dishes, she was that tired. Let the roaches do their worst, she thought, and went to bed.

Death was out when she arrived. If his receptionist were to be believed he'd left only moments before, though Jill's appointment (it was written down on his calendar too, clear as a pistol shot) was for eleven o'clock, and that's what the big, businessy clock on the wall said it was, precisely eleven o'clock. For a while Jill was content to listen to the soothing not quite monotony of the receptionist transcribing from a dictaphone. The foot pedal would go *snick*, and there would be a silence about six heartbeats in duration. Then another *snick* followed by a burst of typing.

When Death was fully half an hour overdue, Jill admitted to being bored and paged through the waiting room's magazines until she'd found a nice angry article in *Cosmopolitan* to reinforce her own nice anger. It had never been an easy emotion for Jill to get to, but when she did, ah, what bliss. Her stale body would begin to tingle, to become a fountain of adrenalin that overflowed out into the weary, workaday world, every molecule of which would then begin to move a little faster until it all began to look (which it never did otherwise) as interesting as the very best Hollywood movie, starring, for instance, George C. Scott and Glenda Jackson and Liza Minelli.

"One o'clock," Jill observed aloud, not quite accurately. "Son of a bitch."

The receptionist grimaced sympathetically. "Don't I know."

"Do you think he's going to show up at all?"

"You never can tell. Though there's one way I could guarantee it—if I go out for lunch. Then he'd be up on the next elevator. Happens every time. He's psychic or something."

"There's no one but him to relieve you?"

"The other girl left Friday. Cashed her check and disappeared."

"If you'd like to go out and grab a bite I can hold down the fort here. I mean, I'm not about to do anything else."

"*Would* you? I am famished. I'd have something delivered, but the one time I did *that*, Lord! A lousy tunafish salad sandwich—you would have thought it was the end of the world."

"Go eat."

"If anyone calls write down their name and get their number and say we'll call right back. If anyone comes in, tell them to wait. Basically, that's it."

The receptionist went off to lunch, and Death arrived on the very next elevator. He would have walked right past Jill into his office if she hadn't called attention to herself by throwing her *Cosmopolitan* at him.

"Oh! Miss Holzman!" He let go the doorknob. "You startled me."

She glowered. She had every right to.

"I thought you were my secretary."

"I said I'd relieve her so she could have lunch. You're two hours late, you know. Two *hours*."

"Some unexpected difficulties," he mumbled.

"The usual difficulties?" she asked sardonically.

He sighed.

"Once," Jill reminisced lazily as she sprawled on the vinyl couch in Death's inner office, "when I was seventeen, I had to have a root canal job. The nerve in my tooth became infected and I had to keep going back and back and back. It was weeks before the tooth was drained and sealed. The dentist told me later that I'd set a record for him—thirteen separate sessions of work on a single tooth."

"Believe me, Miss Holzman, our experience has been most atypical. I don't know what the matter is, but I assure you it isn't your fault."

"Thanks a lot."

"If you wish to come back tomorrow I'll cancel all my other appointments."

"I'm not sure I *do* wish to."

"That's perfectly understandable."

"I don't do this for my health, you know. Candidly, I regard this whole business as odious and demeaning and *medieval*. The fact that it has *also* been unsuccessful only makes for a very salty wound. For all the good *you've* been able to do I might as well have taken sleeping pills. Or arsenic, for heaven's sake!"

"If you'd like me to strangle you, or take you out in my boat. . . ."

"Don't be disgusting."

As usual, having reached the apogee of her rage, Jill found herself relenting. Death seemed truly contrite. Was he to be blamed, after all, for his failures? Rather might she pity him. She *did* pity him. It was wonderful.

So, when as a gesture of reconciliation he offered to take her to lunch at the Peking Park, she needed the merest nudge of persuasion—a "please," no more. And when, after a dilatory and scrumptious meal, he asked her to fill the vacant position at his office, it was only a matter of another nudge. It was either this, she reasoned, or going the rounds of the agencies, than which she dreaded few things in life more.

That it was life could not be denied, but there were compensations. The salary was good, the hours agreeable, and her relationship with her employer—once it was clear that her service would be strictly limited to only such tasks as the New York State Employment Board would have approved—coolly congenial. In any case, Death did not seem eager to resume their earlier intimacies. It was a job, and she did it. If you couldn't be dead, this was the next best thing.

✄ *Displaying the Flag*

Leonard Dworkin had been, till the age of thirty-four, a leather queen. Mostly he'd managed to confine his aberration to the privacy of his own apartment, but when his company moved him to New York he began to frequent, as discreetly as he might, the leather bars along the waterfront. When discretion failed, psychoanalysis was of no help: he would lay out a whopping seventy dollars for a session on Friday afternoon and five hours later there he'd be, in his black leather jacket and his studded boots, attending what looked like the twentieth anniversary class reunion for *The Wild One*, feeling idiotic and lustful.

Years ago he'd contacted a behavioral clinic in Manchester that had been written up in *New Scientist* for its dramatic cures of all major deviations. Their technique seemed foolproof. Every time you were aroused by whatever you no longer wished to be aroused by, you received a huge electric shock. In a very short time you weren't aroused, nor ever again. Despite the commendable logic of this method, despite its impressive successes, Leonard had felt reluctant, but on the day his company promoted him to a vice-presidency he decided that the time had come. He took off three weeks, flew to England, and turned himself in.

He came back a changed man. Not only was he rid of his perversion—he'd stopped smoking as well. Leonard Dworkin, who'd been at the two-packs-a-day level for half his life! His analyst's ironic prediction—that instead of being turned off by his old fetishes he'd only have acquired a supplementary taste for electrocution—proved unfounded. The merest tremor, blocks away, of a motorcycle engine could turn his stomach. As for leather, it was as much as he could do to wear shoes. To think of all the years he'd wasted jotting down his dreams! To think of the money!

As for sex in its more pedestrian forms he felt no urge toward that, as yet. Just being free of his hangup—and of course his conditioning had eliminated any undesirable tendencies above and beyond leather—was all the happiness he asked for now. It was incredible, the energy he had! He felt as though he were eleven again, all bounce and boundless ambition. He did wonders at his job, and in only two years he'd received another promotion and been transferred to head the company's chief research division in Atlanta. His photograph appeared in *Fortune* as one of the hundred leading prodigies of American industry. That was 1966.

By March of 1968 he'd been canned.

His downfall began on a Thursday, shortly after his arrival in Atlanta. He had promised to lunch with Clayton Rusch, his chief programmer and one of the few people reporting to him who understood not only what the division was doing but its potential dollars-and-cents consequences as well. Most of his staff, brilliant as they might be, were resentful of the fact that their research was considered, by other departments of the company, purposeful. Clayton, like Leonard himself, got round this hurdle by refusing to think of business as being in any way less abstract than math. The two men were well on the way to what they both would have called friendship.

The executives' cafeteria, which Leonard had been frequenting, was a bright, low-ceilinged room with bright, lowbrow prints of ducks and dahlias. The food ranged from innocuous to wretched, and there was no bar, no beer, nothing. Understandably, few executives ate there. "So," Clayton explained, "where we should go is Kuczka's."

"What is Kuczka's?"

Clayton smiled mysteriously. "That's hard to explain . . . but seeing is believing."

For one soaring paranoiac moment Leonard thought: a leather

bar! But no, there wouldn't be leather bars in Atlanta, and if there were, Clayton wouldn't be taking him to one for lunch.

They set off in Clayton's statusy little XKE (the two of them filled it to bursting) and drove through a more central and dowdy part of Atlanta than any Leonard had seen till now, without bougainvillaea, without even trees. Kuczka's was a classic working-man's bar tucked between two warehouses, with draft beer in glasses or mugs, Planter's peanuts, cellophane-wrapped sausages, a fluorescing jukebox, and slogans painted on pine, thumbtacked to the woodwork, taped on the mirrors. One booth was left. They took it.

Leonard kept waiting for the punch line, but Kuczka's went on in its average, noonday way like a shaggy dog story. A waitress brought a menu, beers, napery. Clayton insisted on ordering for both of them. Then, apropos his glass of beer, he launched into the story of his uncontrollable weight.

Leonard agreed—dieting was beyond him too.

"You!" Clayton, who tipped the scales at two hundred sixty-eight, had to laugh. Ho! Ho!

"Honestly," Leonard insisted. "In just the last two years I've put on thirty pounds." Then, slyly and compulsively (for a half-truth is so much more comfortable than secrecy and lies), he told about his cure: how his doctor had told him he had to stop smoking, how, and how often, he'd tried and failed, and how at last he'd gone to Manchester.

"And that worked, the shock treatment?"

"Like that." Leonard tried to snap his fingers. "But afterward, I guess as a kind of compensation, I started eating more. I wasn't even aware that I was doing it. It's the old story of driving out one devil and seven others taking his place. And this vice I'm stuck with. I can't go back to Manchester and ask them to cure me of eating."

On this cue the waitress brought their orders: two giant liberty-burgers (Kuczka's specialty) and double portions of french fries. A libertyburger is a hamburger garnished with a special hot catsup (red), chopped onions (white), and blue cheese. A paper flag on a toothpick waved from the bun. Clayton and the waitress waited for Leonard's reaction.

"It's . . . beautiful."

Clayton ho-hoed, and the waitress, smiling, went about her work.

"What did I tell you?" Clayton asked. "Is this incredible? And the whole place is more of the same. The paper napkins, look —red, white, and blue. And the regulars who come in here? Hoo-ee!" He took a great bite out of his libertyburger and shook his head expressively, chewing.

"Patriots?"

"You said it, by god. The real give-me-liberty-or-give-me-death kind of John Philip Sousa patriot. Haven't you been reading any of these signs they've got tacked up here?" He pointed to a peace symbol on the back of the cash register; across it, as a kind of exergue, was written, "Track of an American Chicken."

Leonard smiled noncommitally. "Yes, I'd noticed a certain—"

The jukebox came on—Kate Smith belting out "God Bless America." (The bartender's own dime.) Grinning, Clayton took the toothpick flag out of his libertyburger and waved it in time to the music.

Leonard was uncertain whether he was expected to laugh or sing along. He supposed Clayton was poking fun at Kuczka's, but there was something in his manner of a Catholic making jokes about the Church. A liberal himself, when he stopped to think about it, he'd been careful since coming to the Atlanta office not to utter even the mildest of his opinions. Even in New York, that bastion, he'd gone out of his way during the last terrifying election not to rile the three or four of his associates who'd worn Goldwater buttons. And Georgia was one of the eight states that Goldwater had actually won!

He removed the flag from his libertyburger and put it in his buttonhole. Let Clayton deduce what he would from that!

For the rest of the day, alone in his office, he played with the little flag, twirling it between his thumb and forefinger nervously, abstractedly, not yet consciously thrilled.

During Leonard Dworkin's high-school years in Madison, Wisconsin, he had been required for one period each day, five days a week, to take physical education. Small for his age, careful of his glasses, and totally lacking in confidence or coordination, he'd stood at the edge of all the compulsory games, so diffident that often you couldn't tell if he were watching the game or playing it. So now, on the days that he returned to Kuczka's, he would stand at the bar and, despite the bartender's best efforts to shape the conversations to include Leonard, have nothing more to say for himself than a mild "Goddam," or a noncommital "Is that so."

Nobody knew what to make of him. His Yankee accent and his well-cut, somber New York suits marked him as an alien, but his manner was so deferential, not to say friendly, that it was hard to take exception. "One of the guys" he wasn't, but there was something irresistibly flattering in the close, serious attention he gave to the opinions of, for instance, Buddy Truitt, who loaded trucks for Georgia Eastern Stores and earned, if he was lucky, one-fifth the salary of a Leonard Dworkin. Both sides of their ambivalence was expressed in the nickname they'd given him, "the Professor." Professors are, in general, a suspect lot, but this Professor was coming to *their* school to learn from *them*.

Leonard, for his part, was in transports. Kuczka's beat the leather bars hollow. They had been the upholstery of which this, in a sense, was the stuffing, and though he'd recognized what was happening early on, this didn't get in the way of his enjoyment. His conditioning didn't extend beyond overt homosexuality; every degree of patriotism was permitted to him.

At first he didn't regard it as a vice. He didn't actually get a hard-on. It was more a kind of tingling, over his whole body, which reached, at apogee, a feeling as of swooning away. Sex, in his past experience, had been highly specific and teleological; this was diffuse and . . . heavenly: a sensation halfway between the "Eureka!" of mathematical exaltation and a voluptuary's sigh. He couldn't get enough of it. It wasn't long before he was as familiar a sight at Kuczka's as the plaster of Paris eagle clutching its thunderbolts and olive branch above the top row of bottles behind the bar.

With familiarity came courage, which no less an authority than General Patton has defined as "fear holding on a minute longer." Leonard found that standing on the sidelines was less exciting than joining in. Oh, not in a starring role, not at first. Just little things, at first. He fed dimes into the jukebox for such all-time favorites as Red Skelton's recitation of the Pledge of Allegiance or a ballad by Pat Boone. He bought a small ceramic flag, which he pinned to his lapel just before he went into the bar, just as previously he'd waited till the last possible minute before fastening the loops of chain to the epaulets of his jacket. He picked up a copy of *National Review* and began, cautiously, adding his own authoritative tidbits to the discussions. Was it, he would ask ironically, the function of the CIA to shield traitors in the State Department? Or was this, instead, the responsibility of the U.S. Senate? Then, slipping deliciously into a homelier style, he'd drop certain slang words into the stately flow of his pronouncements: "pinko" and "kike," "comsymp" and (most delectable because most forbidden) "nigger." And all these words would pass as though unnoticed, as though Leonard were entitled to their use, as the owner of a Harley-Davidson (and only the owner of a Harley) is entitled to wear that company's emblem on his belt buckle, his T-shirt, and his cap.

Leonard was officially accepted into Kuczka's inner circle on the evening of January 10, 1967. On that day Lester Maddox had taken office as Governor of Georgia and the U.S. House of Representatives had barred Adam Clayton Powell from his Congressional seat. Leonard had outdone himself on both subjects, and just before closing time Butch Carney (which really was the bartender's name) presented Leonard with a bumper sticker that said: "America—Love It or Leave It!" He could have kissed Butch then and there had his conditioning allowed him to perform so questionable an act.

The next morning he had to get up half an hour earlier in order to scrape the sticker off. Then before he could return to Kuczka's he had to scout all round the city to find an accessory store that stocked the same stickers. He bought two dozen. His new double life was becoming almost as complicated and inconvenient as his old one.

For he had not allowed his patriotic passion to intrude into his *real* life. At the office he was still scrupulously neutral in political discussions, and in his heart he was still a convinced

Eastern Establishment Liberal. He realized that the opinions he espoused at Kuczka's were pernicious and immoral, and the day-time, Dr. Jekyll side of his soul utterly rejected them. Was *he* to blame for the behavior of Hyde? Yet it was not only at Kuczka's that he surrendered himself to his vice. Sometimes, driving along the freeways or at bedtime in his sumptuously spartan apartment, he would entertain fantasies of the most abandoned conservatism. He imagined himself in a voting booth, the curtains closely drawn, voting for Barry Goldwater! Or for *Wallace* (who was then threat-ening publicly to run in the '68 election)! He trembled to think how he would jeer at peace marchers and civil rights demonstra-tors. He took out a subscription to *American Opinion*, Robert Welch's magazine. Welch, who had founded the John Birch Society! He imagined—and why not, since it was only imagina-tion?—*joining* the John Birch Society! The American Legion! The Minutemen! But not the American Nazi Party, for their uniforms touched his sore point.

Inevitably his secret was leaked. One sweaty evening in July of 1967 an electrical engineer, a young PhD not so far down the organizational chart from Leonard as not to recognize him, brought some out-of-town visitors into Kuczka's for the amuse-ment of libertyburgers. Leonard was in full spate on the topic of the niggers then rioting in Detroit and what he felt they deserved. The presence of his co-worker intensified the basic excitement of his patriotism exponentially. He became limp, he trembled, he raved, and the young engineer listened, aghast.

From that day forth Leonard no longer bothered scraping off his bumper sticker every morning before he drove to work. Indeed he had soon graduated from "America—Love It or Leave It!" to the full glory of "Impeach Earl Warren." He flaunted his lapel pin everywhere. He became known among his co-workers as Yankee Doodle Dworkin—and he was proud of it.

Such is the strength of Mr. Hyde.

Martin Niles III, the graying eminence of the board of directors and a man, besides, of some small political consequence in his home state of Connecticut, visited the Atlanta office in March of

1968 and asked, which no doubt he would have done in any case, to speak with Leonard privately. Their talk progressed smoothly along the main thoroughfares of official concerns until Mr. Niles, steeling himself for combat with a few nervous tics, the civilized remnants of his animal nature, observed: "I see, Leonard, that you've become a supporter of Governor Wallace."

Leonard's fingertips caressed the button (an inch and a half in diameter) on his lapel. "Oh, down here, you know, Marty—" (who had been, till just this moment, "Mr. Niles") "—we all feel strongly that something has to be *done*."

"Even in our northern states, I gather, that's a common feeling. Or should I say failing?"

Leonard, breathing heavily, forced his hand down from his lapel to the polished wood of the conference table. "A recent candidate for high office in this land once said (and please correct me if I'm wrong): 'Extremism in the defense of liberty is no vice.' And I guess I've got to agree with him. I take it that this isn't just a theoretical interest, though. You have some particular bone to pick with me?"

Mr. Niles flexed his brow, cleared his throat, and stared. "As a matter of fact, Leonard, I've been hearing some remarkable stories about your conduct of this office. You've changed so much since your days in New York that when these complaints first began coming in we simply refused to give them credence."

"You might say I've changed. I think of it myself as my having 'come out.' Certainly I've gained the courage of my convictions."

"You might say courage. Myself, I'd call it folly."

Leonard bowed his head, acknowledging Mr. Niles's right to his own erring opinion.

Between them, on the bright mahogany, Mr. Niles placed a small decalcomania of an American flag. "Do you recognize that?"

"Yes, sir! It's the flag of the United States of America. And long may it wave, if you'll permit me to say so."

"Oh, recite the Declaration of Independence if you wish. But then I'd like you to tell me if you sent these out enclosed in the company newsletter. With a signed note urging all employees to put them on the windshields of their cars."

"I did. Is there a company ruling against honoring Old Glory?"

"Old Glory! Lord God!"

"The flag then, if that seems gauche. Down here, you know—"

"Let's not pussyfoot, Leonard. You know as well as I do that the flag has become a kind of political counter, and the elements of the radical right have adopted it as their badge."

"No, I'm afraid I haven't been keeping up with the *New York Times*, so I didn't know that. But I do know that 'elements of the radical left' "—(he imitated Martin Niles's elitist pronunciation) "—or what *I'd* call Commies, like to burn it, spit on it, and trample it underfoot."

"Well, I won't presume to denigrate your respect for the flag. I only wish to point out that in the present political atmosphere your action smacks not so much of patriotism as of honest, old-fashioned, American bullying."

Mr. Niles then brought up the matter of *Sex Education—or Seduction?* the documentary film Leonard had had screened in the employee lounge and at the Harlan B. Lewissohn Memorial Lunch. Several managers and heads of departments had complained to the New York office about this.

"I'd like to explain," Leonard said.

"Please do."

"You see, Marty, you not living in this community, you couldn't be aware of the danger, which is very real in Atlanta and very immediate. Even here too many people would rather just stick their heads in the sand and leave the problem to the so-called experts. So there was a need to inform the public as rapidly as possible. And the memorial lunch happened to come along at just the right time."

"Leonard, the 'public' you've been educating on these matters consists of at least sixty-three PhDs. There's not a man-jack of them even at middle management level who don't have a year or two of college. They resent you using your authority to shove your opinions down their throats. Opinions with which, I might add, many of them strongly disagree. Perhaps you're not aware of the trouble we had in selling the idea of Atlanta as a modern, progressive, enlightened community. You are making it look like some benighted, redneck company town. Some of the people here are *frightened*."

"With all due respect, that sounds like a step in the right direction—for some of those bastards. I know that sounds harsh, but let me just show you the sort of thing we're trying to combat."

He took out of his breast pocket a frayed, folded piece of paper and handed it to Martin Niles III. Unfolded, it revealed a chaste line-drawing of the uterus, its components neatly lettered and labeled: A. Fallopian tube. B. Ovary. C. Wall. D. Cervix. E. Vagina.

"Well?" Mr. Niles asked.

"Well! That filth is from a textbook that these sex-ucationists are trying to introduce into the high schools of Georgia. There are two possibilities, as I see it. Either perverts have got a hold on the textbook manufacturer—" (he smiled grimly) "—which I wouldn't doubt. Or else it's the familiar Commie ploy of corrupt and conquer. Or both. Probably both, since the Commies know how to bend perverts to their will."

Mr. Niles abandoned his entire armament of flaring nostrils, chin juttings, and arched brows. "You're crazy."

"It's interesting that you should say that, Marty, because the mental health smear is always the weapon of last resort, isn't it? As you may recall, Robert Kennedy tried to use it against General Edwin Walker. A government psychiatrist, who never even examined Walker, declared him 'mentally ill.' We know what *that* means! That was on October the first, 1962. They thought they'd keep him buried for two or three months anyhow, but only eight days later Walker was released. He was just too big for that kind of legal kidnapping. But I'm much smaller fry. Maybe it *would* work on me."

It was like flying. Not the bland, rational flight of a plane, but the heady, darting, wingborn flight of Icarus. Like Icarus too, there was a limit to the altitude he could reach before he was shot down.

Mr. Niles rose. "Leonard," he said equably, "this has been most illuminating."

Closer than this to saying outright that Leonard was fired

Mr. Niles would have found distasteful. Leonard took his meaning as readily as if it had been an ax, and they shook hands on it.

But this was far from being the end, or even the turning point, of the Leonard Dworkin story. His was no tragic fate. He had found in his new way of life a sense of personal freedom and release from self that the blackest, most heavily encrusted leather had never offered him. A Hell's Angel driving in his full regalia down Madison Avenue at lunch hour, dripping with swastikas and black with tattoos, could not have experienced so intensely his own abandoned self-display as did Leonard Dworkin when he addressed a group of his fellow citizens from the courthouse steps of Chester or Good Hope or Lexington, Georgia. The newspapers reported his speeches, and he was photographed, hand on heart, leading the assembled Savannah chapter of the DAR in the Pledge of Allegiance. He could be seen in every attitude of patriotism—kneeling at graves, shaking the hands of soldiers, saluting chiefs of police—and, always, surrounded with flags, swaddled in flags, waving, as it were, from the top of every flagpole in every town in the sovereign and glorious state of Georgia, which, in appreciation of these services, elected him to the House of Representatives of the United States of America in November 1972.

Feathers from the Wings of an Angel

A Prize Story

All night long the cold snow fell on the roof of the tiny little house in Parsons, West Virginia, the house where Tom Wilson lived. In the morning the dazzling heaps of snow were everywhere the eye could see, in the pine trees, on the icy pond, like a gigantic blanket of immaculate purity that covered everything.

Somewhere there might be laughter, somewhere there might be song and merriment, but in the house of Tom Wilson a mother lay dying. Time has scattered the snowy flakes on her brow and plowed deep furrows on her cheek—but is she not beautiful now? The lips are thin and shrunken, but these are the lips that have kissed many a hot tear from childish cheeks, and they are the sweetest cheeks and lips in the world.

While the fleecy white clouds raced past the sun, a man of careworn aspect—it was Tom—wrung his toil-stiffened hands and divided his glances between the dying woman and the little girl asleep in the trundle bed, whose rosebud lips seemed to be touched by a celestial light. What happier days, vanished or still to come, filled her innocent repose with loving dreams? What foreshadowings of an unearthly happiness did she glimpse?

It cannot be that the earth is man's only abiding place! It cannot be that our life is a mere bubble cast up by eternity to float a moment on its waves and then sink back into nothingness! Else why is it that the glorious aspirations which leap like angels from the temple of our heart are forever wandering unsatisfied? Why should the radiant brightness of human beauty be so swiftly taken from us leaving the thousand streams of our affections to flow back in alpine torrents upon our hearts? There must be a realm, somewhere, where the rainbow never fades!

The scene in which these events took place was the homely cottage of a family that has never known splendor or riches, the dwelling of "common" people, and yet it possessed a beauty that many a millionaire would have traveled far to find. The simple pine boards of floor and walls gleamed with a radiance that was not the radiance of gold or silver. The patchwork quilt that the woman clutched every so often to her bosom, repressing the spasms of coughing that her little darling might still sleep and dream, had been sewn by those same hands, oh many years before, and though it was somewhat faded and worn, like herself, it was no less beautiful now than at the moment when it had been only a bright fancy, a vision of butterfly wings and gardens gay with flowers.

Somewhere church bells began to ring, and Tom looked up, like the sleeper who wakes from his dream. Before him on the table lay a stub of pencil and some sheets of lined paper torn from a child's schoolbook. His handsome eyes were darkened by some abiding pain. What thoughts had the tolling of the bell brought to his troubled mind?

The callused fingers, which have known for so many years the honest grip of a miner's drill, picked up the pencil clumsily. Can he hope to set down on paper the tumult of emotions that is in his heart? Biting his lower lip with intense concentration, he began to write:

FEATHERS FROM THE WINGS OF AN ANGEL
A True Story by Tom Wilson

There he paused. The little figure has arisen from the trundle bed and stretched two precious arms in the clear morning light.

Her blue eyes—they were her mother's eyes—turned trustingly to his, and whispering she asked: "Is Mother still asleep?"

Despite the start of pain her innocent question awakened, he answered with a smile. "Yes, my love. We must try and be quiet."

"And will—" (A tear rolled down from one of those blue eyes) "—and will she soon be well again, Poppa? Like she used to be?"

"Yes, my darling, soon she will be much . . . much better."

"Why then, you have the medicine! Oh, Poppa, how happy we shall be!"

Tom shook his head sadly. "No, my love. As I have told you, I cannot get the medicine unless I have money. And—" (His strong voice choked with sobs).

"And there is no work for you. I know."

"Because the mine is closed, you see."

"The mine has been closed so very long, Poppa. When will it open again?"

"Soon, my darling, soon."

The little girl pressed her pale cheek against the single pane of glass that looked out across the snow-jeweled hills. "The window is so cold this morning," she said in a puzzled voice. "As though it had turned to ice."

"It snowed last night, my dear child, and now the window is frosted."

The child sighed. "Ah, the snow! How lovely it must be, all white and gleaming! How I should love to be able to see the snow!"

Then the whole sunless, darkened life of the fair little being came up once again before Tom's mind. All beauty shut from her forever! For her no foliage-strewn, flower-studded scene to follow the bleakness of winter. No looking with awe into the mysterious depths of the night sky, sparkling with glittering, twinkling star-gems. For over those blue eyes the Creator, in the mystery of His designs, had hung the impenetrable veil. No expectant gaze toward the mother's face for the gentlest smile that ever soothes a childish trouble; only the blind passage of the little hand over and over those features, for one moment's sight of which the little one will often, and often willingly, offer years of existence.

And yet to think that sight might be hers! To think that the sun *could* rise to banish that endless night! But if Tom could nowhere find the few dollars that would save the life of his darling's mother, how was he to provide the thousands that were required for the delicate optical surgery? Ah, the torture of these vain hopes! Nevermore must he entertain these painful yearnings!

Unless. . . .

Once again his eyes sought out the printed announcement tacked to the wooden boards of the wall, a page torn from *Life* Magazine. The renowned publication was sponsoring *a story contest*, and the writer of the winning story was to receive a prize of ten thousand dollars.

Ten thousand dollars! It would be enough to provide the very best medical attention for his wife *and* the operation that would restore his daughter's sight.

Tom was no storyteller. He had only one story he could tell, and that was the story of his life. But if he told that story honestly and truly, surely there was a chance that it might win its way to some sympathetic heart? Oh, it was a desperate hope—he knew that—but it was the *only* hope he possessed.

With one more fond glance at the two beings he loved most in the world, Tom once again took up pen and began to set down, in simple heart-felt words . . . the story of his life. At first the words came slowly, and he feared he would never be able to write it all down in time. For the deadline was January 1, and this was . . . yes, this was Christmas morning!

"Tom?" It was the voice of the dying woman, hushed, and yet one knew there was great strength in that voice, and natural dignity.

"Yes, my dear heart?"

"Are you writing the story for that contest?"

"I'm trying to, but I fear I wasn't born to be a writer. There are so many people cleverer than I."

The woman was racked with a deep cough, and then she spoke again. "Tom, you must promise me you'll finish that story and mail it to New York. No matter what happens. Lying here this morning and listening to the church bells, I felt a strange sensation, a feeling I cannot explain. It was as though, somewhere, a wonderful promise had been pledged to me. But I know this. Tom—you must write that story, you *must!*"

Tom nodded, fighting to keep his voice steady. "I promise you, my love. For your dear sake I *will* finish my story."

The woman smiled.

And now the words seemed to pour out onto the paper like a mountain torrent, and, with them, more than a single tear.

The clouded light of another morning was streaming through the magnificent French windows of an elegant penthouse apartment in New York City, where a man and a woman were sitting at a long table laid with silver and fine linen. Nothing could have been more different from the uncalculating simplicity of Tom Wilson's rude home than this abode of wealth, and yet there was a chill in the air of these vast rooms that no central heating devices could ever dispel. It was the chill that settles upon hearts that have forgotten how to love.

The man and woman, both of middle years, sat without speaking. Sometimes the woman would lift her eyes to the man's face, as though about to break the silence, but each time the stern cast of his features prevented her words, and she returned her unhappy gaze to the cup of tea steaming fragrantly before her.

The man was glancing hastily through a pile of papers laid out by his secretary for his attention. What he read in these papers seemed greatly to displease him, for he cast them aside, one after another, with always the same grunt of displeasure. After several such disappointments, he picked up a thick sheaf of papers fastened together with a pin and laughed. "Now, will you look at this!"

The woman glanced up at him expectantly.

"A manuscript handwritten on lined paper! And there isn't even a stamped and self-addressed envelope! Someone must be playing a joke on me." He tossed it at the wastebasket, but it fell short and lay face up on the expensive brocade carpet.

"Aren't you even going to look at it?" the woman inquired.

"If I looked at every manuscript that came in looking like

that, I'd be kept at it till Doomsday." He laughed with chilling cynicism. "There are thousands of stories that come in thus, un-typed, ink-splattered, with errors of grammar. The secretaries are paid good money to weed them out."

The woman sighed. "I suppose you're right. Although—" (her voice dropped to an inaudible whisper) "—it does seem a pity."

The man continued with his work, which seemed to consist of no more than leafing through sheets of neatly typed papers contemptuously and gradually shifting the pile that stood on the right-hand side of his plate to the left hand side. The woman re-mained at the other end of the table, although her tea had grown quite cold in its delicate porcelain cup.

She shivered suddenly, as though the abiding chill of the room had penetrated to her very heart—or *as though a ghostly hand had been lain upon her shoulder*. She lifted her eyes once again to look at her husband's face, and as she did so she glimpsed, floating down in graceful arcs from the ceiling of the room, *two small feathers of dazzling whiteness*. She traced their descent with a bewildered admiration, unable to imagine how these two feathers could have found their way into the dustless, filtered air of her city apartment.

The feathers settled gently on the topmost page of the dis-carded manuscript. The woman arose from the glittering table and approached the papers lying on the carpet.

"Oh, don't bother with that," the man advised, glancing up. "The maid will take care of it."

But the woman stooped down as though she had not heard, and there was something like reverence in this gesture. In just such a way would a woman long unaccustomed to prayer bend her knees and clasp her hands at that moment when the scales have fallen from her eyes. She brushed aside one of the feathers to read the title of the manuscript, and again that same ghostly shiver ran through her.

"Feathers," she whispered softly, "from the wings . . . of an angel." And though it had been many long years since *she* had believed in angels, not indeed since her own dear angel had been taken from her, she began to read.

When she had finished, her eyes were filled with tears. Her

husband was just rising from the table, having expressed his contempt for all writers and everything they had ever written.

She laid the tattered manuscript before him and said, in a voice at once stern and pitying: "My dear, I beseech you, by the love of one who was dearer to you than anyone in this world, do not leave this room until you have read this story."

The man looked up at her strangely, for it was an unspoken rule between them that *that* loss should never be named between them. Then, he began to read.

Many snowfalls had covered the roof of the little cottage in West Virginia, and many times the sun had risen unseen by those blue eyes Tom Wilson held so dear. January had come and gone, and February too. Every day Tom has trudged along the long snow-laden road into town to ask if maybe there is a letter for him today, and each day his only answer is an impatient shake of the head, and when he has asked at the grocer's for credit to buy a bit of flour and lard, he has received the same answer. Each day it is a harder and harder task for a little girl to bring a smile and a word of good cheer to her father's lips, for her innocent heart does not comprehend that to do this she must hide her own tears!

"And was there no mail today, Poppa?" the dear one asked, as she heard the rude door open and felt the icy blast across her withered cheek.

"Not today, my precious, no."

"Surely, then, it will come soon. Last night I dreamed that an answer would come today. Is it wise, do you think, to believe such dreams?"

"If we do not believe our dreams, my pet, there is very little left to believe in."

Even the child could recognize the bitterness concealed in these words, and she could think of no reply. She struggled up from her little bed, where her father made her stay in order to keep warm in the unheated cabin, and found that dear rough hand, which she pressed to her own feverish lips. Tenderly her father wrapped the quilt about her shivering body and sat with her so throughout the long winter afternoon.

At dusk the snow began to fall anew, and Tom rose to prepare a simple supper of cornmeal mush fried in the last of the drippings. There was but a scant inch of meal left at the bottom of the tin. After that was eaten. . . . He dared not think ahead to that dreadful day.

After the frugal supper—the child could not, of course, see that her father ate nothing himself—they resumed their places before the empty fireplace.

"Tell me again, dear Poppa—what shall we do when you have won the contest? Tell me of the lovely clothes I shall wear, and all the wonderful places we will visit together. Tell me of the rainbows and flowers and butterflies I shall see then."

Tom raised his hands to his head, like one distracted, and, all unbidden, a long groan rose from the depth of his being.

"Poppa! Poppa! What is the matter? Surely you do not think that. . . . You read me your story, and it was so beautiful! Surely when the editors at *Life* magazine read it, why then. . . ."

"Do you really believe that, my love?" Tom asked, still unable, despite a mighty effort, to repress a tone of bitterness.

"Mother believes it will, and therefore *we* must."

Tom raised his eyes to the single candle that flickered on the table. "Yes, of course," he agreed in chastened tones. "We *must*."

At the very moment that Tom said this there came a heavy pounding on the door.

"Oh, Poppa! Who can that be? Is it. . . . When I dreamed. . . . No, it must be some wayfarer who has lost his way in the blizzard. How fortunate that he has found his way to our door!"

Tom opened the door to admit a familiar figure in a blue uniform—it was the postmaster! He handed Tom a special delivery letter. Tom opened the envelope with hands that trembled as much from excitement as from hunger, for he knew that this letter would answer all his hopes—or destroy them.

Like some great radiant feather, the check for ten thousand dollars fluttered to the floor, but Tom's attention was fixed upon the letter that accompanied this check.

The letter read:

My dear Mr. Wilson,

My husband, the director of Life magazine, has asked me to write this letter for him to inform you that your story, "Feathers from the Wings of an Angel," has won first place in the Life magazine story contest. I wish to congratulate you on his behalf, but even more, Mr. Wilson, I want to thank you for having awakened in the hearts of my husband and myself—and, I am sure, in the hearts of all future readers in ages to come—an ineffable and enduring sentiment, a pang of yearning sympathy and of a sorrow sweetened by the hope of some future happiness in the beyond.

There may be those who affect more artificial and "advanced" views of life and duty than yours, Mr. Wilson. Among two hundred millions the vast sea of public opinion must be foam-tipped, as well as underlain by ooze and decaying matter, but the mighty depths are crystalline, pure, and unvexed. The judges of the contest have not awarded the prize to you according to arbitrary standards of "literary taste" and deceiving brilliance, but because your true life-story seeks out the latent, earnest emotions of myriads of readers of Life magazine. Your story has heart-value, and heart-value is in the end the supreme test by which men and art must fail or become immortal.

Yours—with love and gratitude,

"A Mother"

Tears fell from Tom Wilson's eyes—tears of happiness and joy.

"Poppa! Poppa! Tell me . . . is it—?"

"Yes, my darling, my own, my dear love, it is! We have won the contest sponsored by *Life,* and you shall live to see . . . to see. . . ."

Tears of sorrow streamed from the face of the blind child. For though she knew that she would live to see many beautiful things, it would never be given to her to see that most beautiful sight of all—a mother's loving smile.

✍ Getting into Death

Part I

1.

Like another Madame Defarge, fat Robin sat there knitting a sweater for her dying mother, who, from her two-hundred-dollar-a-day bed, regarded the pudgy, industrious fingers with a complacent irony. Just so (Cassandra fancied) might an artistocrat, at the height of the Terror, have looked down from his tumbril, then leaned across to the pretty duchess accompanying him to the place of their execution to whisper some pleasantry. But the duchess, distraught, could no more have caught his drift than poor dear Robin could catch hers.

"Anyhow." Cassandra squeezed her little finger into the top of the pack to tickle a crushed Chesterfield loose from the far corner. "To get back to what we were saying."

"Mother. You know you shouldn't."

"It's all right so long as I don't inhale." She lit it, inhaled. "*Anyhow*. You'd think that having to deal continually with the actual physical fact of it would make a difference."

Robin, apart from not giving a hoot for the inner life of undertakers, thought it extremely poor taste for her mother to be forever harping on, of all subjects, this. Death (she believed), like sex, requires circumspection: a fond unspoken understanding, a few unavoidable tears, and then a stoic and polite silence. "*Mother*. Please!"

Cassandra trampled on these finer feelings. "But possibly the people who go into it as a profession have already lost most of their capacity to respond. Like the boy who could feel no fear. What I wonder, though, is—have I?"

"Mother, don't always be *thinking* about it. Goodness!" She shook out the bold zigzags of heather and gold to signify, as in a Noh play, her agitation. In justice to Robin it may be said that she'd begun this particular sweater well before Mrs. Millar's semi-fatal stroke. Whenever she was doing nothing else Robin knitted, and fully half of what she knitted went to her mother. Mrs. Millar's closets and cupboards brimmed with her handiwork, and every room of her Lenox Hill apartment displayed some token of Robin's overwhelming need to please and smother—even the bathrooms, where the spare roll of toilet paper was camouflaged by a crocheted cosy resembling a gay little baby bonnet without any opening for baby's face.

"I'm *not* always thinking about it—that's what worries me. That's what I meant about my being in the same category with undertakers and forensic specialists. Maybe if I'd written poetry all along, instead of murder mysteries, I might be able to face my own death now with some dignity. I'm jaded. I've filled myself with cheap candy, and now that it's dinnertime I have no appetite."

"Would like me to bring in some poetry?" Robin asked, desperate to change the subject.

"No, I've stopped reading."

"You?"

"As part of my preparation. Books can't help me now, can they?"

Robin unrove a course of stitches to where she'd skipped a beat, unrove her benign chatter back to: "Margaret sends her love, did I mention?"

"Margaret can go fuck herself." Mrs. Millar, though not habitually obscene, had always taken a malicious, unmotherlike pleasure in rubbing Robin's nose in these proprieties she'd picked up in god only knew what clandestine Methodist Sunday school.

"She said," Robin continued blandly, "she would have come along with me last Friday, but she didn't think you'd— she thought you'd *rather* have just me. You and she were never exactly pals."

"So what did she want to come here for? To jeer?"

"You know why? I think she feels—" (another flourish of the zigzags, signifying judgment) "—guilty."

Guilty? Margaret, the second Mrs. Millar, was a cocktail pianist at the other end of the George Washington Bridge. Robert had moved on to a third wife long ago, but Robin, then in her junior year of high school, had remained with her stepmother in New Jersey, for which Cassandra had never felt anything but gratitude. "Guilty?" she asked.

2.

She was reading *Remembrance of Things Past*. She had been reading it for seven years, having surmounted the initial barrier of "Combray" during a long visit to Wilmington, Delaware. She was intermittently bored and ravished by this dullest and best of all books and would have finished it long since except that she kept losing copies or leaving them behind in restaurants, in the bathrooms of inaccessible friends, or under a stack of *Newsweeks* at her farmhouse in Vermont.

She was determined to finish it before she died. Whenever she was left alone she'd slog on through the small print of her fourth new Random House edition. She'd reached page four hundred and seventy-eight of volume two and had six hundred and forty-six pages to go. A week? Or less.

Once Proust was taken care of an entire little desert island of masterpieces awaited her in the enamel cupboard beside her bed: Virgil, Cervantes, Rabelais, Montaigne, the Bible.

But not *Clarissa*. She despaired of *Clarissa*, and to that degree she was resigned to her death.

3.

The Catholic chaplain was a smoothly handsome, stupid priest in the preconciliar style of the forties. Any Catholic who'd grown up believing in Bing Crosby could have died comfortably in his muscular arms; but beyond the promise of a prayer he didn't have much to offer Cassandra. He disapproved of her too ecumenical spirit (she had checked off all three possibilities on the hospital's religious information card), and when his Protestant counterpart arrived, the priest committed her to the consolations of *his* religion with evident relief.

Reverend Blake lacked the sex appeal of the Catholic chaplain and was not much more articulate. But he did try. Theologically he seemed to favor a Pauline fundamentalism, redolent of brimstone and redeeming blood, but the severity of his creed was moderated by the hesitance of his manner. His exortations suggested the rote sales pitch of a young man just cured of a speech impediment and liable at any moment to relapse. Whenever he stumbled to a stop, Cassandra would ask another intelligent question about the product, which he would answer dutifully and with great effort. At last he came right out and asked whether she was buying any.

"I'd like to. I really would. It would be such a comfort to be able to believe . . . what you've been saying."

There was apparently an answer to this objection, for he started in again: "Faith is a gift, Mrs. Millar, that's true. But—"

"Yes, I think I do understand the concepts. But I can't feel them—here." She placed her hand, gently, on her defective heart.

The Protestant chaplain bowed his head resignedly, as though he'd been told she already had a set of his company's knives or encyclopedias. Such an objection was unanswerable.

"There is one thing, though. A favor you might do me. Though perhaps you wouldn't care to. I mean it's only curiosity on my part."

"Whatever I can do, Mrs. Millar." He pulled his chair closer to the bed and regarded her suspiciously.

"Are there other people here who—people like me—terminal cases, that is—who *do* believe?"

"Yes, of course. A few."

"Could you tell me something about them?"

Reverend Blake lifted an eyebrow but held his tongue, sensing that a sale might still be possible.

"You could give them different names, of course. For the

protection of the innocent. But I *would* like to know how other people in my situation are taking it. Whether they're mostly afraid or regretful or what. And to know how their feelings change from day to day."

"Mrs. Millar, I'm afraid that would be absolutely. . . ."

"Unprofessional?"

"To say the least."

"But it might be the instrument, you know, of leading me to Christ."

Reverend Blake assured her that he would pray that her heart should be touched and her eyes opened, but he could not, in all conscience, act as her informer. She thanked him, sullenly, and preferred, when he renewed his visit the next day, to be alone.

4.

Cassandra Millar wrote two kinds of books: gothic romances, under the pseudonym of Cassandra Knye, and her "seriouses," the mysteries, thrillers, and Chinese puzzle boxes of B. C. Millar. (The B stood for Bernelle, a name she hadn't answered to since entering the fourth grade of Miss Bennet's School for Girls in Harrisburg.) The gothics, which she wrote with a blithe, teasing contempt for her readers, were far and away the more successful. Five years ago, at the height of the craze for gothics, Signet had reissued eight of the Knye books with uniform covers in murky pastels representing the same windblown, distressed young lady in front of a variety of dark buildings. They went through printing after printing, sweeping along after them her other gothics, scattered among various lesser paperback houses. *Blackthorn* became a movie; *Return to Blackthorn* went to the Literary Guild; and the whole saga, with all five generations, its various family curses and threatened brides, became the basis of a daytime serial on ABC. Cassandra earned literally a million dollars.

By contrast, B. C. Millar seemed barely to scrape along. Most of *her* books were out of print, though they were championed by certain older critics as the chief avatars of the deductive mystery. Her cleverest notions were forever being borrowed by other mystery writers, Miss Knye most notoriously. Once she'd won an Edgar, for *The Imaginary Logarithm*, and one title, *Panic in the Year 1964*, had been an Alternate Selection of the Mystery Guild. Usually, though, she was happy if a book earned back its modest two thousand dollar advance. The sad fact of the matter was that for all the incidental drollnesses, for all the ingenuity of her plots, for all her vaunted irony, B. C. Millar couldn't write. Her characters were wooden, her dialogue false, her prose a solecism. As a stylist, even Cassandra Knye put her to shame. Miss Knye gushed, she fluttered and cooed, but she was, however vulgarly, alive. As much could not be said for B. C. Millar.

5.

She had been put to sleep at her dentist's office, preparatory to a minor filling, and woke in the hospital several hours later. She owed her life, as much as was left, to her dentist's unusual presence of mind, for at the first sign of arrest he'd placed her on the floor and performed external cardiac massage while his receptionist, who was always so rude on the phone, applied mouth-to-mouth resuscitation. By the time a doctor had been called down from the next floor her heartbeat was restored.

When she woke, her own doctor was beside her, Alec Dotsler. She had known him socially and, as B. C. Millar, had consulted him on a variety of medical problems connected with her murders. One of these, *The Purloined Tumor*, had almost amounted to a collaboration. They had had pleasant conversations at parties about the fine points of medical ethics: with whom one must be candid, with whom one may equivocate, and when a lie is all right. Cassandra demanded to know the worst, and three days later she did: the natural flow of her blood, bottlenecked by a critical valve stenosis, would lessen until advanced hypotension produced another and another failure of her heart. Surgery was impossible, drugs useless. When she asked how long she had, he hemmed and hawed, insisted there was no knowing, and gave her, finally, another month. "With luck," he added.

It would be painless.

6.

Laurie Nolde, the stepdaughter she'd acquired by her third marriage, flew in from San Francisco the weekend after Mrs. Millar's admission. She brought a Skippy peanut butter jar of good grass and three wee orange tablets of LSD.

"No, Mom," she said when Cassandra reached for her purse. "This one's on me."

"I call that sentimental."

"Call it my Christmas present." Laurie smiled, and her pale, thin lips became invisible.

Laurie, thanks to her work at Grey Havens, had an affectless, no-nonsense attitude toward death. (Grey Havens rehabilitates the heroin addicts of Haight-Ashbury.) Through their first joint and well into the second she listened tolerantly to her stepmother's account of her difficulties in coming to terms with death, with the *idea* of death.

"Because that's still all it is to me, an idea. Maybe pain is the answer. Maybe instead of just floating off on a breeze, I ought to feel its teeth. Like natural childbirth."

"But you can't ever expect it to make sense."

"Maybe not. But I might be able to fool myself."

"Seriously, Mom." She took the last drag, held up the roach questioningly.

"Just wash it down the sink."

"Seriously." Laurie let out her breath. "You are—" (and took another) "—about as well equipped to die as anyone I ever knew."

"That's very sweet."

"No, I mean it. Think of the life you've had compared to most people. The freedom? The fun? Two loving husbands."

"And Lewis."

"So? How long did that last? A month? What's a month. And Lewis can't be all bad, he's still your agent. Which is another way you've had it easy—money."

She stopped short, as if she'd bitten her tongue. Money was for Laurie what sex or death were for Robin—an unmentionable. She felt the fiercest curiosity to know how much people earned and the rents they paid and where they shopped for clothes, but she would no more have thought of asking such questions than

Robin would have let herself be seen at a church supper reading *Valley of the Dolls*. So, shifting into reverse, she led the conversation (Cassandra being too knocked-out to do anything but follow) from her stepmother's many advantages to her own handicaps (the largest being that she couldn't really "open up"), and thence to the question of whether or not to marry her fiancé. In his favor she cited his correct opinions, good looks, and malleable disposition; on the other hand, he was a loser, though Laurie didn't come right out and say so. But ought that to be a consideration? Laurie wondered; should the future even enter into it? Clearly, she wanted Cassandra to tell her that it should.

"What, to be absolutely cold-blooded, does your true love *do*?"

"Now? He's a dish washer. But before that he made vests, fringed vests. Only, the shop he was making them for went out of business."

"It's the recession," Cassandra said.

"That's what I said. The *ideal* thing would be if he had his own shop somewhere. The restaurant gig is just something he's doing till he qualifies for unemployment." It was an unconvinced apology. Laurie seemed to think it possible her fiancé *liked* to wash dishes.

"You want my advice, you should marry him. Marriage is an art, and one's first husband shouldn't be too difficult. Time enough, once you've learned to handle washers, to move on to earls."

Laurie frowned.

"A pun," Cassandra explained. "I'm very, very high."

Laurie's feelings had been hurt, but she went on anyhow to weigh the pros and cons of her decision. At length, Cassandra was obliged to pretend to fall asleep to be rid of her. She'd never liked Laurie, not since she'd met her as a precociously deflowered sixth grader, but she'd had no better grounds for her dislike than that the girl seemed so often to parody her own never so explicit hedonism. Yet Laurie answered her stepmother's coolness with something approaching affection. She was drawn to Cassandra as to a mirror in which she could see herself thirty years older and still swinging, still balling, still rolling along; and still, for a wonder, worth looking at.

7.

Every night she would wake up between three and four and not be able to get back to sleep till dawn. Her condition prohibited the use of barbituates, and the night nurse prohibited reading. What better time to think of death? *Death*, she thought. *I am dying.* As well might she have told herself she was in love, or mad. Was *this* a form of defiance? or resignation? or only incredulity?

She tried to picture her own body decaying in the grave, all wormy and forlorn. Nothing.

She tried to think of the spaces between the stars, of timelessness and nonexistence. But such notions affected her no more than stories of the war in India.

Finally she gave up trying and did what she had always done on nights of insomnia: she plotted new mysteries.

8.

Rabbi Yudkin took the Bible out of the enamel cupboard and found the passage in question. Ezekiel 18; 32: *For I have no pleasure in the death of him that dieth, saith the Lord God; wherefore turn yourselves, and live ye.*

"Turn yourselves and live: for my money that's the last word on the subject."

Mrs. Millar appeared to doubt this. "Perhaps. But a person in my circumstances may have some difficulty applying such advice."

"Some people might, but *you're* not doing so badly."

She thought for a moment he was being sarcastic about her having begun a story. But no, it was only his style of comfort. She neither disputed the compliment nor dug for another. Instead she asked after Mrs. Hyman in ward D. Mrs. Hyman, after a life lived unexceptionally on the surface of Scarsdale, was suffering a death of exemplary anguish. Seedlings of cancer swarmed through her flesh, blossoming everywhere into pain. She wept for the doctors, screamed at her husband, abased herself to Rabbi

Yudkin, denouncing herself, her family, the hospital, God. It was Tolstoyan, and Cassandra envied Mrs. Hyman's least kneejerk of dread. She questioned the Jewish chaplain about her interminably, both as to her suburban past and her daily progress toward their common goal.

9.

She blatted out the story in two days. It was about the widow of a famous writer (Hemingway, though she had to disguise that) who persuades one of the master's least competent imitators to forge a series of posthumous novels which the widow releases year after year to her own great profit and the annihilation of the writer's reputation. All done, including the widow's comeuppance, in two tidy scenes that came out, reasonably, at four thousand words.

Lewis phoned to say (what else could he?) that "Revenge" was the drollest thing she'd ever done. He was sure that the *New Yorker* would take it. She'd never sold a word to the *New Yorker*, and she never would. As well might she lust for Cary Grant.

10.

A letter arrived from her father, who had moved to Arizona to escape the pathos of the seasons. He excused himself from attending her deathbed. "But," she wanted to say, "I didn't *invite* you." Aside from the condescension of her Christmas checks (always cashed and never acknowledged), she'd had little to do with him since he'd ridden off fifteen years ago into the sunset. Robin, it must have been, who'd informed him, convinced the old man would veil his malice decently before so major an institution as death. In this Robin had underestimated the strength of her grandfather's character. His letter, scrawled on the back of a humorous greeting card ("Get Well Soon/—Or Else!"), stopped just short of overt self-congratulation. He was sending her, but not by air, an inspiring book by Smiley Blanton.

The letter ended: "Yours sincerely, Uylsses Barlowe." "Sincerely" was underlined.

It was some comfort to think she'd never been trapped into caring for the old bastard. Twice as B. C. Millar and once as Cassandra Knye she'd had the satisfaction of killing him off in books that had detailed his minor crookednesses as a justice of the peace and his larger connivings in the capitol at Harrisburg. She would have liked, for a last fling, to tear into him again, but there was no help for it now. She was forgiven; *he* had the last laugh.

11.

Except in *The Seventh Codicil*, which was a virtual textbook of testamentary law, B. C. Millar had always rather scanted wills as motives for her murders. Cassandra Knye had necessarily more to do with legacies, entails, and such, but even for her these matters had been only so much gothic lumber, in a class with secret passages, mute servants, and mysterious footsteps.

But now, ah! Now she had actually to write her own. Her money would become someone else's. Her money, which she'd meant to spend on jewelry and geriatric treatments! Here was occasion for an elegy. People were no more than the compost in which dollars grew, ripened, fell, and grew again.

Despite his most plausible arguments, she couldn't bring herself to sign the model document her lawyer had drawn up. Half a million dollars to Robin? Inconceivable! Trust funds for nieces, for nephews, for second cousins?

But who or what else should she lavish herself upon? Ex-husbands? Charities? Some foundation, like Shaw's, to advance some freakish cause of her own.

"Couldn't I just give it *all* to the government?" she pleaded.

Mr. Saunders shook his head.

Finally she came up with a formula that satisfied both herself and him. All three hundred and forty-nine names on her last year's Christmas card list were to receive absolutely equal shares in her estate. This would give each heir a little less than four thousand dollars. Robin was to get, additionally, the farmhouse in Vermont and its furnishings.

Mr. Saunders called the next morning to ask: "The Lenox Hill Liquor Store?"

"Yes, they've always been very nice to me there. Cashing my checks. And every year they send me a calendar."

"Is there a particular person there?"

"Oh, I see what you mean. No, divide it up."

"And at Doubleday's, is it Miss Bergen, or Berger? The letter is typed over on the list."

"Who?"

"Bergen. Or Berger."

"I don't think I can remember any such creature at Doubleday's. Maybe you should call them."

"I did. There's one of each, and both are editors."

"Well, if it's going to hold things up, let's give them both a share."

The will ran to forty pages. She signed it, and Mr. Saunders and Dr. Dotsler were witnesses.

12.

From her notebook:

THE DEATH TAX
(or "Death and Taxes"?)

An old woman dying, her family gather in next room, wait for her to be off. Then error is discovered in payment of "death tax." She can't die until her sons have cleared this up at appropriate government office. Much hugger-mugger with red tape, rubber stamps, old birth certificates, etc.

Italy?

13.

Rabbi Yudkin asked how she had passed the night.

"With the Godzilla of all nightmares. Usually I don't remember what I dream, but this one—oh, boy!"

"Shall I interpret it for you? As I think I told you, my first vocation was to psychoanalysis, but my parents didn't have money to send me to med school."

"Here it is, then. But first I have to explain that back when I started writing for the pulps I used to go to this special dentist, who worshiped writers, Dr. Blitzman. I found out about him through my first husband, who was one half of Bud Dorn. The Western writer? My teeth were in horrible shape, and I'd go in once a week, for months it seemed, and he'd drill a well in one of my teeth and then while my filling dried he'd give me one of his manuscripts. There he was, a perfectly happy successful dentist, and the only thing he wanted to do was to sell a love story to the *Saturday Evening Post*. I'd read his manuscript, and then when my mouth was rinsed out I'd give my professional opinion. Which was that his story was promising, but like my mouth it still needed work. I still have some of the same fillings, but he's dead now."

"That was your dream? Or reality?"

"Reality, but the dream didn't add much. I was back in Blitzman's office, in his chair, with these clamps in my mouth to keep me from closing it, and he was reading me this absolutely terrifying story. Aloud. I'd had Novocaine, and my whole body, everything, was numb, except I could still feel the saliva drooling out of the side of my mouth."

"And what was the story about that he read to you?"

"That I don't remember."

She reached for her Chesterfields. Yudkin looked askance.

"Turn yourselves therefore and live ye," she reminded him. "And anyhow I don't inhale."

Yudkin's interpretation of the dream was straightforward, uninteresting, and probable. The dentist represented Death, which Mrs. Millar feared. Death was the undiscovered country from whose bourne no traveler returns, and therefore she couldn't remember what happened in the dentist's story.

Cassandra agreed without a trace of sarcasm that she might very well be afraid of death. Then she asked after Mrs. Hyman, who had developed a last-minute enthusiasm for spiritualism. Each morning a medium visited ward D to help her get in contact with the other side. They'd reached a spirit called Natalie, who was to be Mrs. Hyman's guide once she entered the spirit world.

"Does it help?" Cassandra asked.

"More than I ever seemed to. Would *you* like to try it?"

"Not yet, no. When I'm riper, perhaps." She winked to make it clear that she was joking.

Part II

1.

Within moments of her swallowing the acid there was a tapping on the door, a wee small "shave and a haircut, two bits," like a mouse coming to visit a rabbit. Who could it be at eight o'clock of a Wednesday morning? Who but Robin?

The knob turned. She closed her eyes, forgetting to remove the sunglasses, and composed her hands, deathwise, across her breasts. Mysterious footsteps entered the room.

I am asleep, she thought determinedly (yet without crinkling), and must on no account be awakened.

The footsteps went here and there, filled a jug at the sink, sat in the sighing vinyl chair, and gave up. When the latch clicked shut, she opened her eyes, and there on the dresser, doubled by the mirror, was a massive bouquet of long-stemmed red roses. Who in the world? she wondered, and decided it must have been one of her two Bobs—Millar or Nolde—since roses were so explicitly a sexual attention.

She slipped on her mules and shuffled to the dresser. The card said only: "Best wishes. Ira Seidemann."

Ira Seidemann?

Then it connected: her dentist, Dr. Seidemann. Not only had he saved her life, but he must have spent no less than fifty dollars for all those roses! Cassandra was flabbergasted.

2.

Page 789.

335 pages left.

The *Remembrance* was a long train ride through provincial France, a lulling orderly journey with an occasional glimpse of some astonishing artifact: a cathedral spire, a Roman aqueduct, an avenue of trees extending, like hexameters, all the way to the horizon; then for half an hour nothing but wastes of mud, gray farms, rows of cabbages.

She'd forged ahead ten more pages before her marigold bookmark became more interestng than Proust's prose.

"Heigh-ho!"

The roses nodded in their silly vase. *Yes*, they were thinking, *here we go!*

3.

Against the glory of dying young, any living thirty-year-old must appear as drab as the fashions of five years ago. So there was much *Weltschmerz* (a boistrous poignance, like a college reunion) in listening to the "Sgt. Pepper" tape and thinking back to the balmy days just after she'd run out on dear decrepit Nolde. Cassandra at least possessed the satisfaction of mourning a *second* youth.

The Beatles, however, were only to be the cheese dip before a full formal banquet of Beethoven, Mahler, and Bach. But of all this sublimity she heard but one single, strangulated groan, as her tape machine, a brand new Webcor from Lafayette, gobbled up the first few yards of *"Das Lied von der Erde"* and stopped. The reverse button didn't do anything and the forward button added more tape to the snarl until, having created a giant chrysanthemum-style bow, nothing would budge. The same fate met *"O Ewigkeit, du Donnerwort,"* and *"Gottes Zeit ist die allerbeste Zeit."*

Her trip lay ahead of her like a desert without a camel, a portion without an outline, Shit Creek without a paddle.

4.

As an aid to levelheadedness she put on pantyhose, a bra, a blouse, and her tweedy authorish suit from The Tailored Woman.

Looking at herself through the roses (roses!) she felt as neat and crisp as a parenthesis. Here was the one and only Cassandra Millar, back in her clothes and immortal as ever. Death? A pink night-gown crumpled on a tape recorder.

5.

High winds rasped wisps of Persian from the edges of dream-sicle clouds that rode eastward against the current of the sunlight. The poems disintegrated, line by line, into the tense, the trembling element. It is the air that one sees. That is blue. Whereas the sky is black.

A single bird flew up from the parking lot. And up!

Nature.

6.

The nurse, leaving, had left the door ajar, and bits of talk snagged on the thorns of Cassandra's voracious attention. A numinous veal chop and broccoli warred with the roses. A wedge of noonday light, aswarm with motes of dust, was spread across the foot of the mussed, empty bed. She, the focus of all these data, sat on the visitor's chair, and thought:

Death will be like this. Death is what people talk about when one leaves the room: not oneself, not the vanished, pitiable Albertine, but *their* business and appetites. They could care less who *we* slept with in our time.

She sat so still and listened so intently, for a little while, that she fancied she might be dead already; a whimsy.

7.

She got the window open, and the colder outdoor air swept in and filled the room with messages. Her skin turned to Coca-Cola. She took the jacket off. Sunglasses. The shivering blouse.

Rings and hairpins. Ishtar at apogee. She closed the window, the door, the eyes, and let her living fingers feel, falling back across the bed, her self. She peeled back the calyx of her pantyhose and headed straight for the source. Her fingers pressed past petal after petal like Fabergé bees whose wings (rose-enameled nails) whirred and beat against and bruised the delighted, anguished flower. It was everything magnificent, but even as the twenty-eight flavors spilled and flickered over the top of the opal dam she had enough irony left (she always did) to think, Now more than *ever* seems it rich to die!

8.

Once she'd started on this bowl of heavenly popcorn she couldn't stop, though even as Pelion was heaped on Ossa she sensed that she was missing the boat. Her previous trips (three with Leary himself) had been models of goal-oriented ecstasy, cornucopias of awareness. Finally, forlornly, she looked about her tumbled bedclothes and saw—

Imagine some dumb widow who's just blown all the insurance money on a suite of shoddy furniture and a fake-fur coat. Imagine her entering her living room a year later and looking in the mirror. The gilding of the stucco frame is turning brown. The so-called mink is shedding. There's no chance now to take that secretarial course. And the money's gone. What does she think? Cassandra experienced an analogous regret.

So when Robin came tap tappy-tap-tap, tap tapping on the door it was like the Marshall Plan coming to the rescue of a devastated Europe.

"Who is it?" she asked.

"Me. Robin."

"Oh, Robin, I'm all sticky. What I mean is, not now, darling. Come back at, what time is it now?"

"Three-thirty."

"At four. Okay? Or four-thirty."

"Okay. But."

"Yes?"

"I brought you some books. From your apartment. They're awfully heavy. Can't I just—" (as she asked, the door peeped open and a Bloomingdale's shopping bag crept into the room) "—slip them inside?"

Robin had brought her all the poetry she owned.

9.

"Yes," Yudkin said, "I've read several of them. *The Castle and the Key*. And the one with the Nazi general disguised as his own grandmother."

"You mean *The House That Fear Built*."

"That was a real shocker, that one."

"But those are all by Cassandra Knye. I don't count them as *my* books."

"I've read some of the others too, but I guess I prefer the more romantic ones. Most people do, don't they? Mrs. Hyman, for instance—when she heard that Cassandra Knye was right here in the same hospital, you should have seen the expression on her face. I didn't tell her your real name, of course, but that only added to the glamour of it."

"Mrs. Hyman?"

"She's read everything Cassandra Knye has ever written. In fact, the reason I brought this up, she asked me if you'd sign a copy of one of your books for her. I have it here." He took a battered, book club edition of *Blackthorn* from his briefcase. "You're laughing. At Mrs. Hyman? At me?"

It was a pantomime rather than real, physiological laughter. She opened the book to the flyleaf, thought a moment, and wrote: "To Mrs. Hyman, Till we meet soon, in those Gardens where the summer never fades, please accept my very heartfelt best wishes—and say a prayer for—Cassandra Knye."

Yudkin read the inscription. "Oh, she'll treasure that."

"It's not too much?"

"Too much?" he asked, as if this were an oxymoron. "Oh, not for Mrs. Hyman." Then, furrowing his brow and deepening his voice from light social to medium serious: "Have you ever thought

why it is that most readers do prefer the one kind of book—
'gothics,' you call them?—to the other? Oh, I know you'll say because most people are stupid—"

No: she shook her head violently. He was right. "Oh, I
wouldn't."

"—and that may be half of it. We're all like my own children
in a way. When they know they like a story they want to hear it
over and over. Which must lead you writers to writing things to a
kind of formula. But why this—" (He tapped the spine of *Blackthorn*) "—particular formula rather than the one that *you* like,
the detective formula?"

"What Lewis says—my agent, Lewis Whitman—is that the
reason my mysteries don't catch on is that I don't have a con-
sistent point of view. I can't invent a detective that anybody cares
about, that *I* care about. They're like computers. In fact, one of
the books I'll never write now was going to have the murder
solved by a computer. Whereas I *can* invent a believable victim.
A gothic is almost the reverse image of a mystery. Instead of some
brilliant Sherlock Holmes pouncing on each little clue, what you
want is some pretty featherhead like Nan Richmond who can *miss*
all of them. The plot is set up so that no matter how thick the
readers may be, the heroine is a little thicker. Oh, excuse me, I
didn't mean to say—"

Yudkin waved the apology aside. "All that may be so, but I
think it leaves the essential thing unaccounted for. People read
Cassandra Knye to be frightened. The scene at the end of this
one, for instance, where Nan is dancing with her nephew out on
the dark terrace: terrifying. But I don't see why it should be. She
isn't in any immediate danger. Why should—"

Suddenly there came a tapping.

Robin entered in her big brown bag of a coat and began at
once to leave. "I didn't mean to interrupt."

Yudkin insisted *he* was leaving, and Cassandra, rescued in the
nick of time from having to explain the danger that Nan had
been in, made no effort to keep him by her bedside.

Robin asked after her mother's health today relative to yesterday, admired the roses, and sat down to work on the sweater,
which only wanted one sleeve to be complete.

10.

Underpinning Cassandra Knye's practice was a theory that women regard sex with a fear so overmastering that it can only reach consciousness disguised as a rational and seemly terror of death. This hypothesis seemed strengthened with each successive success of the books based on it, until, with the triumph of *Blackthorn* (the plot of which was based on the summary of Tyce's classic study of patterns of endogamy and exogamy evidenced in the fantasies of one hundred twenty female inmates in a Des Moines mental hospital), she felt as secure of her theory as any Ptolemy.

But now (six-thirty of that same Wednesday), as she stirred the hospital's notion of chicken chow mein around and around and around, it occurred to her that there might be a Copernican alternative that would fit all the facts just as well.

Death, it must be allowed, is a natural metaphor for the act of love; it represents the loss of one's ultimate cherry. Just as virgins are forever pondering what it would be like to go all the way, so the living try (with no better success) to imagine death. From this similitude proceed millennia of romances: Ariadne mistaking Bacchus for Dis; the less fortunate confusions of Tristan and Isolde, of Romeo and Juliet, of Byron, Keats, and Shelley; and, last and least, the potboilers of Cassandra Knye.

But couldn't it just as well be the case that Cassandra, by convincing herself that she was writing about sex, had been enabled to deal with the subject that actually terrified her? that actually *is* terrifying? After the bridal night and a bit of practice, most of us may come to terms with love, but death remains a mystery. We think we hear him walking in the corridor, but when we open the door it's only Midnight playing with a ball of yarn. We think he's at the window, but when we go there his rapping proves to be a dry branch tossing in the wind. Yet he is there, in the shadows, waiting to cut in and waltz us out onto the dark terrace, whirling us about, like leaves. And we know what he intends, then.

These were such pretty ideas and so capable of development that Cassandra longed to have someone at hand who thought at her own speed. She called Lewis, but his answering service had no idea where he was. When she phoned his other number, no one answered.

11.

Robin returned with four cartons of real Chinese food from Woh Ping and cold beer from a deli. They ate voraciously, praising the food and making toasts, when they'd slowed down, to the great meals of yesteryear: the holiday dinners and home-cooked pies of the forties; from the fifties (when the money first started coming in) their extravaganzas at restaurants on Robin's weekend visits into the city; crowning all these, the glories of Robin's own devising now she was grown up with a kitchen all her own—the creamed mushroom omelettes and shrimps polonaise, the sweetbreads and shortcakes, the crêpes and souflées.

Robin began to cry.

"Robin!"

"I'm sorry. But it's just—so awful." She swallowed, took a sip of beer to help it down, and smiled a ghastly smile. "There— all better."

"Darling, what is it?" (Had the fact of her death, her inevitable death, finally broached Robin's defenses?)

Robin denied that it was anything.

"Tell me and you'll feel better."

After further cajoling, Robin confessed that their talk of food had upset her. "I know other people find it offensive. No, don't say they don't. They do. And I just—" She shook her head dismally. "You see, I *want* to stop, I try to, but—I go a day, two days, and then it comes over me. Like another person takes control. And then afterward I just hate myself. I feel so awful. I mean physically I feel awful."

It developed, after more tears, that Robin had tried to become a nurse, had even been accepted into a school—conditional upon her losing fifty pounds. Since her acceptance she'd gained fifteen.

"I've never heard of anything so cruel and . . . preposterous! Why didn't you tell me before? I'm sure we could have found another school. I'm sure we still can. What you weigh, Robin, is a matter for your own—" ("conscience"? decidedly not) "—for *you* to decide."

"No, Mother, they were right. I'm dangerously overweight. And anyhow, that's all in the past. I'm happy with the job I've got. I wouldn't want to be a nurse now. It's only coming *here* every day, walking through the corridors, and seeing all of them, seeing the way they look at me."

This confession was the prelude to the whole, woeful story. Robin was in love. The man was married; his wife was Robin's best friend (they'd met at Weight Watchers); all three of them were wretched.

Cassandra was aghast, never having imagined any other existence for Robin than this, in which she ate, played cards, knitted socks, and paid visits to her mother, who (this seemed to have been the understanding) had been the source of whatever was actual, vivid, and passionally alive in the diminished family of mother and daughter; a mistake.

12.

From her notebook:

Murder Mystery to be told from the point of view of the corpse. Someone like Mrs. Hyman, very acrimonious, bitter. Doesn't know who murdered her: *Victim is Detective!* Pov limited to room in which she's been killed (visual) and immediately adjacent rooms (audio) where police question suspects. She's suspicious of everyone, shocked by their revelations about herself. Gradually learns to free herself of "fleshly bonds." (Research: spiritualism, auras, out-of-body exp., planes of spirit existence.) By the time she's solved the murder, she's able to forgive murderer. Who?

13.

She dreamed that night again of a dentist's office. Not Blitzman's; a dentist long before—Dr. Skutt, who'd extracted her baby teeth in Wilmington and signed her first dental cards. Dr. Skutt had been a harelip, and from her first visit to him at the age of eight she'd had an obscure sense of consonancy between the man's defect and his occupation, as though he were revenging himself on other people's mouths for the horror of his own.

In the dream, she was strapped to Skutt's dental chair, and he was pleading with her to open her mouth. She refused.

He showed her the little mirror on its long silver handle. "Please, open up now, Bernelle. I only want to *look*."

Still she refused, and his anger rose from his tense fingers to his gray eyes. He bent nearer, insisting, and nearer till his lips met her own. But still she kept her jaw clamped tight shut. Skutt's tongue pressed hard against her rotted teeth, which splintered, crumbled, and collapsed.

Part III

1.

Having lived two days beyond her allotted month, Cassandra developed a cursory interest in the actual mechanical processes of her disintegration and sent Robin on a reluctant errand to fetch the relevant medical books from her apartment.

Robin left the sweater behind. It was finished but for the cuff of the left arm, which hung limply over the top of the knitting bag like the stump of some unfortunate creature who'd tried to climb into a full lifeboat. Cassandra held back as long as she could. Then she got out of bed (by now, no mean accomplishment) and, after first wiggling the needles from their loops, unraveled the sleeve back to the elbow.

Robin, on returning, made no mention of this vandalism. Loop by loop, she fit the needles into the right courses; then, patient as a spider, she began to knit again.

2.

The next morning she altogether neglected Proust for the sake of B. B. Milstein's *Cardiac Arrest and Resuscitation*. Milstein told of case after case—"a woman of 53," "a man of 64," and even "a child of 6"—whose hearts had stopped or gone into spasms. Often a thoracotomy was performed to enable the surgeon to reach into the chest and massage the heart, either directly or through its pericardial sac. The various steps of what would very likely be done, next time, to Cassandra were illustrated in photographs: the thoracotomy incision, a cleft running from midchest all the way round to the back; next, the surgeon opening the incision forcibly, with the same strenuous grip one exerts against the halves of a subway door that's trapped one's foot; lastly, the actual process of massage, with the heart, a small glistening thing no bigger than a medium-sized green pepper, resting in the surgeon's fingers. She pored over these few pictures with the same awed satisfaction she'd felt long ago in the Wilmington library riffling through travel books and *National Geographics* for glimpses of beggars and holy men on the other side of the world, where elephantiasis and the worship of god were able to transform human beings into something wonderfully else.

As fascinating, if not as affecting, as these photographs were the case histories. Case Twenty-seven, especially; a fifty-three-year-old woman whose heartbeat was restored after fully five minutes of massage. Thirty-six hours after the operation she awoke demented, the result of anoxic brain damage. She could remember only her childhood and, when asked to sign her name, wrote her maiden name in a childlike scrawl. She thought the medical staff were policemen and could hear sea lions outside her room.

Cassandra could face the prospect of sea lions bravely, not to say eagerly. About a second childhood she wasn't so sure. She dreaded the diminution of her intelligence and would much rather have been dead than stupid and an object of pity to the likes even of a Mrs. Hyman.

3.

Since her dream about Dr. Skutt on the night of her trip she felt she'd done her duty by self-awareness. The dream proved that she was terrified of death. If that terror were not always at the forefront of consciousness, so much the better. She could relax, happy in the knowledge that at least once she'd made an appropriate emotional response to her death.

She'd recounted the dream to everyone: to Dotsler, Yudkin, Robin; to the nurses; to anyone who phoned. They'd all agreed that it was terrifying and, with the exception of Yudkin, urged her to forget it.

4.

Even now, every time she opened a package of cigarettes, she felt a twinge of guilt. Since the publication of the Surgeon General's report in 1964, Cassandra had swayed reedlike in the opposing winds of appetite and moral resolve. One of B. C. Millar's last books, *Death in Its Holiday Package,* had been a veritable tract against cigarette smoking. All the while she was writing it she'd smoked two packs a day.

5.

Cassandra looked at her lunch. She felt as though she'd been flying back and forth across the Atlantic endlessly, never getting off the plane, and eating the same mild meal day after day, mile after mile, like one of the poor vultures condemned to dine on Prometheus' liver.

That afternoon (the seventh day of her second month in the hospital) she began working on *The Dead Detective.*

6.

"It really was," Yudkin said, " a beautiful death."

"Really?"

"Really. And to be perfectly honest, I was surprised."

"It was lucky you happened to be there then."

"Lucky for me, perhaps. Such moments are my chief reward.

Not that I can take any of the credit for *her* good death. But just the knowledge that it's possible—that's something."

"It happened this morning?"

"A little before eight. Ward D faces the river, so that the early light is direct and very intense. The explanation may be as simple as that."

"And what did she say?" Cassandra asked once again.

" 'The light! The light is blinding.' "

"It *sounds* like she may have wanted you to lower the blinds."

"But she was smiling so as she said it. A smile like—well, I can't describe it."

For the rest of the day Cassandra felt alone and slightly panicky. She'd come to depend on Mrs. Hyman in so many little ways. Her hysteria and credulity were the foils to Cassandra's own coolness and rationality. All of her anguished writhings, as Yudkin had reported them to her daily, had been an admonishment not to go off down the same steep road herself. It galled her that Mrs. Hyman, who'd actually had some hope of recovering, should beat her to the exit; it was insufferable that she should do so with such panache. "The light!" indeed! she thought grimly. Who did Mrs. Hyman think she was? Goethe? Little Nell?

7.

There was nothing, next morning, in the paper. Mr. Hyman was a prominent toy manufacturer on 31st Street: surely his wife's death rated a mention in the *Times,* if only her name and age and whom she was survived by. Cassandra herself was counting on four column inches, and though Mrs. Hyman couldn't have asked for as much as that, this total neglect seemed tantamount to being left unburied, out on a dung heap, like Antigone's brother.

Later, when the aide came in to change her sheets, she asked her, "Miss Rooker, do you aides only work in one ward at a time? Or do you get assigned to all different parts of the hospital?"

"Sure," Miss Rooker said, with a warm smile.

"What I want to know, dear, is if you've worked, lately, in ward D."

"Ward D?"

"Yes. What I'd like to know is this: which way does it face? Does it face *east* to the river? Or *west* into the city?"

Miss Rooker paused amidst her sheets to think. "I'm sorry, all the different floors and letters, they get jumbled up. And I don't go up into that area too often."

"Then you wouldn't know the friend of mine who's there— Mrs. Hyman?"

"In ward D?"

Cassandra nodded.

"Not in ward D, I don't think." She affected to giggle. "Ward D is for all the old gentlemen, the ones who can't take care of themselves. There aren't any women there."

8.

Rabbi Yudkin was not to be blamed for having invented Mrs. Hyman (hadn't she almost demanded it of him?)—only for having allowed his audience at the high point of his tale to fall into disbelief. Her death had been too nice, too merely decorative. If only he'd baited his transcendental hook with some engaging, toothsome detail, Cassandra might never have thought to doubt his story. If, for instance, toward the end Mrs. Hyman had tried to destroy her charge-a-plate, or got the hiccoughs, like Pope Pius XII. But to bathe her in that blinding light, to have practically sent down a ladder to her from on high! That showed a want of tact.

9.

She had phoned down to the cashier's office, and, when Yudkin called by for his afternoon chat, she was ready for him.

"When is the funeral?" she asked.

"Not till Friday."

"Here? Or in Scarsdale?"

"In Scarsdale. It will probably be quite a production. Mr. Hyman seems to be in his element again, organizing things."

Cassandra beckoned Yudkin closer to her bed. "Here," she said, pressing the envelope into his hand. "I want you to do a favor for me. A little deception."

He looked doubtful.

"A wreath. I want to send her the very best wreath you can get."

"Oh. But."

"The card needn't say any more than—'With sincere sympathy, Cassandra Knye.' "

"Impossible. I mean—" He looked into the envelope. "Oh, Mrs. Millar, this is far too much!"

"For a wreath? Nonsense. I called a florist and asked. And don't try and tell me they don't want flowers. I know Scarsdale!"

"But—"

He was caught. Either he'd have to admit that Mrs. Hyman didn't exist, or he'd have to take the money.

"I would have sent the wreath myself, but then, you see, they might have been able to trace it back to *me*. I want to be the person I always love in a story—the anonymous benefactor. And I know I can count on you to preserve my pseudonym. But if there's some reason you'd rather not, I *could* get Robin to send it."

"No! No, I just questioned the—" He held up the bulging envelope.

"The propriety of it?"

"Yes. To be frank."

"But it isn't really disproportionate when you think of all I've got. Oh, say you'll do it."

Yudkin wavered, sighed, and pocketed the envelope.

"I knew you would." She leaned forward in the bed and pinched his cheek. "If you could *see* the way you're blushing!"

10.

She'd made her pile by telling people what they seemed to want to hear—that Death was a gentleman whose kisses were gentle even as he threatened rape, that one may venture out onto the terrace with him and come back (a bit sadder, a bit wiser, but intact) to the party. In fact, there are no survivors of that waltz, and so the heart of every one of her books had been a lie, her latest, *The Dead Detective*, being the most whopping of them all.

But what of that? Her readers had wanted it, and now at last she wanted it too. For Yudkin had invented Mrs. Hyman in response to her expressed, her almost strident need, and Cassandra had been his more than willing dupe. She wanted no further knowledge of *real* people, of how they were cheated, cornered, betrayed, ignored, and themselves driven to cheat, entrap, and betray in turn. She could have killed Robin for reminding her of the processes of love—the anguish of being rejected, the guilt of rejecting, the desolations of loneliness. No, she craved fiction. "Reality," as one of her old buttons had proclaimed, "is a crutch." If this were a lie, well then, she needed what help she could get.

And so did everyone.

Yudkin had done the right thing. He'd told the lie his duty had demanded and persisted in it, even at the expense of self-respect.

Cassandra could do no less.

11.

That same afternoon she contacted Mr. Saunders to revoke her first will and have him bring in his model document, which he did that evening.

To her father she wrote a rich, ripe heartthrob of a letter, telling him what, in the last analysis, a wonderful father he had been, and how much, at bottom, she'd always loved him.

Then she wrote to both Bobs (identical letters) along the same bittersweet lines, though tempering the language to their more discriminating tastes. She couldn't think of any plausible tale to tell Lewis except that he had a wonderful mind and she loved him.

She phoned Laurie to reveal what she'd so desperately tried to ferret out on her visit to New York—how much she was coming in for from her stepmother's will. Had the Christmas tree in Rockefeller Center collapsed on her, Laurie could not have been crushed by any larger happiness. Her whole life, she swore, would be changed.

But letters and phone calls were easy. Forthright, uncomplicated plagiarisms from The Best-Loved Lies of the American People. The real test would be Robin, who, for all her prissy pieties and pretended deafnesses, was her mother's sternest audience and cruelest judge.

12.

In the summer of '45 Bob and Cassandra and Robin and Bob's cousin Margaret Millar had all driven west in a Kaiser station wagon to see the actual country Bob had been writing about all these years. The culmination of the many misadventures of the trip came when Bob and Margaret contrived to be lost for four days in Grand Canyon National Park, leaving Cassandra with Robin, the dying Kaiser, and eight dollars. At that time Cassandra had been a haggard twenty-six, Margaret a dazzling nineteen.

Time and affluence had improved Cassandra; the same amount of time and too much liquor had made of the second Mrs. Millar a shipwreck of her former self. Conscious of their reversed fortunes and without considering that they were about to be reversed again, Margaret was abjectly complimentary. How wonderful Cassandra looked! What a lovely negligee! How lucky she was to have a private room!

"When *I* was in the hospital," she said, "I was in the general ward. With all these colored women? You can imagine what *that* was like. Hackensack! But this! This is more like a hotel room than a hospital. The furniture! Though you would think for what you're paying you'd have a room with a view to the river. Still it's not a *bad* view. In fact, it's nice."

"Would you like a cigarette?" Cassandra asked.

"I shouldn't. But thank you, I will." The knuckles of Margaret's hand were swollen, the flesh puffy, the skin coarse. To think she was still able to play the piano! "Chesterfields! You don't see many of them nowadays."

"No, you don't. Bob used to smoke Chesterfields. I must have picked it up from him."

This was the first mention of his name since Margaret had come in the door twenty minutes ago.

"Do you hear from him?" Margaret asked.

"Not often. He lives in London. And he's married again. But that's old news by now."

Margaret screaked with laughter. "Always the gay Lothario!"

It was her chance. "Yes," she said softly, "he was that."

Margaret, who had prepared herself to unite with Cassandra in vilifying their ex-husband, was dismayed now to hear him so eloquently praised, so candidly cherished. Cassandra wanted (she said) only to remember what had been good and live and warm and tender: the laughter they had shared, the growing and deepening sense of mutual discovery, the love. But who could describe love? One could only experience it.

"You loved him too, didn't you?" she said, catching hold of Margaret's hand as soon as she'd stubbed out the cigarette. "Oh, of course you did! How could you have helped it? How could I?"

Margaret tried, gently, to pry her hand away. (It was such an ugly hand.) "But I always thought—"

"That I was jealous? Oh, at first I may have been. But how could I have gone on feeling like that after all you've done for me? You brought up Robin. You were the mother to her that I was too busy and too selfish to be."

"But wasn't I—"

"Yes?" Cassandra let her free her hand.

"Wasn't I just as selfish, in my own way? For years I lived off the money that you and Bob sent me for Robin."

"Oh, money!" She waved her hand through a column of cigarette smoke: that's all money was. "The important thing is that you brought up Robin to be the dear, beautiful person that she is, and for that I'll always be grateful."

Margaret looked up doubtfully, but already, even with those doubts unresolved, the tears had started to her eyes. "Do you really love Robin then?"

"Love her!"

"She always wanted you to, you know. So badly."

"I guess I never knew how to express it."

"That's what I would tell her. But this last week, Mrs. Millar—" Margaret stopped short.

"Cassandra. Please."

"This last week, Cassandra, she's been so happy. She's been another person."

"Has she? I'm glad. I was so afraid that I'd have . . . passed on before I had a chance to . . . make her understand. And that's why I told her I wanted to see *you* too. I don't want to leave *any* bad feelings behind me. Oh, when I think of the time I've wasted, the love I've thrown away. You and I, Margaret—you and I!"

Margaret seemed to consider this deeply, but could do no better than meekly to echo, "You and I."

Cassandra elaborated: "We had so much in common."

"Oh, Mrs.—"

"Bob thought so too, you know. He said to me once, years and years later, that he thought we were like two twins, you and I. Not physically, of course, because you're much prettier than me, but deep down, where it counts."

By now Margaret was thoroughly rattled. Cassandra's revelations had exceeded all her capacities as a spectator. She'd lost track of who the characters were and what relationships were presumed to exist between them.

Cassandra leaned forward, to cup Margaret's rouged jowls in her fine hands. She looked lingeringly into her bleary, fuddled blue eyes and then, with a more than sisterly emphasis, kissed her mouth.

"There!" she said, returning to her pillow with a sigh. "That's what I wanted to do the moment you came in the door."

She had arrived at what she thought would have to be her last word on the subject of death, and it was as astonishing in its way as the detective's announcement, in the last chapter of the book, that *none* of the suspects were guilty.

It was just this: Death is a social experience; an exchange; not a relationship in itself, but the medium in which relationships may exist; not a friend or a lover, but the room in which all friends and lovers meet.

She reached for the Chesterfields, took one, offered the pack to Margaret, who accepted one after a tremor of hesitation. A flame flicked from the lighter, and Margaret inhaled.

Then there was a knock on the door. Tap tappy-tap-tap. Tap. Tap.

"That will be Robin," said both Mrs. Millars together.

The Joycelin Shrager Story

When people asked what he did, Donald Long's standard riposte was, "I'm a mechanic of the dream." Meaning, he was a projectionist. Actually, few people had to ask, since Donald had been around since the first black-and-white flickerings of the Movement early in the fifties. With the money he earned at the Europa he produced *Footage*, first as a quarterly and then a bi-monthly. For years it was their only magazine, but gradually as success changed the Movement into the Underground, *Footage* was supplemented and then surplanted by newer, more commercially oriented magazines. Donald Long's reputation as the Rhadamanthus of the underground film was undiminished, and possibly enhanced, by reason of this failure, but there was one consequence to be regretted—he had to continue full-time at the Europa, from one in the afternoon till the early evening, six days a week, in order to support his magazine and himself.

The Europa is on 8th Avenue, just below 49th. Originally it had been a showcase for Russian, Polish, and Estonian movies not otherwise distributed in the city, but then, imperceptibly, without a change of owner (or, so far as Donald could see, of clientele), the Europa drifted toward a policy of nudism and the exposure of organized vice, especially the white slavery traffic. By the end of '69, the Sexual Revolution had swept the October Revolution into oblivion.

Something of the same thing had been happening in his own life. Donald was forty-two, and after decades of honest homeliness he was finally coming into his own. What had been even ten years ago a bony kind of face was now rather striking in a severe way. No longer did he dissemble his baldness with a few iron-gray strands brushed up from the sides. No, he let it declare itself, and what hair still was left to him he grew, boldly, down to his shoulders. But best of all his somatype had become trendy, and he was able to fit into all the skimpy pullovers and striped pants that most men couldn't have attempted after the age of thirty.

Not that he became a satyr quite. He simply began taking advantage of the opportunities that had always offered themselves to him from time to time. At parties he was less diffident. He would even dance. (He had gone to a Reichian therapist and redirected some of his energies from his head down to his balls and, concomitantly, his feet.) He got rolfed, and laid.

But he didn't fall in love. He kept waiting, alert as a seismograph, for some tremor of affection, warmth, whatever. All he ever felt was a great glow of health and, toward his partners, benevolence, a degree of gratitude, a lesser degree of curioisty. But love? Never.

He knew what love was. Twice before he'd been in love. The first time, at twenty-one, he'd made the mistake of marrying his love-object, the black actress Cerise Miles. That was 1949, the year of Kazan's *Pinky,* and among enlightened Manhattanites love conquered all. By 1951 Donald and Cerise had come to hate each other much more passionately than they'd ever loved. As a result, his memories of the early, positive period of the relationship resembled, in its deliberate fuzziness, the one film Donald himself had ever made, *Tides of the Blood.* Among much else, *Tides* was a record of his marriage's collapse. (And, by implication, of Western civilization's.) Cerise had played herself, improvisationally, a performance that, even after Donald's editing, was considered a limit-case of what underground cinema could do along the lines of honesty.

The second time he was luckier and fell in love with the wife of his best friend, Gary Webb. The necessity of concealment kept Donald and Grace Webb in a state of zesty suspense and made their few rare moments alone together lyrical in the extreme. Then, after the adultery had gone on some two years, Grace felt she had to tell Gary. There was no question of divorce, since both Webbs were renegade Catholics who still believed in the sanctity of the marriage bond and the natural law. It was just her unconquerable candor. Gary was wretched and furious by turns, and Donald and Grace were rapturously guilty and more in love than ever.

Gary Webb was at that time (the late fifties) the most prolific (and, according to *Footage*, the best) director in the Movement. Film for him was less an art than a religion. He was its priest, and his camera was the sacrament he carried through the world, hallowing it. He filmed everything: snowfalls, muggings, Grace in *hal asana* position, trees in Washington Square, football games on channel five, a friend's stoned, staring iris (a shot he was sure Hitchcock had plagiarized in *Psycho*), a dripping faucet, cars on the street, and the natural births of all six of his sons. He also filmed, with Grace's connivance, representative moments of her adultery, and this footage became the basis of his most revolutionary and well-known film, *Reel 168* (1959).

The affair ended when Gary inherited his grandfather's farm in western Kansas. The Webbs moved west, with their cats and children and cameras, and in a few months Grace had been absorbed into the irrecoverable past. Years later he was to get a postcard from either Grace or Gary, he could never be sure, to which was glued a snippet from the ad for *The Great Gatsby*: "Gone is the romance that was so divine." The card showed a motel outside of Lebanon, Kansas.

On Sunday mornings, thanks to its owner, Norman Brodkey, and to the tax laws that make such transformations so profitable, the Europa became the Foundation for Free Cinema. The foundation's screening policy was egalitarian, even kindly in a careless way, mixing established old masters like Anger and Brakhage with whatever else happened along, and throwing in an occasional reel of the Europa's indigenous beavers when their directors or actors had credentials in the Movement. This policy usually guaranteed a minimum attendance of twenty-five or thirty, comprised mainly of fledgling filmmakers, their casts, and close friends.

On this particular Sunday, May 17, 1970, the foundation was showing two works by Anna Congdon: *Stigma* (1954, 48 min.) and *Dreams of Eurydice* (1967, 73 min.). As the combined running times precluded more than a token representation of films by the foundation's regular customers, as well because Miss Congdon had never ventured from her native Australia and so lacked the social leverage by which to muster the fiction of a coterie, and finally because the weather was more than ordinarily unacceptable, the turnout stopped just one short of none at all. That one was Mike Georgiadis, whose oeuvre, long since completed, shared a common mythopoeic strain with Miss Congdon's, and at whose urgings Donald had at last agreed to give the old girl her crack at America.

Mike was propped on the stainless steel ledge of the ticket booth, coughing, joking, and smoking fifteen-cent El Productos. It was an evil, evocative cough, but pardonable when you knew that Mike was dying of emphysema, had been dying of emphysema now for all of fourteen years.

They passed the rainy minutes gossiping about colleagues, the waxing and waning of their incomes, marriages, entanglements, and reputations. Mike, who was firmly established at the waning end of all scales, had a knack for interpreting any scrap of news so as to make his friends seem morons, martyrs, or, if the news were incontestably good, thieves. Donald, whose style was to be magnanimous, praised whom he could and forgave the rest. Donald's exculpations incited Mike to ever fiercer judgments, and these in turn provoked Donald to still more ingenious charities. They worked well together.

A damp, large, lardy girl in a yellow vinyl poncho with a Bolex Rex-4 pendant from her neck like some mammoth ankh had parked herself before the foundation's mimeoed schedule, which was Scotch-taped over the glassed display of stills for *Lust Party*. As she read, her mouth and eyebrows ticked an unceasing commentary of pouts, sneers, frowns, and grave suspicions. "Disturbed" was the word that came to mind.

Mike vanished into the theater.

Donald couldn't take his eyes off the girl's Bolex. Its fittings were rusty, the leather was peeling from its sides, and its carrying strap was a doubled length of twine: a camera as woebegone as the wide, wet, hungry eyes of a Keane puppy. He was smitten.

She looked at him and looked away. She scrabbled in a tie-dyed cotton satchel and brought out a dollar bill compactly folded into sixteenths. She undid the dollar regretfully and pushed it into Donald's cage.

"Has it started yet?" she asked.

"No, not yet. We've been waiting for more people to turn up."

"Then maybe you could do me a favor?" She bared her small brown teeth in a defeated smile, like a teen-age panhandler's or a Scientologist's, that no rebuff could dismay.

"Certainly," said Donald.

"I'm making a film." When he did not contradict her she went on. "And I need some footage of me coming down the street to the theater here. All you have to do is aim the camera at me and look through here." She pointed to the viewfinder, from which the eyeguard was missing. "And touch this when I say to. Otherwise it's all wound up and ready to shoot."

Donald consented to be her assistant. He came out from the ticket window and took the wounded camera in his arms.

"Be careful with it," she thought to insist, seeing that he was careful. "These things are very expensive."

Then she walked up to the corner, turned round, fussed with her poncho, squared her shoulders, and fixed her wide, meaty lips in a smile representing an irrepressible buoyancy.

"Now!" she shouted.

Through the viewfinder he watched her advancing toward him with a sinking certainty that Fate had come in at the door without knocking. He knew she was not beautiful. Indeed, her face and figure and bearing passed beyond mere homeliness into the realm of absolutes. She was sinfully ugly. Nevertheless, his whole frame was in a tremble of sexual anxiety such as no beaver had ever roused him to.

When the film had run out, she said, "You're Donald Long, aren't you?"

He admitted he was.

"Wow, that's terrific. You know, I've read every word you've ever written?"

"No kidding."

"Yeah." She nodded her head solemnly. "So this is really an important moment in my life." Then, offering her hand: "I'm Joycelin Shrager."

Joycelin's film, *The Dance of Life* (or rather, this latest install-ment, for *The Dance of Life* was conceived as a *film fleuve*, ever flowing on, the unexpurgated and amazing story of her life), was screened by the Foundation for Free Cinema three Sundays later. There was a good turnout. One reason was because this was an open screening, and where there is hope there is good attendance. The other reason was because Donald had been sending out signals and his friends had rallied round, as to Roncesvalles. Jesse Aarons, a director who was making a name in porn, had come, and Ed Gardner, who reviewed sometimes for the *Voice*; Louise Hiller, the modern dancer who had rolfed Donald, and her latest boy friend, Muhammid Kenzo, a black painter who'd had a painting in the Whitney; the Bachofens, of the Bachofen Gallery, and their son Arnold; Mike Georgiadis, Helen Emerson, and Rafe Kramer (surviors from the older, Maja Deren era of the Art Film); Lloyd Watts, the conceptual artist who'd come to doing street signs and traffic lights by way of his underground movies about cars, and three poets from St. Mark's, one of whom had had the bad fortune to be wearing the same lime-green leather pants as Jesse Aarons. In all, an imposing assembly.

Joycelin's three best friends were also at hand, eager to see themselves as stars on the Europa's screen. There was Murray, a tall, lean, aging, gay Satanist with frizzed hair; his roommate, Eric, an office temporary; and Doris Del Ray (her stage name), who'd met Joycelin at a New School film history course in 1968. Doris now studied jazz ballet with a teacher in Brooklyn Heights who had studied at Jacob's Pillow, long ago, with Ruth St. Denis. Consequently there was always a special sequence featuring Doris Del Ray, with choreography by Doris Del Ray, in each new in-stallment of the work in progress. There she would be in her black tights, clawing at the air or convulsed into an expressive ball of pain or solemnly mounting and descending staircases swathed in remnants of sheer rayon, her long hair unbound, a priestess. This time it was a kind of temple scene, with Murray wearing his satanic vestments, on the steps of the Soldiers and Sailors Monument in Riverside Park. Murray also had a longish moment reading the Tarot. The camera studied each card intently while the soundtrack continued to play the temple theme, "Anitra's Dance." Eric's big moment came after the Tower was turned up. He picked up the card, scowled, and returned it to the deck. The music changed to "Ase's Death." He looked still grimmer: slow fade to black. As Eric's most salient character trait was an uninflected, sullen resentment that Murray regarded as butch, in *The Dance of Life* he symbolized Death and other negative vibrations. He never did much more than smoke and glower, but there was always a moment of him doing that somewhere in the middle of each reel, like Harpo's musical interludes in every Marx Brothers movie.

Contrary to the practice of Gary Webb, who scrupled, God-like, to efface the evidences of his own directing presence (even editing out footage into which his shadow might have strayed), Joycelin appeared abundantly in *The Dance of Life*—was, in fact, nearly coextensive with it. Here she was, at the start, striding down 8th Avenue toward the camera and into Donald's life. Now (with Donald still aiming the camera) she was fiddling with the dials on the phonograph (in tribute to the *Orpheus* of Cocteau). Holding up the record sleeve of *Revolver*. Feeding a squirrel in Central Park. Standing in the empty band shell and clapping her hands with enigmatic ill temper. (They'd had their first argument, and she was making fun of him.)

Here was Joycelin gluing acoustical egg cartons to the walls of her bedroom, and regluing them as they fell off. Here she was coming down 8th Avenue again. You could see the smile being jarred from her mouth as she walked. The expression that lingered in the closeup was one of mild, moist avidity. Someone in the theater (it sounded like Helen Emerson) actually snickered, but then it was time for Doris and Murray to do their thing on the temple steps, a sequence so typical of the foundation's offerings that no one dared say boo.

Joycelin next accepted a bouquet of pilfered tulips from Doris's hand, Doris having become a statue. Cut to Joycelin's favorite M. C. Escher poster, then pan down to Joycelin arranging the tulips in a glass. Then, in a moment of understated candor, the camera (with Joycelin guiding it now) examined Donald's clothing draped over a semideflated inflatable chair. Clouds scudded, Squirrel Nutkin nibbled away, the Hudson flowed softly by, and she ended her song with a reprise of herself advancing in slow motion down 8th Avenue, while, voice-over, she intoned a stanza from a poem she'd found in *Strengths*, a mimeo magazine of feminist poetry:

> *i love you*
> *for the way you see*
> *Innermost Me*
> *i love you*
> *for the strong caress*
> *of your fingers in my heart*
> *& how they always seem to know*
> *what parts are spoiled*
> *& pass them over*
> *to pull out treasures*
> *that I never knew were mine*
> *until you gave them to me*

The terminal closeup of Joycelin's face slowly faded to white. As the last wisps of eyebrow evanesced, a wee small voice went on:

> *i love you*
> *for the self-beauty*
> *i behold*
> *gleaming like diamonds*
> *in the priceless setting*
> *of your eye*

The applause stopped short of an ovation, and after that, in the discussion period, no one had anything to discuss. Ordinarily Donald could have got the ball rolling, but the poem, which had been added to the soundtrack as a last-minute valentine surprise, had thrown him off his usual moderating form.

He started the next movie, a slapstick parody of *Star Trek* by a ninth-grader at the Bronx High School of Science. People laughed at it perhaps more than it deserved. Joycelin got up in the middle and left the theater. After a short argument with Eric, Murray followed her out.

One forgets, during one's own romances, that it is a curse to fall in love. This time, for Donald, this had been apparent from the start, nor would it ever cease to be apparent. He was appalled at his heart's election. But there it was—he loved her. Worse, he lusted after her continually with the fixated, somnambulistic desire of Peter Lorre in *M* or a bride of Dracula. Waking he thought of her, sleeping he dreamed of her. It was the real thing, which there is no resisting.

After hours at the Europa, if he were not in demand at her apartment on East 13th, he would watch, entranced, reel after reel of *The Dance of Life* (which earlier had borne the title *Dance of the Moon-Girl*) and wonder: why? why me? why Mimi?

Mimi was his pet name for her (Squirrel Nutkin was hers for him), after Puccini's Mimi, and in particular after the Mimi of Marguerite Ruffino, of the Ruffino Opera Company, which put on grand operas at an Off-Broadway theater on Monday nights, when it was closed. The company was financed by Marguerite's husband, a retired fireman, and in every production she sang the leading soprano role with a headlong, blissed-out inadequacy that kept her fans coming back steadily for more. Donald had seen her in *Aïda*, in *Norma*, in *Così fan Tutte*, and in *La Gioconda*, but her greatest role, surely, was Mimi. No *Bohème* had ever been sadder, or truer to life, than the Ruffino's.

Pity—that had been Donald's downfall. All his life he had loved losers, losing, loss. At zoos his favorite animal was the yak, yearning hopelessly behind its bars for the peanuts no one wished or dared to feed it. He had pretended to find a higher wisdom in the more kindly varieties of ignorance, a Woolfean beauty in faces that were unarguably ill-formed and hidden forces throbbing in the filmic daydreams of the weak, the lazy, and the incompetent. Seeing this vice apotheosized in the love he felt for Joycelin did nothing to diminish his passion for her, but it did enable him to see how thoroughly he resented everyone else who took up space in his life. His friends! He wanted nothing but to be rid of them. No, even more he wanted a revenge for the decades he had spent praising their meritricious work—and he began to see how, beautifully and without a single overt betrayal, he might obtain it.

Unless she were filming and needed the light, Joycelin slept till two or three o'clock. This, together with the penchant of most twenty-year-olds for self-examination, allowed her, even after a second bout of love-making, to go on talking all night long— about her past, about her latest ideas for *The Dance of Life*, about what she'd do with his apartment if it were hers, about Murray and Doris and her boss at May's department store, where she worked four nights a week in accounts. Her boss had it in for her.

"Because," she explained one night, "I'm Jewish."

"I didn't know you were Jewish."

The burning tip of her cigarette bobbed up and down in the dark. "I am. On the side of my mother's grandmother. Her name was Kleinholz."

"But that doesn't necessarily mean—"

"People think Shrager is Jewish, but it isn't."

"It never occurred to me to think so. You don't *look* Jewish."

"People can sense it in me."

She was fired three days later. Proof, if any proof were needed, that anti-Semitism had struck again.

She was certain that Donald was concealing his true opinion of her. The books in his bookcase, the records on his closet shelves were unlike her books and records. Chance remarks required long footnotes of explanation. His friends were inattentive, and she didn't find their jokes funny. He said their humor was just a shorthand form of gossip, but that was no help. If they talked in riddles, how could she ever be sure it wasn't *her* they were gossiping about? Anyhow (she wanted him to know), her friends didn't care much for *him* either. Murray thought he was a phony. He'd done a chart of Donald and found out terrible things.

The easiest way to calm her at such times was not to urge the sincerity of his admiration, but to make love. She seemed to take his uxoriousness as her due, never offering any of those erotic concessions that a typical underdog believes will earn the ravished gratitude of the beloved, just lying back and yielding to his ardors. It astonished him, in his more reflective moments, how accepting she was of her own substandard goods. A Nigerian tribesman who has come into possession of a Land Rover could not have been more reverently admiring of his treasure than was Joycelin of the machineries of her flesh. Mirrors never fazed her, and she could pass by any shop window in the city and instantly translate its mannikins into images of self. She wasn't (she knew) pretty, not in any conventional way at least, but the fairies who'd presided at her birth had made up for the lack with other gifts, and the light of them shone in her eyes. This was how her father had explained the matter to her in the once-upon-a-time of Cleveland, and that mustard seed had grown into a perduring, mountain-moving faith.

And yet she was uneasy. She revealed that in high school she had been known as Miss Bug. Once she'd taken a beginners' class with Doris's teacher in Brooklyn Heights and realized that the woman was making fun of her behind her back.

"That's what hurts, you know. Because you have to pretend you haven't noticed. Why couldn't she just come out and criticize me in the open? I know I'm no Pavlova or anything, but still. With a little more encouragement I'd have got the hang of it. I'm a born dancer, really. Murray thinks I must have been a ballerina in one of my previous lives. There's certain pieces of music that when I hear them it's like *The Red Shoes* all over again."

"You shouldn't let one person's opinion get you down like that."

"You're right, I know. But still."

She waited. He knew what she wanted from him, and it aroused him to be able, expertly, to supply it. It was easy in the dark. "You know, Mimi, the simplest things you do, just walking across a room maybe, or sitting down to eat, they have a kind of strange gracefulness. It *is* like dancing."

"Really? I don't try to."

"It's probably unconscious. Like a cat."

"Yeah?"

She wanted more, but he didn't have any immediately at hand. All he could think of was Cupcake, his super's fat, spayed calico, who rode the elevator up and down all day in the hope of getting to the garbage in the basement.

"Penny for your thoughts," she insisted.

"I was thinking about us."

An egg carton fell from the wall.

She waited.

"I was thinking how sometimes it's as though there'd been a disaster, like in *The Last Man on Earth*, if you ever saw that."

"*I* feel like that at times. Completely alone."

"Except in my scenario you're there too. Just you and me and the ruins."

"Why you dirty old man! You're the one who's like a cat— an old tomcat. Stop that!"

"I can't, baby. Anyhow, we've got to get the world repopulated again."

"No, seriously, Squirrel Nutkin. You've just given me an incredible idea for the next part of *Dance*. And if I don't write it down I might forget."

She was up till dawn. Scribble, scribble, scribble.

He would arrange get-togethers with his oldest, dearest, so-called friends and let the fact of Joycelin sink in as they ate her parsimonious stews and meatloaves. Then, when the dishes had been cleared away, they'd watch *The Dance of Life*. With a soldierlike pleasure in his own remorseless fidelity, he squeezed wan compliments from his boggled colleagues. There were years and years of debts to be collected in this way, and Donald was careful never to exact more than the interest on the principal, so that in a few months he might press for renewed courtesies.

With Joycelin, increase of appetite grew by what it fed on, and when the first faltering praises trickled to a stop—the strained comparisons to Merce Cunningham or tantric art—she would nod demurely (making a note of such novelties in her mental notebook) and then ask for *criticism.* She admitted she was young and had rough edges. While in one sense her faults were part of her Gestalts (and therefore sacrosanct), on the other hand she was still growing and learning, and so any advice was welcome. For instance, in the long tracking shot of Doris, did the degree of jiggle perhaps exceed the ideal? Did the uncertainty of what was happening detract from the Vision she'd meant to get across? Most guests survived these minefields by adopting the theory offered them—that all their hostess needed was a little more know-how vis-à-vis equipment, a little polish to bring out the natural beauty of the grain.

However. There were, inevitably, a handful who lacked the everyday aplomb to conceal their honest horror. Of these Mike Georgiadis was the most shameless, as well as the most cowardly, for he didn't even wait for the bedsheets to be tacked up screen-wise on the wall before he was in flight, leaving poor Helen Emerson and Rafe Kramer to cope on their own. Helen in her day had soaked up god only knew how many fifths of Donald's Jim Beam, and Rafe had been dumping his little abnormalities into Donald's all-accommodating psychic lap for half their life-times, like an eternal festival of the murky, lubricious movies for which he had once won, with the wind of Donald's reviews in his sails, a Ford Foundation grant, no less. Even *they* betrayed him that night. Helen first, by bursting out, at the end of the jug of Gallo hearty burgundy, with the awful pronouncement that Joycelin's case was hopeless. That she was not an artist. That she never could be an artist, and that surely in her heart of hearts she must know this too.

In the face of such gorgon truths, what use was there talking about camera angles, shooting ratios, film stocks? Joycelin became tearful and appealed to Rafe.

Rafe was mute.

Helen, with implacable good will, said was it so important after all? People fussed too much about art. There were other things. Life. People. Pleasure. Love. Enlightenment.

Joycelin turned to stone.

Donald bit the bullet. "Helen," he said, echoing her tone of creamy reasonableness, "you *know* that what you're saying just isn't so. When you consider the budgets that Joycelin has had to work with, I think she's made better films than any of us. They're utterly honest. They're like doorways straight into her heart."

"Better than any of us?" Rafe insisted with mild amaze.

"Damned right."

"We're the has-beens," Helen declaimed, slipping into her English accent. "The bankrupts. The burnt-out cases. Isn't that so, Donald?"

"*I* didn't say it."

"And Gary?" Rafe demanded. "Is he another has-been?"

"You know how much I've always admired Gary's work, Rafe. But yes, I do think *The Dance of Life* is right up there with the best things Gary Webb has ever done. And Joycelin's still growing."

It was enough. Joycelin's composure was restored, and she it was who smoothed these waters with the assurance that nothing was worth old friends losing their tempers over. The Sara Lee cheesecake must be thawed by now. Why didn't they eat it?

The September issue of *Footage* had a long essay by Donald about *The Dance of Life*. He waited till it was in print to show Joycelin. As she read the article, a look came into her eyes. A look such as you might glimpse on a baby's wholly contented face, when its every need has been fulfilled: the understanding, for the first time, that there is a Future and that it will suffice.

Afterward he regretted that he hadn't thought to film her at that moment, for he was beginning to think of *The Dance of Life* as his own movie too, and even, in an odd way, to believe in it.

Donald had three rooms in a brownstone around the corner from the Europa. Since he'd been there time out of mind, his rent was less than Joycelin's, though she had only a narrow studio with a bathroom that she had to share with Murray. Donald's apartment, though no less ratty in its essentials, was of a less effortful kind of grunginess than hers. The furniture was off the streets or inherited from friends. Never had he deceived himself into attempting improvements, not by so much as a pine bookshelf. Things piled up of their own accord, on window sills and table-tops, in corners and closets, and increasingly they were Joycelin's things: her stereo (after it had been repaired); her paperbacks; her seven coleus plants; the Escher poster, a rug, a chair; most of her clothes; even the precious Bolex Rex-4 and the rest of her equip-ment, since his neighborhood was marginally safer and the windows had bars.

At last, after a serious talk, they agreed they were being ridiculous in keeping up two apartments. Even if it meant for-feiting her two months' deposit, wasn't that better than paying rent forever for a place that they spent so little time in and that had never been more anyhow than a temporary expedient?

So they borrowed Lloyd Watts's station wagon, and early one Tuesday morning they loaded it with whatever was still worth salvaging from East 13th Street, which was not a lot. Most painful to relinquish was an armchair that Joycelin had schlepped all the way from Avenue A, but she had to admit it was too bulky and probably (serviceable as it still was) full of roaches. There was a problem too with the toaster and the electric coffee pot, since Donald already had the best Korvette's could offer. But you can't just leave armchairs and appliances behind, like the old bags and paint cans under the sink. So, even though he didn't answer his door, it was determined that Murray was to be the inheritor of these and other orphaned articles: a lidless blue roasting pan, some empty flower pots, a can of turtle food for the turtles that had died, a wealth of coat hangers, and a bicycle pump. Joycelin didn't have a key to Murray's room, but she knew how to jimmy his lock.

The room was painted a uniform, satanic black—floor, walls, ceiling, window—and all the light bulbs were gone from the sockets. They might very well have moved in all the presents with-out seeing Murray at all if Donald hadn't thought to light the room by opening the refrigerator door.

Their first thought was burglars. But burglars would not have dressed Murray so carefully in his cabalistic coat and hat and left him in the middle of a pentagram. No, it was Nembutals, as it had been twice before.

The reasons were not far to seek. Only a week after meeting

Jesse Aarons at that fateful Sunday screening of *The Dance of Life,* Eric had got a part in a gay porn feature called *The Boys in the Bathroom,* and now he was living in a sado-masochistic commune in Westbeth. He wouldn't even talk to Murray on the phone. At the same time, more delicately but no less definitely, Joycelin had left Murray in order to mount the ladder of *her* success. He couldn't even be her cameraman now because of Donald. What was left?

They got him to Bellevue in the station wagon, and his stomach was pumped out in time. All the way back to 13th Street, where they'd forgotten to close the doors, Joycelin couldn't get over her awesome intuition. What force had led her to Murray at his darkest hour and made her break down his door?

Then she remembered the Tower. Right there in *The Dance of Life* was the answer, plain as day. From the moment he'd turned up that card, she should have known. Perhaps (was it so impossible?) she had!

Next day she was back at Bellevue with Murray's billfold (he needed his Medicaid I.D.), a pillowcase full of fresh underwear and socks, and the old Bolex Rex-4 around her neck. The guard wouldn't let her into the elevator with her camera (these were the days of the Willowbrook scandal, and warnings were out), and so the only footage she could get to illustrate this momentous chapter of her life was some very dark shots of the lobby and her argument with the nurse, and a long, careful pan of hundreds and hundreds of windows, behind one of which, unseen by Joycelin and never to be seen by her again, a pacified Murray in clean blue pajamas was playing dominoes with a Jehovah's Witness, who had threatened to jump from the balcony of Carnegie Hall during a Judy Collins concert until an usher convinced him not to.

At Christmas, Donald spent a small fortune on Joycelin, his jo. In addition to such basic too-muchness as perfume, an amber necklace, and a Ritz Thrift Shop mink, there was: a cased set of Japanese lenses and filters, a four-hundred-foot magazine for the Bolex with sixteen giant spools of Kodak Four-X, a professional tripod with a fluid pan head, three quartz lighting heads in their own carrying case, a Nagra ¼-inch tape recorder, assorted mikes, and a mixer. He'd stopped short of an editing machine, reflecting that there'd be time for that extravagance later.

When all these treasures had been neatly wrapped in the most expensive gold paper with bushy red satin bows and stowed beneath and about the Christmas tree, itself a monument to his fiscal incontinence, he felt, supremely, the delirium of his own self-inflicted loving-madness. *O sink hernieder!* And he was sinking. At last he could understand those millionaires in Balzac who squander their fortunes on floozies, or those doctors and lawyers in Scarsdale and White Plains whose savage delight it is to see their money transmogrified into tall gravestones of coiled hair surmounting their wives' irredeemable faces, into parabolas of pearls declining into the dry crevasses between two withered dugs, into the droll artifice of evening gowns, whose deceits, like the sermons of Episcopalians, no one is expected to believe.

The unwrapping began as a responsible masque of gratitude and surprise and ended in genuine anxiety infused with disbelief. Without working out the arithmetic, she could not but wonder how, unless he were a stockbroker in disguise, Donald could have afforded all of this.

At last, when they were sitting down with their eggnogs in front of the electric yule log, she had to ask.

"It's simple. I sold the magazine."

"You sold *Footage*. That's terrible!"

"I'm keeping my column in it. That's down in writing. All I'm giving up is the drudgery, and Jesse is welcome to that."

"Jesse Aarons?" she asked, as he snuffled in the loose flesh of her neck.

"You see. . . ." He curbed the stallion of desire, leaned back in the nest of handcrafted pillows that had been Joycelin's merry gift to him, and exposited. "Jesse had the idea, some while ago, that there should be a *serious* magazine about skin-flicks. Something that would do for porn what *Cahiers* did for Hollywood, make it look intellectual. At the time I'd used a couple of his articles along those lines, but I couldn't see taking the whole magazine in that direction."

"I should hope not. But then why—"

"Five thousand dollars."

Joycelin set down her eggnog on the new Nagra and became serious. "But just last week, Donald, Jesse *borrowed* eighty dollars from you."

"The money doesn't come directly from Jesse. Harold Bachofen was the purchaser, but his name won't go on the masthead. Though Arnold's will, of course. Harold screwed Jesse out of the profits on *Ear, Nose, and Throat* last year, and he's giving him *Footage* by way of an apology. I think he wants a slice of his next feature now that Jesse's star is on the rise."

"I still don't think you should have done it. I mean, *Footage* was worth a lot more than five thousand dollars. It's the most respected magazine in the field."

"Every issue of that respected magazine puts me two hundred dollars in the red. When I'm lucky. We've got better things to do with our money."

"You should at least have waited to find out whether I get my CAPS grant or not. If Helen Emerson can get a CAPS grant, I don't see why I can't."

"Absolutely, Mimi my love. All in good time. But meanwhile, five thousand dollars is five thousand dollars." He poured the last of the eggnog into her glass.

She sipped and thought. Fake firelight from the yule log rippled over her Art Deco negligee. She struck an attitude—elbow propped on the arm of the couch, chin resting on the back of her hand—suggestive of close attention to music not audible to other ears than hers. At such moments Donald was sure she was thinking: "Is he looking at me now?" But this time her thoughts had truly been on a larger, philosophic scale, for when she came out of it, it was to declare, with all the hushed solemnity of a presidential press secretary, that Donald had done the right thing and that she was proud of him. And very happy.

The first issue of *Footage* to come out under Jesse Aaron's aegis had for its cover a still from *The Dance of Life* that showed Eric in a denim jacket, squinting at the smoke of his cigarette. It looked every bit like a face on the cover of a real magazine.

Joycelin gazed and gazed, insatiable. There was also another nice little mention in Donald's column.

"I wonder. . . ."

"What do you wonder, my love?"

"Whether I shouldn't try and get in touch with Eric again. I mean, he has been so much a part of *Dance* right from the start. Just because he isn't with Murray any more—"

"What about Murray? Did you ever find out his address?"

"No, and I don't care if I ever do. The bastard."

Murray had gone off to San Francisco without ever saying good-bye, much less thanking her for his life. The transition between concern for Murray's mental health to bitterness at this snub had been difficult to accomplish.

"Bastard?"

"Well, I wasn't going to tell you this, but you know how Murray was always telling everyone how he was a Scorpio? He's not. When I had to bring him his things to the hospital, I looked in his billfold. Where it says date of birth on his draft card, the date was January 28, 1937. An Aquarius! His *moon* isn't even in Scorpio, for god's sake. I looked it up, and it's in Capricorn."

"He probably thought he'd be more interesting as a Scorpio."

"Of course that's what he thought. But that doesn't make it right, does it? There's one thing I can't stand, and that's a liar. I mean, if your own friends *lie* to you, how can you believe *any-thing?*"

The wedding was in June, at St. Mark's on the Bowery. Joycelin's parents were to have come, but at the last moment (not unexpectedly) her mother came down with shingles, so Harold Bachofen acted *in loco parentis* and did very well. Joycelin's gown was a collaboration between herself and Doris Del Ray—a white silk muumuu swathed in tulle, with a veil and train that were one and the same. Donald dressed white tie, as did Harold Bachofen. Everyone else came in whatever they regarded as regal, which included, in at least one instance, drag.

The theme of the wedding, in any case, was not to have been fashion, but *film*. Everyone who owned or could borrow a camera was told to bring it to St. Mark's and shoot, the resulting trousseau of footage to be incorporated into a single grandiose wedding march in *The Dance of Life*. Since the invitation list included everyone in underground film who hadn't actively snubbed Joycelin, the results were gratifyingly spectacular. Donald stopped counting cameras at twenty-three. As a final dollop of authentication, a news team from *Eyewitness News* appeared just as the bride was being led to the altar. (Donald's former brother-in-law, Ned Miles, was now an executive at channel seven.) The wedding, alas, was squeezed out of the news that night by an especially sinister double murder in Queens, but the news team made it into *The Dance of Life*. They were the only people in the whole church who seemed at all astonished at what was happening.

And Joycelin? She was radiant. True movie stars, Donald had theorized once in *Footage*, actually receive energy from the camera, or from the cameraman, like plants getting energy from the sun. They become more alive, more definite, more completely who they are, like the dead on the Day of Judgment when they arise, wartless and cleansed of all the local accidents of character: the skeletons of their essential selves. So too Joycelin, whose special and enthralling awfulness always awoke to greatest vividness when she was being filmed. And today . . . today, with cameras springing up like daisies in a field, today there was no reckoning her transcendancy. Roland Barthes said of Garbo that her face represented a kind of absolute state of the flesh, which could be neither reached nor renounced, a state in which "the flesh gives rise to mystical feelings of perdition." In this respect Joycelin and Garbo were much alike.

The filming continued at The Old Reliable, where the reception was held. As Donald had been temporarily overwhelmed, Joycelin and Doris took it on themselves to collect the contributions to the Foundation for Free Cinema, which was what they'd requested in lieu of conventional wedding gifts. People got drunk too quickly, a crush developed, and Jesse Aarons got into a fight. The bride and groom left early.

Joycelin was kittenish, not to say petulant, in the cab, and when they arrived home she insisted on a bride's prerogative of having the bedroom to herself. Donald undressed down to his shorts, and then passed the time drinking from the bottle of Asti Spumante he'd rescued from the reception. It was flat. He didn't feel so wonderful himself. Great and long-awaited events do take it out of you.

He tried to get into the bedroom but Joycelin had locked the door, so he watched *Eyewitness News*. They showed the actual bloodstains in the stairwell where the woman had been stabbed. Forty-seven times. And the woman's niece as well.

At last she said to come in.

The dear old Bolex, on its new tripod, with its four-hundred-foot magazine in place, was set up facing the bed. The quartz lighting heads blazed down on the turned-back sheets like the desert sun.

"Surprise!" She was wearing nothing but the one-piece veil and train.

He could not pretend to disapprove on either moral or esthetic grounds. Joycelin had not only seen *Reel 168*—she'd read Donald's reviews of it. The principle was the same. But still.

"Mimi, darling. . . . I don't think I can. Not at this moment."

"That's all right, Donald. Take your time."

He went and sat at the foot of the bed, facing the eye of the lens. "Any other time, but not tonight. That reception got me down, I think. Seeing all those people I haven't seen in so long."

"You don't have to apologize to *me*. Just sit right where you are and say what you're feeling. Whatever it may be. Now that we're married it's like we're just one person. *Dance* is yours now as much as it's mine. Really."

She started the camera rolling. Unconsciously he'd placed his hands in front of his listless crotch. He could not look up.

She held out the directional mike. "Just say anything. Whatever you're thinking. Because whatever *is*—is right."

He was thinking about failure, which seemed, tonight, the universal fact of human life. But he couldn't say that. His thoughts were sealed inside his head like the documents in the cornerstone of a building. They could never come out.

"Hey there! Squirrel Nutkin! Look at the camera, huh? Say cheese."

He looked up at the camera and began to cry. For her, for him, for all his friends—for the dance of life.

Let Us Quickly Hasten to the Gate of Ivory

The cemetery lay at some distance outside the city, but in such fine weather it was a pleasure to be able to escape into the country. The blue of the sky was emphasized by a few scattered clouds which obligingly kept well away from the sun. The morning warmth touched, but did not penetrate, the surfaces of the scene, the fields, the winding road, the muddy trenches on either side, and the tall weeds. In such a landscape, on such a day, they (Mickey and Louise) figured only as decoration: one shepherd, one shepherdess. Louise, in her best pastoral mood, smiled and allowed her hair to be ruffled by the wind.

They parked the Volkswagen in a large lot of matt-black asphalt enlivened by a herringbone pattern of whitewash and authoritative traffic arrows, which (since the lot was empty) they ignored. She took the bouquet from the back seat, two dozen white and red roses. Three times during the drive out here Mickey had asked her how much she had paid for the flowers. Mickey wasted not and did not want.

"Aren't you taking your sweater?" he asked.

"On such a nice day?"

Mickey, the father now of two children, a man of responsibilities, frowned. "You never know."

"True, true." She took her sweater, draped it over her shoulder, stretched.

"Did you lock the door on your side?"

"I don't know."

Mickey went back and locked the right-hand door. Then he unlocked it, rolled up the window, and locked it again.

Just inside the brick gate, beside a bed of tulips, was a rack of flower vases—all of them, like so many empty milk bottles, of the same squat shape and tinny green color. Mickey paused a moment to select one.

FROM THEIR LABOR
NOW THEY REST

The grounds of the cemetery swelled and dipped agreeably. The young leaves and the grass insisted, this early in the year, rather too much on their color, and even the pines had been caught up in this naïve enthusiasm: their branches were tipped with that same vivid lime.

"I hope you know the way."

"Pretty well," Mickey said. "We go over that high hill there—" (pointing west). "From the top you can see a second little hill beyond, and it's on the other side of that, about halfway down. Between two fir trees."

"Is it very big?"

"Not very. About up to my knees. Mom chose it herself."

They started up the path. Louise was very conscious of the crunch of her heels on the gravel.

"Have you been here a lot?"

"No. Not since the funeral, in fact. We've had a rugged winter. And Joyce gets too depressed."

"I suppose it would be depressing in the fall, but it's lovely now. More like a golf course than a cemetery."

At these words the memory of their summer evening trespasses on the golf course returned to both of them, and they exchanged shy smiles of complicity. In the winters they had gone sledding on those same illicit slopes.

With his smile as her sanction Louise caught hold of Mickey's free hand. Obediently his fingers curled around hers, but with the same gesture his smile vanished.

"Oh, we can, you know," she assured him. "Holding hands *is* permitted between brother and sister."

SACRED
to the Memory of
CECELIA HAKE
Aug 15 1892–Dec 2 1955

"It's just that . . . well, it's been so long."

"And that's the pleasure of it. Do you think Joyce would be jealous?"

"Probably, but she wouldn't dare admit it. Joyce is a great believer in family bonds. Do you like her?"

"I might learn to. But I think *I'm* too jealous still. I haven't been able to have you to myself for one minute. This is nice."

"You don't have to leave tomorrow."

"Ah, but that's just it–I *do* have to."

Near the top of the hill the path became steeper. Ahead the tiers of markers and monuments caught the full dazzle of the morning light. Louise had to squint as she climbed on.

From the top, one could see a wide wavering line of hills that graphed, against the blue sky, some very temperate recurrence. An artificial stream reemphasized the cemetery's resemblance to a golf course. Perhaps one would be able to find a hard white ball in unclipped grass at the base of a tree or by the stream's edge. Uncertain how much whimsy her brother would be willing to tolerate in the circumstances, she said nothing.

Behind them the VW was still alone in the parking lot.

The path branched right and left, and Mickey seemed in doubt which to take. "I think it's that hill," he said. She had to follow behind, for the path had narrowed.

"So many," she said. "I had not thought death had undone so many."

"Oh, it's not bad, really," Mickey said. "The real trouble will be in twenty, thirty years' time. . . . It *will* be getting cramped then. There was an article in the paper about it. The population problem."

INTO THY HANDS
O LORD

"Oh, I didn't mean to say it was crowded—just so very *big*. I mean, there was a time when they could fit everyone into a churchyard."

"Doesn't sound sanitary," he observed.

"It wasn't. That's why they had to start building big cemeteries like this. The ground used to rise up outside of the church until it came right up to the windows. Really."

"Where'd you ever pick up a story like that?"

"From Lesley. He was full of morbid knowledge."

"Oh." Mickey quickened his pace to avoid any larger response. Louise's divorce was still a sore point with the Mangans, staunch Catholics all, though (as she had pointed out to her other, less-favored brother, Lawrence) her marriage could not have counted for much in the eyes of Mother Church, having never been consummated. Neither Louise nor four years of psychoanalysis had been of much benefit to Lesley.

"Oh, dear," Louise said. "It *won't* be a perfect day."

Mickey turned around. "Why?"

"The sun's gone under. Look."

In
Loving Memory
of

MARJORIE EDNA
NOYES

who fell asleep May 6 1911
Aged 5 years.
Also of Clement Hoffman
Uncle of the Above
who died Jan 24 1923, aged 41 years

"Are you sure it's this hill?" Louise asked. "Didn't you say between two *fir* trees? These are all pines."

"To tell the truth, I'm not sure of anything now. It all looks so much alike. It never occurred to me how hard it would be to find again. Maybe it was the hill farther to the right."

"That one? Or would it be farther back by now? You'll have to keep playing Virgil, I'm afraid. You know me—I can get lost on my way to the Laundromat."

"Let's try it, anyhow. It's easier than going back to square one. Or would you rather rest for a moment?"

"Rest? I'm good for hours yet. Though I am glad I wore low heels. What does it look like, exactly, the stone?"

"Just a plain slab, like most of these, a rectangle with the edges rough and the face polished. Granite. Marble would have cost twice as much, and it doesn't last so well."

"Did you use his initials—or his full name?"

"Mom gave them the whole works—Edward Augustus Mangan. I argued with her about it. He never liked people to know his name, but she felt it wouldn't be Christian, just the initials. She's down as Patricia, Wife of the Above."

"It sums her up nicely."

Mickey always remained neutral in Louise's quarrels with her mother, and so (was it not the special purpose of this day that these misunderstandings should be patched up once and for all?) he steered the conversation toward safe pieties:

"Why *didn't* you come, Louise? If it had been only a question of money, I'd have been glad to pay for your ticket."

Louise saw no reason to express any doubt of this very doubtful statement. Ever since high school, Mickey had been touchy on the subject of his stinginess. She replied in the same slightly unctuous spirit of reunion, "I wanted to, of course, but it was so soon after the divorce, and I was only inches away from a breakdown. Besides," she went on, unable to repress her legitimate grievance, "except for the announcement, none of you had written to me. And in Dad's case, you know, I didn't even receive the announcement. It was almost by accident that I ever did find out."

"HE GIVETH
HIS BELOVED SLEEP"

"I'm sure we sent one. Perhaps it got lost in the mail. That was the time you were in England, or one of those places."

"Well, it doesn't matter—I'm here now. Let's hope *they* are."

At the base of the hill the path branched once more, both forks going off, by Mickey's calculations, in wrong ways. They left it and walked on the trim grass toward a row of newly planted poplars. Bouquets of spring flowers, some withered, some still fresh, decorated the gravestones, which in this part of the cemetery seemed rather statelier and (she observed) older. She didn't point this out to Mickey, who was now visibly irritated at his failure to find their parents' grave. It would hardly do to tell him that it made no difference to her, that she'd come for his sake, not theirs.

Beyond the poplars there was an unexpected dip in the ground. Pink hawthorn filled the small valley from end to end. The shaded blossoms gave off a pallid glow, and she remembered how, only five days ago, the plane had risen above the cloudbanks into such a sudden pink luminescence as this.

STEPHEN BLYTHE
MARY BLYTHE
"Loved by Everyone"

"Damn all!" Mickey said. It was an admission of defeat: they were lost.

"Oh darling, what does it matter that we've come a bit out of the way? If we hadn't, we would have never seen this. And it's lovely!"

Mickey looked at Louise strangely. "Darling" had possibly been the wrong thing to say: it exceeded the limits he assigned to a sisterly affection.

"We can't just turn our backs on this, you know. We *have* to go down there. It won't take five minutes."

Mickey looked at his watch. "We shouldn't be late for lunch."

"Just a sniff of those flowers. Then we'll go back to that first hill and start fresh."

"They are pretty, aren't they?" he conceded.

"It must be an accident. Cemeteries aren't supposed to be as pretty as all that. Who would bother going to heaven?"

That was rather overdoing it, she thought, but it seemed to work, for Mickey grinned and offered her his hand, quite voluntarily, as they stumbled down the slope zigzagging between the marble angels and the elegant sarcophagi.

In Dear & Honored Memory of

GERALDINE

Cherished Wife of Martin Sweiger
who Departed this Life
February 4 1887
Aged 54 years

"I am the Resurrection and the Life."

The view northward across level ground terminated at the distance of about a mile in a violet haze; in all other directions extended a depthless continuum of hills as tall as or taller than this on which they stood. Nowhere were roads or buildings to be seen, only the green hills pocked with white, the stands of pine and poplar, fir and willow. No other persons, and no sound but their own heavy breathing and, now and again, the caucusing of unseen jays.

"It's impossible," Mickey said in the same matter-of-fact tone in which he might have spoken of an unbalanced equation in one of his students' exam papers.

"It's silly," Louise agreed. "It's perfectly silly."

"Cemeteries just aren't this *big*."

"Of course not."

"Joyce is going to be furious."

"Won't she, though? Imagine trying to explain to her that we got *lost* in a cemetery. It's impossible."

This seemed to exhaust the possibilities of the topic. Once anything is firmly established in the category of the impossible it eludes further discussion or analysis. They had abandoned any pretense of looking for Mr. and Mrs. Mangan's gravestone an hour ago, though Louise still clung to their commemorative bouquet as to some fragment, a Miraculous Medal or a scapular, of a discarded faith. The wax-paper wrapping had frayed, and she had to be careful not to be pricked by the thorny stems. And the flowers themselves. . . . With a grimace she threw them away, as earlier, in his first fit of temper, Mickey had thrown away the squat tin vase.

MIZPAH

Initially they had conceived of their project as finding their way back to the parking lot, simply that; now they were just trying to get out, by any exit, in any direction.

"There's no one here, have you noticed that?" Louise asked. "I mean, there aren't even gardeners around. *Someone* has to cut the grass. And someone comes around with these flowers. We keep seeing fresh flowers everywhere."

"Mm, yes."

Mickey's eyes avoided hers. Perhaps the same point had already occurred to him, but he had not spoken out of a sense of delicacy. He knew her too little to be able to gauge her susceptibility to panic. She, for her part, could not gauge his. The consequence was that they both remained remarkably cool.

"It would be all right, you know, if this were a *wood*. People do get lost in woods, brothers and sisters especially. But not in cemeteries!" She essayed a careful laugh, conscious, bounded, calm.

"Well, which way do you think?" he asked.

"For plunging on? East, I suppose. I'm still convinced that that's where the car should be. But which way is east?"

Mickey regarded the sun, now at its zenith, and consulted his wristwatch. "It's twelve-thirty, and we're on Daylight Saving Time. So I'd say *that* would be east, give or take fifteen degrees either way." He pointed to the crest of the highest hill that they could see, behind which gray clouds had begun massing.

"The question is—should we climb it or follow the low ground? It's a bit higher than this hill; we might see farther."

"Not another hill, Mickey, please! I really am a bit bushed. Not to speak of being hungry. I wish now that I could eat those farmhouse breakfasts that you do."

"Yeah. Jesus."

At the mention of food the thought of Joyce returned more vividly to both of them, the dismal thought of the explanations that would have to be made, of the failure of those explanations.

TO DEAR
FLORRIE
FROM HER MOM
SEPT 18 1960

The moment they reached the bottom of the hill the quiet of the day was broken by a mechanical roar that seemed to come from all the hills at once. A *truck!* she thought. The highway! Then she recognized the sound and looked up. A jet flew past westward. It was unusually low. She wondered if the pilot could have seen them down here. Perhaps just barely, if he'd known where to look. She pictured herself stripped to her brassiere, waving her white blouse at the airplane: it would never do.

"Flying that low, he must be coming in for a landing," Mickey said. "But I didn't think the airport was so close. In any case, he should be flying east."

"Maybe he's taking off."

The jet passed out of sight, leaving behind only its white, precise tail that slowly feathered out into the blue.

Louise giggled.

"Something amusing?"

"I was thinking—wouldn't it be funny if they sent out a rescue party for us? It would be in all the papers."

"Jesus!" Mickey said. "Don't make jokes like that."

S. † P.

EUSTACHY TUSTANOWSKI
DOKTOR MEDYCYNY

18.5.1837—8.12.1918

The sprinkler revolved and jets of water arched up in two opposing spirals, fell with the sheen of dull silver.

They broke into a run down the grassy incline. Mickey tripped, and it was Louise who reached the sprinkler first. Grasping the brass tube she drank avidly at the pencil-thin stream of water. She had scarcely wet her clothes.

When she looked up, mouth numbed with cold, Mickey was still sitting where he had fallen.

"Oh, it tastes wonderful! I didn't realize how thirsty—what's wrong darling?"

Mickey was swearing, with great seriousness and small invention. Louise dashed away from the sprinkler, which resumed its duties, and went to her brother. "What *is* it?"

He began to pull grass up around the half-submerged marker over which he'd tripped. The marker read, simply:

CLAESZ

"It's this son of a bitch that's the matter. He tripped me. I think I've sprained something, and it hurts like the devil."

"Shouldn't you try to walk on it now—before it starts to swell?"

Mickey stood up, swearing, and hobbled toward the sprinkler. Before he could catch hold of the revolving brass arm he had been drenched. When he'd had his fill he turned the sprinkler upside down in the grass.

"You know what I want to do?" he said, seating himself on the nearest gravestone and removing his right shoe and sock. "I want to smash something. I'd like to take a big sledge hammer and start smashing in all these goddam tombs."

TO OUR
DARLING
MOTHER
AND FATHER
"IN GOD'S KEEPING"

"Mickey, it can't be *very* much farther to one of the gates. We've been walking for miles, I'm sure we have. It's three o'clock by my watch. *Miles!*"

"I'll bet we've been walking in circles. People are supposed to do that when they're lost in the snow. It's the only explanation."

"But we took our direction from the sun," Louise objected.

"The sun! And what direction would that be? There *is* no sun." And indeed the light now issued from the clouds with such perfect uniformity that this was not any longer a viable strategy. There were a few areas of somewhat more intense brightness, but these seemed to be distributed at random through the prevailing gray.

"Do you know what it's going to do? It's going to start raining, *that's* what it's going to do!" He smiled, a melancholy but triumphant prophet. The sprained ankle had triggered the latent melodramatist in Mickey, whose talents usually had no larger scope than family bickering and the bloodless victories of the classroom. Now, like Lear, he had all nature ranged against him.

"We'll wait it out under a pine tree if it does."

"Wait it out! Jesus, Louise! It's three o'clock. Joyce has probably telephoned everyone we know, asking for us. Maybe she'll even drive out here and see the car parked in the lot."

"Fine. Then someone can start looking for us."

"You don't think they're going to believe us when we tell them we were lost, do you? Lost—in a cemetery!"

"What *will* they think, then?" Louise asked angrily. She

knew he wouldn't dare put it in so many words, and he didn't.

"Jesus," he said.

"Besides, your ankle is a perfect alibi. Anyone can get lost in a cemetery for a *little* while. We got lost, and then you sprained your ankle and couldn't walk. I'll tell you what—I'll go on ahead and find the way out and then I'll come back here for you. I'll be very careful to memorize the way; I'll blaze a trail. What is it you have to do—drop bread crumbs or something like that? And with luck I'll find someone to help you back. How's that?"

Mickey nodded glumly.

She set off up the nearest hill to take her bearings. In this part of the cemetery there seemed to be no paths at all, and the lawn was not so well cared for. Though someone, surely, had set that sprinkler going—and not too long ago, either, or the ground about it would have been muddy. Really, they had been behaving quite irrationally about the whole thing.

Every ten or twelve yards she would glance back at Mickey, who was resting his face in his hands. His pose reminded her vaguely of some painting she had seen. Her year in Europe with Lesley had melted into a single conglomerate blur of churches and paintings and heavy meals. All afternoon, as her hunger had grown, she had chattered on compulsively about restaurants in Paris, in Amsterdam, in Genoa; German sausages, curried chicken, English puddings, the sweet heavy wines of Spain, and the hopeless inadequacy of all European coffees.

GARDENS OF MEMORY AND PEACE

At the top of the hill she rested, out of breath, against a tall oak. The close horizon of placid, swelling lawns, this endless unvarying cyclorama, filled her now with a subdued, almost meditative, horror. The ring of hills seemed to tighten more closely around her with each new prospect.

No, she would not be able to journey off into that blankness alone. Through the unacknowledged panic of the afternoon it had been Mickey's presence that had buoyed her up, and even this brief moment away from him, not even out of his sight, she could sense the encroachment of those thoughts she had so far been able to evade. Even if they could not be evaded much longer, she did not want to have to face them on her own.

"Nothing?" he asked when she returned.

"Nothing. Those hills—they were the same hills we've seen all day. And I just couldn't . . . not by myself."

"You don't have to explain. I was feeling much the same thing as soon as you left. It was like . . . I don't know, like being left alone in the dark."

She squeezed his hand, grateful for his understanding. He no longer seemed embarrassed at her touch.

"It's so absurd, isn't it?"

"Absurd? It's supernatural, kid."

She had to laugh at that.

"Oh, Jesus, it's starting to rain."

"Let me help you as far as that pine. We'll be dry there."

They waited out the rainstorm under the pine, telling each other stories about Europe and the high school where Mickey taught physics and algebra and coached the basketball team, about the whole sick mess with Lesley, and about Joyce's hundreds of spiteful, sponging relations. It was the best talk they'd managed to have since Louise had come to town.

And after the rain the sky began to clear, though, because of the wind that had sprung up, the day remained, permanently, chillier.

ALDRIDGE

LOUIS	ANN	JAMES
1868–	1882–	1905–
1927	1939	

"To live in the hearts of those
we love is not to die."

After so many hours of silence the birds came as a relief. They arrived in a great whirling flock that passed beyond the westward slopes, returning a minute later from the north to settle in the elms on both sides of the hollow. Their clamor had the reassuring quality that can sometimes be found in a noisy bar or a busy street, a pledge of the continuity of exterior event.

During their talk under the pine, Mickey's right foot had swelled so badly that he could no longer squeeze into his shoe, which now dangled by its laces from his belt. He walked with the help of a branch stripped from the same accommodating pine.

They did not talk, for what could they have spoken of but their improbable dilemma? There comes a point when analysis, a too conscious awareness, becomes a liability and hindrance to action, and Louise feared that they had overstepped that point already. Their talk had suggested to her, at least, the central problem in this business of being lost: whether it had its source in the nature of the woods or in the nature of the orphans lost in those woods? In other words, could they be in any sense, perhaps without their knowing it, malingering? Each sequent hour seemed to argue for this hypothesis. The alternative—that the cemetery itself was responsible for their plight, that it was quite as big as it seemed to be—was intolerable and, in the most literal sense, unthinkable. Therefore (because it was unthinkable), they would not speak of it.

SUFFER LITTLE CHILDREN
TO COME UNTO ME

When they came upon the brook, it was a complete surprise. Had they been walking at a faster pace they might have tumbled right into it. The longer grass concealed the brink, just as the chattering of the birds had masked the sound.

"The stream!" Mickey said.

They looked up with one accord, as though expecting to see the parking lot just a few yards on. The brook curved out of sight around the base of a hill.

"It can't be much farther on," Louise argued. "The *only* time we saw the stream today was from that first hill."

"Oh, Jesus," Mickey said with relief.

"And it proves one thing—it proves we haven't been walking in circles, not entirely."

Mickey put his hand in the water. "It's flowing that way." He nodded to the east-lying hill, where tesserae of marble and granite flared in the afternoon's declining light. "Do we follow it upstream or downstream? What do you think? Louise, are you listening?"

This problem had occurred to Louise at the first sight of the brook, and she had been staring in the other direction, against the sun, while Mickey spoke.

"Look," she said.

A crumpled mass of green paper was floating toward them. She stooped and picked it dripping from the water. She smoothed it on the grass.

"Is it the same?" he asked.

"I'm sure it is. See, where the stems have torn it. Do you believe in portents, Mickey?"

"I don't follow you."

"The trouble is, even if one believes in them, how are they to be interpreted?"

"Hey, let's get into gear, sister dear. Which way—upstream or down?"

"Downstream? I'm not a very experienced druid."

"Then downstream it is."

They followed the winding course of the brook for an hour. Louise figured that in the space of an hour they could not accomplish more than a mile at Mickey's best pace.

Though they both believed they had found the thread that would lead them from the labyrinth, they remained chary of talk. Only once did Mickey break the hopeful silence:

"You know, Joyce will be talking about this for the rest of her life."

Louise smiled. "She won't be the only one."

The brook emptied into a small pool that drained into two culverts. The culverts took their course thence under a hill. They climbed the hill, from which they were able to see other hills. The western horizon was an intense violet, veined with pink. The sun had set.

"I think I'm going to scream," Louise said.

Instead, she sat down and began to cry. Mickey put his arm around her, but he couldn't think of anything reassuring to say.

They stayed on the hilltop until it was quite dark, hoping

to see electric lights or at least the nimbus that would hover above a large congregation of lights, but they saw only the stars and the blackness behind the stars. When the mosquitoes discovered them, they started off once again, following the probable course of the culverts.

At night the cemetery reminded them even more of the golf course of their youth. They held hands as they walked along, and sang, together, all the songs they could remember from *Oklahoma!* and *The King and I.*

Here lies
the mortal body
of

LT. JOHN FRANCIS KNYE

only son of
FELIX & LORRAINE KNYE
Who was killed in action
Aug 7 1943, Aged 20 years.

"Taken to his Eternal Home"

Because the grounds were so well kept, it was hard to gather an adequate supply of dry wood. Mickey built up the fire while Louise scouted about the neighboring slopes, foraging. As long as she kept in sight of the flames she didn't feel uneasy. On her third excursion she came upon a veritable windfall—two large fir branches that had come down in a storm some time before and were fairly dry by now, the fir tree itself having acted as an umbrella during subsequent downpours. They were so heavy she had to make a separate trip for each branch. With these broken up and stockpiled they decided they were well ahead of the game.

"With any luck," Mickey said, "someone will notice the glow of the fire and report it. I'm sure fires are illegal in a cemetery."

"Oh, I'm sure."

"I've reached the point where I'd be happy to be arrested. Anything to get out of this place."

"Ditto me. Though let's hope they don't come *too* soon—I'd hate to think I'd gathered all this wood to no purpose. It's a nice fire."

"The day hasn't been an entire loss, I guess. We've managed to have our family reunion after all. Though it may have cost you an extra day."

"As long as I have an excuse that satisfies my conscience, I don't mind the time lost. It's your ankle I worry about. How is it now?"

"All right if I keep still."

"I keep having the funny feeling that the parking lot is probably only a hundred yards away, just out of sight."

"I've had that feeling all day. Warm?"

"The front of me is toasting to a crisp, but my back is a little chilly. What saint was it said, 'I'm done on this side—you can turn me over'?"

"St. Lawrence."

"Lawrence, of course. I'll bet joyce has been phoning him all day. My God, the thought of facing them. . . ."

Most of the time they watched the fire in silence. Mickey lay on his left side, so that he could prop his bad foot on a low marker. Louise sat with her arms about her legs, her chin resting on her knees. Whenever the fire grew low she added another branch, and the flames would leap up to double or treble their height until the brittle foliage had been consumed. At regular intervals white moths would flutter into the flames to achieve a final metamorphosis.

"The one thing I *don't* understand," Mickey said, resuming the talk they had begun under the pine tree, "is why you married him in the first place. You can't blame him for deceiving you."

"Well, he *was* handsome. And very personable. Everyone agreed that we would make a dazzling couple, and they were right, in a way. Then, I suppose a woman likes to think that she can *redeem* that kind of man."

"It doesn't sound as though he wanted redeeming."

"Oh, he did and he didn't. In his own

way he was quite fond of me. Besides, you forget—he was famous. In the set we moved in, most women would have done the same dumb thing. It's a different world."

"And you say that you knew from the first how it would turn out."

"When I thought about it. Perhaps *that* was the determining reason. Maybe it was just the kind of marriage I wanted, a kind of pantomime. It was the kind *he* wanted. Please, let's not talk about it now?"

"I'm sorry. I didn't want to upset you."

"Oh, I'm very hard to upset. Today has proved that. I'm just tired. Mickey, do you still know the names of all the stars?"

"Some. I've forgotten a lot."

"Teach me."

Mickey pointed out the brighter constellations that could be seen despite the glare from the fire. Afterward she laid her head in his lap to see if she could sleep. Untended, the fire began to die out, but they were resigned to this. Eventually they would have used up all the wood in any case. Where their bodies touched they kept warm.

"Mickey? Are you awake?"

"Yes. I didn't think you were."

"When you told me, this morning, to take my sweater— how could you possibly have *known?*"

"Strange, isn't it? I was thinking almost the same thing a little while ago."

Sometimes she stared up at the constellations, murmuring drowsily their renascent names; sometimes her eyes were closed. Mickey's hand was twined comfortingly in her hair.

Tomorrow she would have to fly back, and it would all return to the way it had been. Mickey would write, once or twice, letters about his children's health, the UNTIL terrible winters, his basketball team. THE DAY BREAK And she would eat expensive lunches at hotels, and talk, for hours, with the same people, or with new people who would too quickly become the same people. She would go to their parties, their shows. . . .

Tomorrow.

No. That was over. Tomorrow would find them in the cemetery still. They would walk across the same perpetual lawns. They
were lost. They would continue to be lost. The cemetery would
stretch on and on like—what had he said before?—like a Moebius
strip. The same hills speckled with white rectangles of stone,
striped with gravel paths. The same blue sky. In an almost perfect
silence they would walk through the cemetery, lost. They would
learn to eat tubers and roots and pine nuts. Perhaps they would
find a way to catch small birds. Quite possibly. She fell asleep in
her brother's arms, smiling: it was just like old times.

In Remembrance of
EDWARD AUGUSTUS MANGAN
1886—1967

and of
PATRICIA, Wife of the Above
1900—1968

"Let us quickly hasten to the Gate of Ivory"

The Master of the Milford Altarpiece

What blacks and whites, what greys and purplish browns!

BERNARD BERENSON

Often enough Rubens may have quietly taken stock of all previous Italian art at this time, especially of the Venetian school, the knowledge of which had had so little influence on other northern artists. Though scarcely one immediate reminiscence of Titian can be discovered in Rubens's later work, whether of objects or of single forms, he had learned to see with Titian's eyes. He found the whole mass of Tintoretto's work intact, and much of it still free of the later blackening of the shadows which makes it impossible for us to enjoy him, but he may well have been repelled by the touch of untruthfulness and lack of reticence in him, and by the crudity of a number of his compositions. It is obvious that his deepest kinship by far was with Paolo Veronese; here two minds converged, and

there have been pictures which might be attrib-
uted to either, for instance a small, but rich
Adoration of the Magi which the present writer
saw in early, uncritical years and has never been
able to forget.

JACOB BURCKHARDT

I.

I can hear him, in the next room but one, typing away. An answer to Pamela's special delivery letter perhaps? Or lists of money-making projects. Possibly even a story, or a revised outline for *Popcorn*, in which he will refute the errors of our age.

Wishing to know his age, I went into the communicating room. "Jim?" I called out. "Jim?" Not in his office. I called downstairs. No reply. I returned here, to this desk, this typewriter. Now there are noises: his voice, the slow expository tone that he reserves for Dylan.

He is twenty-three. He will be twenty-four in December. For his age he is fantastically successful. I envy his success, though it isn't a personal thing—I can envy almost anyone's. I need constant reassurance. I crave your admiration. Is candor admirable? Is reticence even more admirable? I want to read this to someone.

Chip said, on the phone last night, that Algis Budrys called him the world's greatest science-fiction writer. I certainly did envy that. Jane said afterward that Chip is coming up here at the end of the week, possibly with Burt. (Burt?) Marilyn is still in San Francisco. I felt resentful.

I don't think I am alone in being obsessed with the idea of success. We all are. But though we may envy the success of our friends, we also require it. What kind of success would we be if our friends were failures?

This isn't the story. This is only the frame.

Pieter Saenredam

Pieter Jansz. Saenredam; painter of church interiors and topographical views.

Born at Assendelft 9 June, 1597, son of the engraver Jan Saenredam. He went as a child to Haarlem and became a pupil in May 1612 of Frans Pietersz. de Grebber, in whose studio he remained until 1622. In 1623 he entered the painters' guild at Haarlem and spent most of his life there. He was buried at Haarlem, 31 May, 1665.

He was in contact with the architects Jacob van Campen and Salomon de Bray, and perhaps also Bartholomeus van Bassen. He was one of the first architectural painters to reproduce buildings with fidelity (that is to say, in his drawings; in his pictures, accuracy is often modified for compositional reasons).

In his bedroom, which also served him as a studio, the curtains were always drawn. The cats performed ovals and sine curves in the bedclothes, a gray cat, a calico cat. Most of the furniture has been removed. The remaining pieces are placed against the wall.

The pleasures of iconoclasm. Destruction as a precondition of creation. Our burning faith.

The same painting over and over again. The high vaults and long recessions. The bare walls. The slanting light. Bereft of figures. (Those we see now have, for the most part, been added by other hands.) Nude. White.

He opened his present. Each box contained a smaller box. The last box contained a tin of Mixture No. 79, burley and Virginia. From that young scapegrace, Adriaen Brouwer (1605–1638).

It was an exciting time to live in. Traditions were crumbling. Fortunes were made and destroyed in a day.

The columns in the foreground have been made to appear much wider and taller, and the arches borne by them have been suppressed.

His first letter:

> RFD 3
> Iowa City, Iowa
> May 66

Dear Mr. Disch—

Twenty minutes ago I finished The Genocides. And should have finished it days ago, but I kept drawing it out, going back over things, taking it a few pages at a time: because I didn't want it to be over with, sure, but mainly because I felt there was so much to take in—the structure, the pitch and tone of the narrative, the interflow of situations—and I wanted to give myself every chance I could. . . .

From a letter two months later:

> . . . I am touched, Tom, by your extremely kind offer. To show my things to Moorcock. If they were only good stories, I'd take you up on it in a minute. But they're not, and I know it, which makes things different, almost embarrassing. But I may still put you in the compromising position, after thinking it over a while. I could use the sale (money, ego-boost, a beginning), and some of 'em aren't really that bad . . . and so on. But for now: I thank you very much. No way of expressing my gratitude—not only for the offer, but for your proffered friendship as well, your demonstrated openness. . . .

And this, when I had asked him for a self-portrait:

His Whilom. Born in Helena, Arkansas. Parents uneducated. Spoiled because was so hard to conceive him, wrecked mother's health to bear him against the advice of doctors. One brother, seven years older; philosopher, PhD, teacher. Spent his youth on banks of Twain's Mississippi and in Confederate woods banking his small town. Became interested in conjuring when about twelve, an interest which persists. During high school edited some small magic mags, composed and formed chamber groups, took music lessons (against his parents' wishes, who thought playing in the band was enough, and regardless of their lack of funds), had few friends. Spent summer between 11th and 12th grade doing independent research under guide of National Science Foundation, it being his ambition at that time to become a biochemist. Was oppressed that summer by the routine boredom of checks and balances, began to write poetry under the inspiration of cummings. In his 12th school year, wrote plays, directed plays, acted in plays, won dramatics prizes, became very depressed about not having the money to go to Princeton, became a dandy and discovered girls. Decided he was a poet.

The Exterior Symbolic. Am tall, very thin with a beer belly and matchstick legs. A disorder of the lower back has left me slightly stooped and given me a strange, quite unique walk. Wear wireframe glasses. Dress in either corduroy coat or black suit, with dark or figured or flowered shirt and black or figured tie. An angular, long face. Black curly hair that sticks out like straw and generally needs a cutting.

Aedicule

The enclosing planes of walls, floor, ceiling. Subsidiary planes in tiers supported by the vertical members—posts, legs, brackets. A light bulb hangs from the ceiling. His room is characterized by rectilinearity. He unpacks his boxes and arranges the books on shelves, tacks prints to the walls, disposes of his clothing into drawers.

Without are trees, weeds, grasses, haystacks, cathedrals, crowds of people, rain, bumps, animals ground into meat, billboards, the glare, conversations, radiant energy, danger, hands, prices, mail, the same conversations.

The artist is obliged to structure these random elements into an order of his own making. He places the ground meat in the icebox, arranges the crowds of people into drawers. He carves a smaller church and places it in the larger church. Within this artificial structure, each figure, isolated in its own niche, appears transfigured. Certain similarities become apparent. More and more material is introduced. New shelves must be built. Boxes pile up below the steps. The sentences swell from short declarative statements into otiose candelabra. Wax drips onto the diapered floor. Styles conflict. Friends drop in for a chat and stay on for the whole weekend. At last there is nothing to be done but scrap the whole mess and start from scratch.

Whitewash. Sunlight slanting across bare walls. Drawn curtains. Vermeer's eventless studio.

He paints a picture of the table and the chair. The floor. The walls. The ceiling. His wife comes in the door with a plate of doughnuts. Each doughnut has a name. He eats "Happiness." His wife eats "Art." The door opens. Their friend Pomposity has come for a visit.

II.

Yesterday, all told, he got three letters from Pamela. Passion that can express itself so abundantly, though it may forfeit our full sympathy, is a wonderful thing to behold. Given the occasion, how readily we all leap into our buskins! And if we are not given the occasion outright, we will find it somehow. Madame Bovary, c'est nous!

When every high utterance is suspect, we must rely on surfaces, learn to decode the semaphore of the gratuitous, quotidian event.

Oh, the semaphore of the gratuitous, quotidian event—that's beautiful.

For a long while I pressed my head against my purring IBM Executive and tried to think of what constituted, in our lives here, a gratuitous event. There seemed far too much significance in almost anything I could remember of yesterday's smallest occasions. I returned most often to:

Raking leaves. Not, conscientiously, into a basket for burning, but over the edge of the escarpment. Like sweeping dust under a rug. Jim came out on the porch to announce a phone call from my brother Gary. He has been readmitted to Canada with immigrant status. Then, back to my little chore. Jim said he hates to rake leaves. "Because it reminds you of poems in *The New Yorker?*" I asked. He laughed. No, because it reminds him of his childhood. Weeding the towering weeds in the back lawn, unmowed since mid-August. The two most spectacular weeds I tamped into a coffee can and set beside our other plants on the table in the bay of the library.

Strings of hot peppers, predominantly red, hanging unconvincingly on the pea-soup kitchen wall. Jane's handicraft. Staring at them as I gossiped with Jim. About? Literature, probably, and our friends.

Judy bought a steak, and Jane made beef stroganoff and a Caesar salad, both exemplary. The flavor of the sauce, the croutons' crunch.

Chess with Jim before dinner, with Jane after I'd washed the dishes.

Jane cut Jim's hair. Dylan was skipping through the scattered curls, so I swept them up and put them in the garbage.

At what point was I happiest yesterday: as I raked leaves and washed dishes or when I was writing this story? At what point was Jane happiest? At what point was Jim happiest?

Was Jane happier than Jim? Was I happier than either? If not, were both, or only one, happier than me? Which?

I spend too much time lazing about indoors. I overeat. I smoke a package of cigarettes every day. I masturbate too often. I am not honest with myself. How, then, can I be expected to be honest about others?

Happiness is not important.

■

The Conversion of St. Paul

The acquisition of certain knowledge (as Augustine shows us) is possible, and men are bound to acknowledge this fact. The knowledge of God and of man is the end of all the aspirations of reason, and the purification of the heart is the condition of such knowledge.

The city is divided by schisms, as by innumerable rivers. His single room on Mississippi Avenue overlooks an endless genealogy of errors, sparrows, roofs. He has, by preference, few friends. He reads, each evening, of the great dispute over the nature of the Trinity. Demons in the form of moths tickle the bare soles of his feet. He fills his notebooks with theories, explanations, refutations, apologies—but nothing satisfies him. Of what solace is philosophy when each sequent hour reveals new portents of a sure and merited destruction, innumerable portents?

He cannot endure the strength of these emotions.

He writes:

To be happy, man must possess some absolute good: this is God. To possess God is to be wise. But none can possess God without the Son of God, who says of Himself, I am the truth. The truth namely is the knowledge-principle of the highest, all-embracing order, which, as absolutely true, produces the truth out of itself in a like essential way. A blessed life consists in knowing by whom we are led to the truth, in what we attain to the truth, and how we are united to the highest order.

That much seemed to be clear.

Often (of this he did not write) the walls of the room warped. The old man from next door came and stared at him as he lay there in the bed. Crook-backed and dirty (a magician probably): the name "Sabellius" burnt into the gray flesh of his high forehead.

In the churches, the gilded sculptures of Heresy and Sedition. Plastic dissembling itself as trees, weeds, grasses; simulating entire parks. The seeming virtues of his friends were only splendid vices. Their faces were covered with giant worms.

He distinguished between the immediate and the reflective consciousness, which concludes itself in unity, by the most perfect form of the will, which is love. Does the Holy Ghost proceed from the communion of the Father and the Son?

Explain the hypostatis of Christ. Tell me you love me. Define your terms.

He fell on his back and saw, in the clouds, the eye of the whale. He saw the river burning and his friends destroyed.

And no one listens to him. No one. No one.

An excerpt from his letter of Sept. '66:

The large, looming discovery: Samuel R. Delany. I had read a few of his books and been quite impressed and assumed he had been writing for three hundred years and was roughly ten million years old. God, I should have known (and if I'd read the jacket notes would have) . . . by the time he was 22, he'd had four books published. The last three of these are a trilogy, and his best work. He's about 24/25 now, with eight books. And he's beginning to think about shorter work. . . . "Chip" has the strongest, most vital personality I've discovered in the sf clan. That young, and writing like that! (This is the larger part of my current depression—that he does it so much better than I.) Read his books and you drown in poetry.

And this, from a letter to his wife:

Glad to hear that you and Tom are getting along so well and things are working out; also, of course, very glad to hear that you're working. I'm really damned pleased that you like him so much. Tom is a fantastic influence on everyone he comes near. I find it difficult to be with him for more than a few minutes without having the urge to get right to work on something better than anything I've ever done before. I don't know if I have mentioned it, but Tom is beyond doubt the only person I know to whom I'd apply words like "genius." In ten years or so, he's going to be quite, quite well-known and quite, quite respected. What is he, and what are you working on; and are you, is he, serious about the poetry magazine? I hope so.

That radiant quality of mind is something he shares with Mike, with John Sladek, and with Pamela.

And then (though not chronologically):

I'm constantly amazed, Tom, at the similarity of our tastes, expression, and ambitions. If we were French poets, I'm certain we'd think it necessary to form a "school" about ourselves: arguing with the establishment and among ourselves, bitching at traditions, j'accusing all over the place, emitting manifestoes, issuing bulls, belching intent everywhere we walked, excreting doctrine and should-be's, generating slogans, shouting what we collectively think, and having a hell of a lot of fun doing it all . . . I don't think anyone has ever done that in sf, have they? Poetry, art, music, other writing reeks with such focused groups (I'm led to think of this by just having read a book on contemporary poetry, in which the movements of the projective-verse poets and deep-image poets were detailed; it sounded like so much fun, and everyone concerned got so much out of it, and you can't argue that they wham-bang turned the tides of poetry).

A Schematic Diagram

Linda began her affair with Gene in high school. Sometimes Linda wanted to marry Gene. Sometimes Gene wanted to marry Linda. Gregory married Lois. Ben married Nancy. Doug married Sue. Linda and Gene took a flat with Paul. Gene married Marion and moved to Montreal.

Bereft, Linda sailed to London on the *France*. At the university she met Ahmet.

Jerry had an affair with Lois. Gregory was almost killed in a motorcycle accident. Jerry went to Europe. When he returned, a year later, to New York, he subleased Paul's apartment. Paul went away and wrote a novel. He returned and collaborated on a second novel with Jerry. They went to London.

Linda wanted to marry Paul. She had an affair with Jerry. The three of them lived together in Ahmet's flat. After an unhappy and brief affair with Bob, Paul went away and wrote about it. Jerry moved out of the flat and had a brief and unhappy affair with Nancy.

Doug and Sue went to London. She hated London and returned to the States. Doug had an affair with Linda. Jerry had an affair with a different, younger Linda. Mr. Nolde had an affair with the first Linda. Linda was very unhappy. She wanted to marry Jerry. She wanted to marry Doug.

Paul returned to the States. He decided to sublease the Williamses' house with Sue. Doug grew worried and returned to the States. Ben was very upset. He refused to give Linda Doug's phone number.

Gene and Marion went to London.

POETS:	Gregory. Gene. Doug. Paul. Jerry. Bob.
NOVELISTS, SHORT STORY WRITERS:	Gene. Doug. Paul. Jerry. Lois. Nancy. Ben. Linda. Sue. The Williamses.
PAINTERS:	Marion. Linda. Sue.
EDITORS, ANTHOLOGISTS:	Doug. Jerry. Bob. Ben. Mr. Williams.
ARCHITECT:	Ahmet.
ART COLLECTOR:	Mr. Nolde.

III.

The artist, when he makes his art, shares a common fate with Rousseauistic man: he begins free and ends in chains.

And other metaphors (for instance, the furnishing of a room) to express the fact that at this point I know pretty well the nature of everything that must follow to the end of "Reredos" (which was the title it preserved through the entire first draft).

Both Jim and Jane are doubtful about the merits of this story. They seemed to enjoy the preceding sections at the première in Jane's studio (she had just finished a handsome gray nude; we were all feeling mellow), but they questioned whether that wider audience who will read my story to themselves, who have never met me and, likely, never will, would find it relevant or interesting.

What a wider audience ought to know (bear in mind, reader, that this is the frame, not the story):

Four years ago, when I was in advertising, I wrote a story called "The Baron, Danielle, and Paul," which portrayed, behind several thick veils of circumspection, my situation during the previous year, when I had been living with John and Pamela on Riverside Drive. That story appeared, revised, as "Slaves" in the *Transatlantic Review*. Before it had come out, I was living with Pamela again, this time in London and with a different John, a recombination that Jim (before he had ever met Pamela) used as the basis of an amusing piece of frou-frou called "Front and Centaur." After he had met her he wrote "Récits," which is a kind of love story and in no way frivolous. (It, too, was taken by the *Transatlantic Review*.) Then Jim came here, to Milford, and almost immediately Jane wrote a story about the three of *us*: "Naje, Ijm, and Mot." Two days ago Jim sent this off, immaculately typed, to McCrindle, who edits *TR*.

In these successive stories there is a closer and closer approximation to the "real" situation. Thence: this. (Which will almost necessarily go to McCrindle too. If he rejects it? *New Worlds?* Jim is co-editor there.)

A bedroom farce with all the doors opening onto the same

library. Stage center, a row of typewriters. On the walls, posters advertising the *Transatlantic Review.*

But beyond the fleeting amusement of our prototypical incests, the story does (should) raise a serious question. Concerning? Art's relationship to other purposes, let us say. Or alternatively, the Artist's role in Society.

Why do I write stories? Why do you read them?

The Semaphore

The maples, whose leaves he would so much have preferred to rake, grew far up the hill, beyond even the most reckless gerrymandering of the boundaries of the backyard. The leaves that he was in fact raking were dingy brown scraps, mere litter, the droppings of poplars.

Jane came out onto the porch. She had just made herself blond. "You shouldn't do it that way," she said.

"How *should* I do it?" he said.

"You should rake them into piles, and then put the piles in boxes, and then empty the boxes into the incinerator, and then incinerate them."

"Do *you* want to rake the leaves?"

"I hate to rake leaves—it reminds me of poems in *The New Yorker.* I wanted you to come in the kitchen and look at what Dylan's found."

Dylan had found a slug.

"It's a snail," she said, "without its shell."

"It's a slug," he said.

"Oh, you're always so disagreeable."

"Snail!" Dylan crowed proudly. "Snail!"

"No, not a snail," he explained, in the slow expository tone he reserved for his son. "A slug. Say 'slug.' "

Dylan looked at his father with bewilderment.

"Slug," he coaxed. "Slug. Slug."

"Fuck," Dylan said.

Jane laughed. (The night before Jim had tried to explain to Dylan the difference between a nail and a screw. Dylan could not pronounce the word "screw," so Jim had taught him to say "fuck" instead.)

"No, slug." But wholly without conviction.

"Snail?"

"Okay, it's a snail."

Jane found a grape jelly bottle and punctured the top with a nail. (Nails don't have threads; screws do.) She put the shell-less snail in the bottle and gave the bottle to Dylan. The snail's extended cornua explored its meaningless and tragic new world.

"Do you want to give your snail a name?" Jim asked. "What do you want to call him?"

After a moment's deliberation Dylan said, "Four eight."

Neither Jim nor Jane thought this a very satisfactory name. At last Jane suggested Fluff.

Even Dylan was happy with this.

Jim went outside to finish raking the brown leaves, while Jane went up to her studio to work. Her new painting represented a single gray body that embraced its thick torso with confused arms. The three heads (which might have been the same head seen from three different angles) bore a problematical relationship to the single torso. It was based on one of Blake's illustrations to the *Inferno*.

Dylan stayed in the kitchen. He uncapped the grape jelly bottle and filled it with water. Snails live in water. The aquarium in the dining room was full of snails and guppies.

Fluff floated in the middle of the water, curled into a tight ball. Dylan, as he watched the snail drown, pronounced its name, its name, pronounced it.

From the letter he wrote to his wife shortly before he came to Milford:

Pardon the typing. My arms are a bit sore from yesterday's struggle with the harmonium, and I'm a little groggy, still, from being up

late last night writing the first of this letter (which, looking back
to, I feel should be torn up and disposed of). And I'm all emotional and everything. (I cried when I got your letter, and the
effects have not yet worn off. I miss you so much. I love you so
much. I want to be with Dylan so badly. You really have no idea
what importance you two are in my life, how central you are
to everything I do. Just after the death of his wife, Chandler wrote
to a friend something like, "Everything I did, for twenty years,
every moment, was just a fire for her to warm her hands by."
Which is rather how I feel. You'd do best, by the way, to disregard
Tom's proclamations on the subject of earthly love. Tom's ideas
of love, as you must surely know, are rather peculiar ones. Never
listen to a renegade Catholic's opinions on love; only listen to
what his work tells you. I do love you. I love you very much, and I
love you more, this moment, this month, this year, than ever I have
before. I do, Jane. There's desperation in it, yes—I need that love,
to hold up against the world—I need it to give all the rest of what
I do some small meaning, a degree, a single degree, of relevance—
I need it as defense, and as reason. But that doesn't make the love
any less real. With Creeley, I'm afraid I finally believe that "It's
only in the relationships men manage, that they exist at all." You
ask me to write of love. But how can one write of love, particularly
our love?—it is absolute, and words are approximations. I have
done the best I can do, here, in this letter. I have tried, in the
poems, to do better. But I do not, finally, believe in the power of
words to do other than distort, fictionalize, and obfuscate. I love
you. Which is the simplest and best way, because every word there,
and there are few of them, is an absolute concept. I love you.)

A Lasting Happiness

"How strange life is," Jim remarked, after a pause during
which he had taken in the stark details of my cramped cell. "Who
would have thought, only a few years ago, that you . . . that I. . . ."

"Those years have been kind to you, Jim," I insisted earnestly.
"Your books have enjoyed both popular and critical success.

Though you cannot be said to be rich, your life has been filled with pleasures that wealth could never buy. The youth of the nation acclaim you and have no other wish than to pattern their lives on yours. And you, Jane Rose, you are lovelier now than when first we met. Do you remember?—it was July, in Milford."

She turned aside a face that might have come from the pencil of Greuze, but I had seen that tear, and—dare I confess it?—that tear was dearer to me than her smile!

"And you, Tom?" Jim asked in a low voice.

"Oh, don't think of me! I've been happy too in my own small way. Perhaps life did not bring altogether everything that I once expected, but it has given me . . . your friendship."

He broke into tears and threw his arms about me in a last heart-rending embrace. "Tom!" he cried in agony. "Oh, Tom!"

I smiled, removing his hands gently from my shoulder to place it in Jane's. "You'll soon have all of us in tears," I chided, "and that *would* be silly. Because I expect to be *very* happy, you know, where I am going."

"Dear, dear Tom," Jane said. "We will always remember you."

"Ah, we ought never to trust that word 'always.' I would be quite satisfied with 'sometimes.' And young Dylan, how is he?"

"He is married, you know. We have a grandchild, a darling little girl."

"How wonderful! How dearly I should like to be able to— but, hush! Can you hear them in the corridor? It's time you left. It was so good of you to come. I feel quite . . . transfigured."

Jane rose on tiptoe to kiss my cheek. "God bless you!" she whispered in my ear.

Jim pressed my hand silently. There were no words to express what we felt at that moment.

They left without a backward glance.

The warden entered to inquire if I wished to see a priest. I refused as politely as possible. My hands were bound, and I was led along the corridor—the guards seemed much more reluctant than I—and out through the gate to the little pony cart.

The ride to the place of execution seemed all too brief. With what passionate admiration my eyes drank in the tender blueness of the sky! How eagerly I scanned the faces fleeting past on both sides! How familiar each one seemed! And the grandeur of the public buildings! The thrilling flight of a sparrow across the panorama of roofs! The whole vast spectacle of life—how dear it suddenly had become!

A sturdy young man—he might, I reflected, almost have been myself in another incarnation!—assisted me up the steps and asked if there was anything that I would like to say.

"Only this—"I replied. "It is a far, far better thing that I do than I have ever done; it is a far, far better rest that I go to than I have ever known."

He nodded resignedly. "Mm-hm."

✄ The Persistence of Desire

"No more shall Walls of Clay or Mud,
Nor Ceilings made of Wood,
Nor Crystal Windows bound my Sight,
But rather shall admit Delight."

THOMAS TRAHERNE

It was a new building, set amid other new buildings. The sill on which her hands rested was a strip of maple. The clear varnished grain was flecked by a single drop of white paint, from when they had painted the ceiling. The sun warmed the sore flesh. Sometimes a breeze breathed across the fingers. It was as though the sill were some strange kind of keyboard, and the silence of the room was the music she created, masterpiece after masterpiece, prodigal as Schubert.

The view was satisfactory, with lots of sky. She liked the weather, but not trees. On Tuesday the 11th, and again on Tuesday the 18th, it rained. Only, that second Tuesday, intermittently; but even so, the women, before they entered the supermarket, had to pause a moment at the door to furl their umbrellas. She was grateful for such weather, and the way the tires hissed on the wet pavements, the way the concrete ledge beyond the sill slowly changed to a darker but still nameless gray.

In the sunlight she imagined the men in overalls slopping through their work. Their laughter, their indifference. A radio blaring, probably. Droplets flung from the bristles of the brush pattered on the stiff canvas spread across the floor. All but this single droplet: she scraped at it with the tip of a nail, but it clung resolutely to the wood.

In June they took out her telephone. Too many long-distance calls. When the man came it was embarrassing. She pushed some of the clothes under the bed, threw some in the bathtub, and drew the plastic curtain of black sea horses and golden bubbles. It must have seemed peculiar to him, coming to such a building as this to take out a phone. She wondered if the super had found out. An Irish name, beginning in O. Not that it mattered, really. Her rent was taken care of automatically.

The turtle lived in a rectangular box of clear plastic. Initially she was aware only of layers of light that vanished as she approached, of shards of rock rising from the shallow water, of the persistence of desire and brief lightning flashes of understanding and despair. This second, supervenient consciousness overlapped the usual view from the bedroom window, sometimes quite sharply, but more often so faintly as to pass unheeded, like the sounds of unseen traffic. Passing the same shop window at different hours of the day, one is at times more aware of what is on display, at other times of one's own reflection in the glass, and there are moments when the two worlds seem to hang in the balance.

She looked at her hand. The torn cuticles. The white, cracked flesh about the knuckles. The skin flaking from the reddened fingers. She blamed the Lysol, or the glove, but of course it was her own fault, for mixing so strong a solution, for going on with the work after she'd felt the leak. She was afraid to touch her face with the raw, red hand, as though it had become a source of infection.

It rested in the sunlight and her will focused, ineffectually, on returning it to health.

As a girl (she recalled) she had tried to start a fire in the woods with a small plastic magnifying glass, creating a series of crisp, black pockmarks on the leaves and occasional wisps of smoke, but never a fire. The glass was too weak.

Then, with the hand still before her, and her attention focused on that hand, and the full force of her will, she saw the turtle itself. With a slight shiver she realized that this was the animal whose narrow world she had caught glimpses of these many days. She closed her eyes; the turtle remained, a green oval ornamented with irregular hexagons, the dull ache of its hunger. It seemed to be three feet below her, or two feet. There was no object in the plastic box by which to gauge its absolute size.

A fetid smell hung over the water. The turtle's wastes and tiny, rotted shrimp. All the rocks here were polished to such a degree of smoothness that no amount of scrabbling up and down would scrape off the filaments of slime that clung to its hind claws and tail.

The turtle was real. It lived somewhere in the building. She was not imagining it. It lived here, and it was dying. Though it might hold on for weeks, or months.

She was aware, approaching the park, of the hunger of the trees pressing upward past the shadows of the buildings, of the other trees. She was aware, in their branches, of the more conscious and insatiate hungers of birds and squirrels. She felt their hurts and diseases in her own body, sudden implacable lusts, endless fear, rages, and a vague sense, like a film of oil shimmering on water and killing the life below, of wrongness.

Eventually she stopped going out on the street. Anything she needed could be delivered to the door of the apartment.

The first thing she had done, moving in, was to take all the plants from the window boxes. Out to the stairwell where she dropped them, clay pots and all, down the incinerator chute. Two of them, a philodendron and a waist-high rubber plant, were too big for the chute. They rode up and down in the elevator all day. The sickly rubber plant lost half its leaves, but it was not, after all, her responsibility. At five o'clock they were gone. Perhaps someone

had adopted them, the way sentimental girls take pity on sick
kittens or birds that have fallen from their nests. More likely the
super had thrown them in a garbage can.

He was an ugly man. Irish, with an alcoholic, Irish nose like
some unpleasant, supposedly edible tuber. A bachelor, he kept
cats. Forbidden to go outside, they would sit daylong beside the
plate-glass windows, staring out, feeling, as she could, what other
creatures felt. But knowing only their fear, never their pain. Fear
was a kind of food to them. The cats, though they disliked and
avoided her, reluctantly accepted her as an equal.

The turtle's shell was going soft. It no longer attempted the
Sisyphean task of scaling the sheer plastic walls of its box, its cage,
its tomb. Warm and dry and nearly as stripped of sensation
as the scrap of carved stone on which it lay, the turtle became
a part of the larger silence of the room. No food was dropped into
the water. The water vanished.

She would have been grateful had these absences been allowed to grow, ripen, and drop from the branch, making the
silence whole. But just as the pain would subside to utter ne-
science, the owner would remember. Fingers would clamp down
on the yielding shell, and the turtle would find itself swirling in
a dazzle of porcelain. Food would appear on rocks that once again
were moist. It would be reawakened to the pain of its dying.
Braced against the smooth rocks, it tried to climb up the wall its
eyes could not see toward the ledge its claws could not reach.

Her hand grasping the sill, she listened to a noise of human
voices. The street below had faded to unintelligibility. As though
the angle of the light made it impossible to see, through the shop
window, whatever lay behind, the bric-a-brac and pretty nothings.
There was only the reflection of her face, her cotton dress, a
parked car, and behind it a blur of traffic in the street.

Her fingernail was broken from overmuch picking at the
speck of paint that marred the wood of the sill. It was still there.
Sometimes the muscles of her neck would tense and she would
feel a fleeting urge to lean forward and attack the speck of
paint with her teeth, with the entire strength of her jaw.

The red tones seemed to have become more vivid, other colors having, in proportion, diminished. So that it looked like meat. It lay there, some two or three feet away, in the sunlight. Throbbing. Full of blood. More like some autonomous creature than a part of her.

Weakly it pulled itself toward the speck of paint. Weakly claws scrabbled at the smoothness of the maple.

The hand in the box waited to be fed. It curled round the sun-warmed stone, as though to press from it the secret of its happiness, its warmth, its beauty. Then its grasp slackened, its attention wandered.

Slowly it crawled across the rocks, trying to escape the world of substances, desiring a world of light.

The Planet Arcadia

It is hard to understand why dawn lands on these hills, exciting the chains of carbon with quanta of light, or why, when we step beyond a particular line traced across the marble pavement of the courtyard of π, we are forced to reappraise certain temporal relationships. It is enough, perhaps, that we should rely upon our captain, Captain Garst Flame, who does not hesitate to resolve dilemmas of this nature with ruthless rationality—even, at times, like Alexander, with an Ax.

There are four continents, roughly equal in area, grouped in opposing pairs, two to each hemisphere, so that a simple W traced upon the Mercator projection would adequately describe our first hasty itinerary, ticklings of the fingers that would soon so firmly *enclose*.

The planet moves in an eccentric orbit about RR, a highly irregular variable in the Telescope. A primitive theocracy governs the Arcadians, whose diet consists largely of herbal salads, milk and dairy products, and a savory spiced meat resembling our mutton.

Even at noon the light of RR is tinged with blue, just as his eyes are always blue: genius is not too strong a word for Captain Flame, of whose tragic fate this is the unique record. To him the indigenes present the firstlings of their flocks; him we of the crew (Oo Ling, the lovely Micronesian biochemist; Yank, our impetuous freckle-nosed navigator; Fleur, who took her double doctorate in Cultanthrop and Partfizz; myself, geologist and official Chronicaster to the Expedition) thrice have raised to the nomenclature of *Palus Nebularum.*

The central massif of the White Mountains describes a broad U above which the sister cities of Hapax and Legomenon form a gigantic umlaut of arcane beauty. Fleur has recorded and analyzed the structure of the Temple. Her breakdown shows that the centers of curvature, marked by the double circles of the three interfaces of the interpenetrating hemispheres, lie *in a straight line,* the same that has been traced upon the marble that paves the courtyard of π. From this it can be proved that the Arcadian mathematics, so primitive in other respects, is based upon a shrewd understanding of the physical properties of soap bubbles. We have spent many hours in the common room discussing the implications of Fleur's discovery. Oo Ling, who is contracted to my bed, questions Fleur's recommendations of clemency, which I am inclined to support, provisionally. How I love to look into the depths of those ianthine eyes, two vernal flowers floating on a skin of cream, to touch the oily quiff that clings, like iron bonded to aluminum, to that noble brow. Oo Ling. I desire you, pressing my fist into my genitals as I pronounce your name, Oo Ling!

But I fear the imminence of our dissent. Your voice will be with Yank's, mine with Fleur's, and the decision will rest with Captain Flame, who has remained through all these bull sessions, impassive, serene, showing to us a smile that mocks every attempt at interpretation.

Captain Flame, it is with tears that I record the tragedy of your fate.

I am extending my orological investigations, assisted by the indigenes Miliboeus and Tityus, sons of the Abba Damon, who holds the staff of π. Miliboeus, as the elder, wears a kirtle of heavy mortling dyed the color of fine glauconite; the younger Tityus, uninitiate to the Arcadian mysteries, dresses in simple dun fluff fastened with leather thongs. My own suit on these field trips is a tough corporal unit of flesh-patterned polyisoprene, which can be activated to simulate any sacral movements, such as walking, running, skipping, etc. This, we have learned, is a useful subterfuge, in view of the Arcadian predilection for natural forms.

.   .   .

On the eleventh trimester of our Conquest, Miliboeus said: "Death sings to us, Abba."

And Tityus: "Just as the clouds struggle toward their disappearance, alas, our hearts contest with our minds."

I replied, in the Arcadian tongue: "Brothers, I do not understand. The sun is at solstice. Your blood courses through your veins swiftly, as water spills down the mountainside. Youth you possess, wisdom you shall inherit, and poetry—"

Tityus interrupted my peroration, slapping an insect that crawled in the fluff of his thigh. He showed me the smear on the palm of his hand. "It is thus," he said sadly.

"And thus," said Miliboeus, licking the smear from his brother's hand.

Astonished, I reached the captain at once by Telstar and narrated this incident to him, while the enlarged image of his hand wandered thoughtfully among the swollen Greek letters of the primary unit. Captain Flame spends all his uncoordinated moments on the bridge now, breathing its metamorphic air, sealing from us all channels except the red and yellow bands. Dammed, our love swells. Moths beat white wings against the protective shell of glass. Images that betoken our more animal nature, which we share, in a sense, with the Arcadians; and I have seen, in the captain's blood, and heard, in his screams, the cost of transcendence.

"I expected this," he said, at red, my narration having terminated.

"I did not expect this," I said. "I did not know that you expected this."

Oo Ling joined our communication: "I expected this too—for these reasons: first, they have kept us in ignorance of their mysteries; second, we are not allowed within the Temple; third, their daily speech is filled with imprecise denotations."

"I object," I replied. "Firstly, it cannot be the mysteries that Miliboeus fears, for he is initiate. Secondly, all primitive cultures observe similar taboos. Thirdly, the inexactness of their speech is characteristic of its emergence from the Rhematic age. I maintain that they are naïve, merely."

"That is probable," the captain said, "and it is this very probability that led me to experience anxiety. Naïveté can be more
counterproductive than active deception and, if intransigent, is
an argument for genocide."

"Do you feel a large degree of anxiety?" I asked.

"I had felt only a small degree of anxiety, but this message
has caused it to enlarge, and it is still enlarging now." He bipped
the image of a swelling iridescent sphere.

Oo Ling descended gracefully to the yellow band. "Have you
had sex today, Garst?"

"No, nor yesterday."

"Maybe you're just feeling horny. Why don't I come to your
bed?"

"Good idea. Are you free now?"

"Yes. I'll finish with these proteins later. I need a good lay
myself." Oo Ling blanked off our link.

"With your permission, Captain, I'd like to observe."

"As you please," he replied, with circumspection in the image
of his eyes, *bleu d'azur, bleu celeste*. The wall irised open and the
floor drove him toward the bed, which puckered to receive that
splendid torso, those limbs tensed with an heroic lust. I moved in
for a closeup of his loins, then followed the rippling, golden flesh
slowly upward, as Cellini's finger might have caressed fauld, breast-
plate, and gorget of his own molding. I tightened my shot to a
single staring disc of *bleu d'azur*, in which I saw, as in a mirror,
the image of Oo Ling. Oo Ling, I desire you, pressing my fist, then
and now, into my genitals as I pronounce your name, as your
image falls and rises on the image of our doomed captain, Garst
Flame.

When you come, I come with you, and we are together
there, the three of us, and then, sighing, I must break the link, and
I find myself sitting, half disengaged from my unit of polyisoprene,
with the two youths, Miliboeus and Tityus, staring at my happiness and pride.

They show me specimens of the rocks they have been collecting, while, at a distance, a lamb bleats with a lamb's naïve anxiety,
and the lurid sunset shifts from peach to mauve to indigo, a
phenomenon as puzzling to me, as arcane, as beautiful, as the expression on his lips when he is not smiling.

This happened on Day Theta/11th trimester of our Conquest of Arcadia, according to the sequence described.

Now, as an eagle will swoop down upon an incautious hare, the strong talons shredding her pink flesh, so dawn's light pounces on the geanticlinal welts of the White Mountains. Yank has noted in his report the presence of certain new faculae on the surface of RR, heralding perhaps some cosmic disease. Light seems uniform, yet is thronged with data: coded histories of all future event dance in its waves like the motes that people the sunbeams, sunbeams that awaken the sheep in their fold, whose glad conclamation then wakes the tardy shepherds Miliboeus and Tityus, as in the age of Dickens and Pope the sound of songbirds might have awakened a poor London chimneysweep, the victim of economic oppressions. The image of their brotherly kisses flickers on the screen of the common room, and the image of the morning sunlight, the bleating of the flock.

I lean across the trough to let my fingers graze the down of your hand and trace the curve (a lituus) of your silken quiff. I whisper in your ear: "And who is *my* brother?"

Shall I interpret your laugh? Shall I admit that your smile is an auspex to be ranked with sunspots and birdsong, with deformations of the liver, the pancreas, and the intestines? You are as solemn as a saraband by Lully, as arousing as Brahms's "Lullaby." When I regard your sexual organ, engorged with blood, I lose all sense of kinship patterns, of teamwork, of philosophy.

And your reply: "Oo Ling?"

And my echo: "I cannot tell you all that I am feeling."

Fleur pokes a finger in my ribs. "You two lovebirds have got to break it up. We've got our work cut out for us today."

Obediently we return our attention to the screen:

The shepherds wake, and walk toward their death, as a young man of good family, in the heyday of the Industrial Revolution, might have ascended the Jungfrau to enjoy one of its many celebrated views. The random motions of individual sheep become, in aggregate, a progress as direct as the path of an arrow.

Simultaneously, at the Temple, the Abba Damon unlocks, with a caduceus-shaped key, the gilded doors. The opposing helices

of the two serpents are of complementary shades, blue and orange.
The key is so shaped and so colored that the slightest motion
seems to set the two snakes writhing.

Unseen, except by our miniature cameras, the twin serpents
writhe in the lock; the doors swing open, and Damon leads forth
the celebrants. The procession follows him in single file along the
line retraced that same morning upon the marble pavements with
the blood of Miliboeus and Tityus. Above the Abba's head sways
his crozier of office, decorated with brand-new orange and blue
Celanese acetate ribbons, the gift of Oo Ling, who, watching this
solemn, scary moment with me in the common room, cups my
breasts in his hands, naming, as they flash past on an ancillary
screen, the names of the amino acids composing the phenylalanine
chain: "Voline, aspartic acid, glutanic acid, voline . . ." (and so
on). Just as once, twenty or thirty years ago (though this seems
probable enough, I *remember* nothing of the sort), a much shorter
Oo Ling might have recited that same litany at my maternal knee.

More affecting, however, than Oo Ling's prattle is the fuss
that Yank is making over the community's coffee pot. Will Fleur
have cream, he wants to know. Will I take sugar? Of course I will!
And thank you very much.

The cameras float up the mountainside in the wake of the
flock, documenting the thousand flowers crushed beneath the feet
of lamb and ewe, tup and yeanling: anemones, bluebells,
cinerarias, and daisies; lush eglantine and pale forsythia; gentians;
hawthorns, irises, and April's bright-hued jonquils; and many other
kinds of flowers as well, all of them crushed by innumerable sheep.
Sometimes, however, Miliboeus would stoop to pluck one of the
more enticing blooms, then knit its stem into one of the garlands,
bucolic and complex, with which he'd crowned himself and his
kid brother.

"Well, there's coffee for everyone," Yank said, with a little
sigh of accomplishment.

"But I see five cups," I pointed out, "and there are only four
of us."

"Yes, Mary's right," Fleur said. "Captain Flame is missing!"

It didn't take us long to discover our leader's whereabouts,
once the dials were properly adjusted. For he too was on that

mountainside, halfway between the two young victims and the procession of priests, who were, already, opening the vault in the hillside—how had it escaped our detection all this time?—from which, with the terrible inevitability of nuclear fission, the Wolf emerged.

Fleur shrieked: "Watch out, Garst! Behind you!"

But he had blanked off all bands and was deaf to our warnings. We observed the events that followed with a mounting suspense, little suspecting that they would lead us, step by step, to a catastrophe of global dimensions.

Concerning the Wolf.

Though not larger than a double sleeping-space and almost noiseless in its operation, the Wolf was expressive, in every detail of its construction, of a sublime rapaciousness, a thirst for dominion so profound as to make *our* Empire, universal as it is, seem (for the moment we watched it) as insubstantial as the architectures shaped by the successive phrases of a Bach chorale, which fade as swiftly as they rise. Here, incarnate in chrome-vanadium steel, was the Word that *our* lips had always hesitated to speak; the orphic secret that had been sealed, eons past, in the cornerstone of the human heart, suspected but never seen; the last, unwritten chapter of the book.

Busy swarms of perceptual organs encircled its crenelated head to form a glistering metallic annulet; its jaws were the toothy scoops of ancient steam shovels; it was gray, as a glass of breakfast juice is gray, and beautiful as only a machine can be beautiful. We of the crew were breathless with astonishment, admiration, and, needless to say, fear.

The Wolf advanced along the path of trampled flowers (anemones, bluebells, etc.), stalking not only the flocks and the two young shepherds but the very Empire itself, in the person of Garst Flame. Did *it* know this already? Had the ever expanding network of its senses discerned Garst's presence on the path ahead, and was this the reason that it seemed now to quicken its pace, as a lover, learning that his beloved is unexpectedly close at hand, will hasten toward her?

What was this creature? Could it have been formed here in Arcadia? In what hidden foundry? What intelligence had wrought so eloquently in chain and cogwheel, engine and frame, the manifest aim of all intelligence? What was it going to do? What weapons would be effective against it? These were the questions we asked ourselves.

All poetry, as Yank once remarked apropos of this brace of sacrificial lambs, is a preparation for death. Tityus tosses his crook—where the wood has slivered, a tuft of fleece has snagged and clings—to his older brother: why, except *we* know the danger they are in, should this playful gesture rouse in us feelings of such ineffable sadness?

Such sadness. And yet, paradoxically, of all the indigenes it is only these two who, like green-barked saplings uprooted and bagged before some terrific flood, will survive, while all the rest, the stoutest oaks, the tallest pines, must be drowned in the waters of a necessary and just revenge. But I anticipate myself.

This is my point: that since we can never know from *his* lips why our captain left his post, we must suppose that he was moved by a sense of pity, and that somehow he had foreseen the danger that had till then been locked within the rocky shells of the Arcadian hills, as chemists at the dawn of the modern age suspected the existence, though they could not prove it, of the intercalary elements.

Through the morning and far into the afternoon, while the dreadful contest between the Wolf and Garst was being fought out on the slopes below, their sport continued, the songs, the jigs, the clumsy, countrified wrestling that was more like loveplay than a form of combat, the pastoral lunch of whey and the snack later of scarlet berries—and all the while, like the tremolo work above a Lisztian melody, that same unvarying brave show of insouciance!

All this is astonishing, true enough, but as Fleur remarked even then, it is also essentially unhistorical. No more of this blather about Meliboeus and Tityus, who are nothing more now than gray, useless, aging aliens taking up bench-space in the Home Office's Park of All Arts, like turkeys manufactured for a holiday that is no longer much celebrated and still gathering dust beneath the counter of some hick store in Gary, Indiana, or like poems that were never translated from French or a song that never got taped, etc., etc. The possibilities for obsolescence are as numberless as the stars.

Dinosaurs quarreling; the customs of pirates, of the Iroquois, of carnivorous apes; the great Super Bowl between the Packers and the Jets; the annihilation of Andromeda III; Norse berserkers hacking Saxons and their horses to bits; the hashish-inspired contretemps of the Assassins of Alamut; the duels of Romeo and Tybalt, of Tancred and Clorinda; killer-dwarves of the Roman arenas; John L. Lewis smashing the skulls of company scabs with his mammoth jackhammer; Apollo flaying Marsyas, slaying the Delphian Python at the very brink of the sacred abyss; bloodbaths, bullfights, drunken mayhem, battle hymns, Schutzstaffel deathcamps, missiles programmed to reproduce themselves in midflight; Germans galloping across the ice of Lake Peipus; Juggernauts and abattoirs; Alexander's delirium at *Arbela*; *Bull Run*; the Romans slaughtered at *Cannae* and slaughtering at *Chaeronea*; *Drogheda* defeated and depopulated; Panzers swarming across the sand toward *El Alamein*; the Carolingian empire dissolving at *Fontenay*; the French victorious at *Fontenoy*; images that can only begin to suggest the weight and excitement of the drama our cameras recorded that day, as nine and a half feet of red-haired, blue-eyed human fury matched its strength and wits against six tons of supercharged, kill-crazy engineering.

Even the cameras and mikes shared in the combat, for the Wolf's busy sense were equipped with their own weapons systems. A methodical destruction of our network began, to which I retaliated (communications being up my alley) with a simple Chinese-type strategy of endless reinforcement. I figured that the more eyes the Wolf used to pursue and destroy the ship's receptors, the fewer it would have available for its fight against Garst Flame.

As in so many deadly contests, the crucial moments were often the least spectacular. By bluff and psychic ambush each sought to win some fractional advantage over the other. Garst would set his corporal unit swaying hypnotically. The Wolf would spin round him in swift circles, braying and honking and clashing his jaws at erratic intervals, hoping to jar Garst from the steady 4/4 rhythm of his wariness.

Then, without warning, Garst unleashed a river of attenuator particles. The Wolf skittered sideways and parried with a hail of yttrium that spanged harmlessly against the tough polyisoprene of the corporal unit.

A teat of the Wolf squirted clouds of antilife gas, but Garst's nerveshields protected him. The priests, who had arrived on the scene moments after things got started, backed away in terror. The spray settled where they'd been standing; the grass withered and turned black.

The Wolf's eyes and ears were steadily demolishing the cameras and mikes that I poured into the area, making reception in the common room ragged and fragmentary. On the other hand, the personnel registers were functioning beautifully, and it boosted our morale a lot to know that Garst's acetylcholine production was down thirty-six per cent with a corresponding fifty-four per cent rise in sympathin. The time lapse for prosthetic response was, in consequence, pared to microseconds.

Then the impossible happened. The Wolf seemed to be taken in by one of Garst's feints, and he was able to run in under the lowest, least well-armored jaw and give it a taste of his circuit randomizers. The jaw turned to haywire—but it had been a trick! Three tentacles, hidden till now in another jaw higher up, blurted out and wrapped themselves around both Garst's arms and his helmet. Ineluctably he was lifted upward, flailing his legs with futile vigor, toward the chomping steam shovels.

It had been to just such a death as now loomed over our captain that the Abba Damon had willingly and consciously fore-doomed his own two sons! Think of *that*, all you moralizers, before you condemn the decision we arrived at (after hours of de-bate) concerning a suitable punitive measure.

To return, however, to that moment of supreme anxiety. It was just then, wouldn't you know it, that one of the Wolf's ears shot down our sole surviving camera, and simultaneously over the audio we heard the roar of a tremendous implosion.

The personnel registers dropped to a level of complete non-being.

To get fresh cameras to the scene I had to detach the network from my own unit. By the time it arrived everything was over. The amazing thing was that Garst had won, the Wolf was dead. And here is the stratagem: once the Wolf's tentacles had glued themselves to his corporal unit and begun corroding the armor, Garst had tongued the trigger for maximum Self-Destruct, then, hoping against hope, had jettisoned himself bang right out of his unit.

He'd landed, unsheathed and soft, at the feet of the Abba Damon. The suit meanwhile destructed and with it every contiguous atom of the Wolf, whose eyes and ears buzzed round the site of the implosion afterward like bees who've lost their hive. Then, without a central, directing intelligence, their programming caused them to knock each other off, as the soldiers sprung from Cadmus' sowing began, as soon as they'd risen, fully armed, from the sun-warmed furrows of Boeotian Thebes, to slash and stab at each other in the madness of civil war.

The Abba Damon stoops and lifts the pale, pained torso with just such a mingling of amazement and acquisitive delight as a collector in the heroic age of archaeology might have shown upon discovering some antique term, an armless satyr from the baths of Titus.

"Take me to . . ." Garst whispered, before the treason of his own lungs, desperate for more, and purer, air, silenced him.

With our captain cradled in his arms the Abba Damon retraces his path down the slopes of the mountain, along the line of blood in the courtyard of π. Again the twin serpents writhe in the lock, and now for the first time, as our camera flutters above the sacrifice like the Dove in representations of the Trinity, we see the Inner Temple.

A piece of road equipment, precious in its antiquity, seems to have been abandoned before the high altar.

A song of woe, Arcadian Muses, a song of woe!

The Abba Damon traces the curve (a lituus) of his staff of office as, with sacramental dispassion, he observes his assistants fastening the cords securely around Garst's genitals. How many times—and with what feelings of tenderness, the charity of the senses—have all of us, Fleur, Yank, Oo Ling, myself, caressed that cock, those balls, the little bush of hair! O Garst! Now we cannot touch you! And never, never again.

Then, as the priests take turns operating a crude windlass, the victim is raised until at last his body swings, inverted, an obscene, pitiful pendulum, above the rusting machinery. I cannot recall this moment, this final image without feeling again the same numbing terror, which shades, again, into the same unspoken collusion, as though, then and today, a compact were being made between us: between on the one hand, the Abba, his priests, that green planet, and, on the other, myself, the crew, our ship, an Empire—a compact whose tragic clauses we must obey, on each side, down to the last remorseless syllable.

A song of pain, Arcadian Muses! Arcadian Muses, a song of pain!

I must mention his screams. His suffering, like the attributes of Godhead, is at once inconceivable and endlessly intriguing, a perpetual calendar of thought, an Ouroboros. I think of that strong and splendid being stripped to the irreducible human sequence of head, chest, gut, and sex, and though usually it is a matter of indifference to me that I am of the female sex, I am glad to know that I need never fear such a thing happening to me.

Sing of death, Arcadian Muses! Sing!

He raises the knife and, murmuring some words to the effect that he does this only with the greatest reluctance, slits Garst's throat from left to right. A brief necklace of blood graces the white flesh that only that morning was banded by the red collar of Imperial office. The blood streamed down across his face to drench and darken the soft curls. His body hung there till the last drop had drained out into the rusted engine of the caterpillar.

Sing, Arcadian Muses! Sing the mystery. For your own death approaches.

The motor turned over once, sputtered, and died. The scoop

lifted a fraction of an inch, and these events took place, our captain's death, the destruction of Arcadia, so that that gesture might be made.

Following these barbarities, the Abba Damon, in pleading for the release of his sons, sought to excuse himself and his people with arguments and "explanations" too laughable to merit the dignity of inclusion in this record. To repeat such tales would be an affront not only to the memory of our leader but also to that of the planet which it was our pleasure, the next day, to wipe out of existence.

Before X-hour each of us wrote an epitaph for him in the log, an ineffaceable magnetic tribute to the man who'd led us to success on so many missions.

This was Fleur's: "Soon we'll be back at the Home Office, back on the red bands, where you were always most at home. Our recall priorities will be adjusted, they always are before reassignment, and that means I'll forget you, except for a couple of memories that won't matter that much. This pain is a ground-mist, and the sun comes up and it's gone. But if I were able to miss you, Garst, I would."

This, Yank's: "The last time I kissed you . . . the rest may have to go, but I'm holding on to that."

And this, Oo Ling's: "I'm sorry that he had to die."

This history has been my epitaph for you, Garst. There is never a last thing to say, unless Oo Ling has said it. One day I told you I loved you more than I loved the rest—and even then it wasn't true. None of us, probably, loved you very much, because if truth be told you weren't that lovable; but we have done that which in your eyes would have been more important: we have done our duty.

Thus, on Day Delta/12th trimester, the Conquest of Arcadia was concluded. Just before blastoff we fired a full charge from the temporal cannon at the heart of RR. Before the sun set that evening on the cities of Hapax and Legomenon, it would have gone to nova.

.   .   .

Arcadia has ceased to be, but other planets await us. The whole great pulsing body of what-is has been tied to the altar, and we advance to tie about its universal neck the sequence of our extinctions, like ropes of pearls, each one a unique, and now demolished world. O glades and rivers, O winds and darknesses, will you mourn, with us, their loss?

✹ Quincunx

"That's just what I complain of," said Humpty Dumpty. "Your face is the same as everybody has—the two eyes so . . ." (marking their places in the air with his thumb) "nose in the middle, mouth under. It's always the same. Now if you had the two eyes on the same side of the nose, for instance—or the mouth at the top—that would be some help."
                    Through the Looking-Glass

Chrysanthemums

The man in the bed has an excruciating sense of humor. It is a very simple bed. Pine. People visited him and left flowers. A Chinese chrysanthemum means cheerfulness under adversity. A red chrysanthemum means I love. A white chrysanthemum is truth. Pine represents pity, but the bed is not pine after all. It is steel, steel that has been painted white, a hospital bed. The man was in a hospital bed. He was sick. This is a story. It represents chrysanthemums.

This is the second time that this man has been here, in the same bed, in the same room, or the third time, or the fourth time. Have you ever been in a hospital? Are you a nurse? What time is it? What time is it now? Seven o'clock. Eight o'clock. Now it is seven o'clock. People in hospitals live lives that are at once more dramatic and duller than, as a general rule, the lives of people elsewhere. Stories emphasize dramatic aspects of existence.

List fifteen stories that take place in hospitals.

Even in his hospital bed Mr. Candolle preserves his excruciating sense of humor. The larkspur is levity; the saffron crocus, mirth. Time is the white poplar. It is seven o'clock. He switches on the bedside light. A vase of chrysanthemums. Various colors. The feeling that something is beautiful. Statements concerning the nature of their beauty, of beauty itself. The nurse enters. Mr. Candolle thinks about the nurse. I am too happy. I change but in death. I die if neglected. I have lost all. I live for thee. I love. I shall die tomorrow. I will think of it. I will think of it. There are men—and Mr. Candolle among them—who can be aroused merely by the sight of a woman in a white uniform. She is like white jasmine, while lilies, white poplar, white rose. He finds it hard to picture this woman engaged in similar tasks in other rooms of the hospital, changing the bedsheets, reading thermometers, her silvery laugh. She vanishes. Mr. Candolle is alone. His various thoughts crawl around on the floor looking for crumbs of food. Shadows of poplar flicker across the blinds as the cars pass by outside.

It is seven o'clock.

His hand touches the light switch, a single finger. Your finger is like his. Touch him. Talk to him. Your silvery laugh. Your softness. Your omniscience. Your isolation, which is not unlike his. Seven o'clock. The bed begins to tell jokes concerning the doctors and nurses, the visitors, the little thoughts on the floor, jokes that fall onto the sheets like damp millet.

"Nurse!" he calls. "Nurse!"

There are thousands of beds, thousands of hospitals, thousands of chrysanthemums, but each of them by being placed in a slightly different context has a unique meaning. Mr. Candolle's thoughts began to eat the chrysanthemums. The nurse sits on the other side of the room, in flickering shadows, and continues to knit, unnoticing. A red sweater for Mr. Candolle. A red pullover. A red ski mask. A red chrysanthemum.

Mr. Candolle thinks: Can time be said to be a fourth dimension?

The nurse thinks: Mr. Candolle is getting worse.

The thoughts think: Red chrysanthemums.

Time eats Mr. Candolle. Time eats the nurse. Time is flat and round and red. Time is a chrysanthemum. It is not a fourth dimension.

Touch me. Kiss me.

It is excruciatingly beautiful.

Representations

It would be expecting too much, Judith, to expect you to understand me. The elegance of my hand will always confound you. You are Semele and I am Jove. Leave me. Walk to another painting and look at that. Think of how, as you stand here in these new uncomfortable shoes, your feet hurt. I despise your shoes. I despise the color of your hair. When I leave you, Judith, I will never come back.

When I said, "I am afraid I will destroy you," did you believe that? Is the easiest thing to say equally the easiest to accept? Look how gracefully she bows her head in acquiescence, the curve of her neck leading to the curve of her shoulder.

Consider, Judith—for I intend to continue calling you Judith as long as I like—consider this plate of lemons and oranges and eggs. Consider their shapes, their colors, the space they occupy. But you are forbidden to touch them or even to talk to them. You are alone and mute in a dress that is far too orange for your complexion. Your volumes are unconsidered. Your head aches. Your name trails behind you on a golden ribbon as you walk away. . . .

I can see you still, through the high arch of the door. A cow seems to be looking out from its painting at your feet, as you stand there in those new uncomfortable shoes, looking at the cow in the painting and wondering why people ever went to the bother of painting cows and plates of fruit, why other people bought the painted cows, what they meant to them *emotionally*. But are you any better than a painting yourself, Judith? Look at you. Stiff velvet draperies squat on your large breasts, hunker down on your thighs, trip your aching feet. The clouds crackle. Wheatfields warp.

You are covered with glass. No one can touch you. No one *wants* to touch you. You are hung so high that no one even bothers to look, and the sentiments that you express are, quite frankly, cloying and incredible.

Yesterday, my beauty, while you were braced within this gilded frame, legs cramped in that rigid, ridiculous contrapposto, I decided to go to the party at the Clarks. We drank cheap wine from expensive glasses. It was duller than even you could imagine. At nine o'clock their child came out in his pajamas, and we gathered about him, admiring his poise, his expression, while his mother interpreted to us his sleepy, sibylline words. Around us the leaves murmured in their Hobbemas, their Sisleys, their Constables.

The sunlight shifts. Your painted flesh regains some of its remembered appeal. If I admit that I am partly to blame, are you willing to try and start over again? Shall we go to my room, or to yours? Shall we give our children the names of Roman gods—or would you prefer the sparer style of Tom, John, Lucy, Rosaline?

Look at me, Judith. I am standing before the Cuyp, but you have left me for Guido, Guercino, Annibale Carracci. The sunlight is fading and the clouds are pink. Take off your shoes. Yes. And now the golden ribbon with your name. Look, we are both as naked as the sunset. We are children again.

The leaves are green and golden, and you are running barefoot toward me through deep grass. How I admire your poise, your expression!

Judith, you are a masterpiece, and so I've saved up this one last surprise. You did not look close enough: that isn't a cow!

Europa, jump on my back!

The Death of Lurleen Wallace

The equinox occurs not long after sunset this evening. The Prince of Abolie plans to observe this event, with a few guests, in his ancestral tower. These luxurious entertainments are regularly mentioned in the *New York Times*. How easily one might become lost on the vast grounds of his estate or in the intricacies of the portrait gallery! Review copies of recent books are scattered with abandon through all the rooms. Once a week the gardener rakes them into little piles and carries them out to be burned.

Her luggage is taken to her room. She is introduced to Miles and Flora. The gravel drive is patterned by the snow tires the Prince has already ordered the chauffeur to put on his Chrysler Imperial. Everyone is nice to her. Everything is commonplace. These morbid fancies with which the children embellish their conversation are only to be expected at their age.

But in the evenings, when she must take her place at table, she feels less certain, less assured. The guests wear masks. Their impassioned discussions of the equinox, of the pollution of the river, of the war, is disquieting. "*Plus ça change,*" the Prince remarks, "*plus c'est la même chose.*"

These fears of the governess, for all that they may be irrational, are nevertheless the very stuff of romance. Secretly, are we not *all* in love with this ruined Prince? No matter what he has done, no matter what he still may do. The suspicion that someone is locked within the tower adds a savor to his caresses. While his hands wander across your body, you listen to his eloquent analyses of the presidential campaign, the polluted rivers, the riots in Chicago. . . .

Vases of flowers. Draperies. These luxuries pursue her through the house like packs of dogs. Merciless. Starving. What is the color of his eyes?

In August treetops, the birds saw the imminence of autumn, and even she must recognize it now, marching down into the valley with its red banners. Day and date are of no consequence. It is autumn. The children hunt for mussels in the polluted river. Splashing, giggling. The governess, bound, her mouth taped shut with Vote for Wallace stickers, watches young Miles caress his sister. The Prince's hands scamper after each other with little cries among the reeds and across the muddy beach. In her imagination she returns to this scene again and again. It is always the same. The river. The masked policeman. The children's little tongues wandering across her body.

Every morning the gardener brings breakfast on a tray to her room. With a sense of almost insupportable luxury she reads the

New York Times. "There is a sickness abroad in the land. It cannot be cured by looking away from it or pretending that it does not exist. The Wallace movement is an evil phenomenon."

The Prince insists that she attend his dinner.

For most of this week daylight and darkness are approximately equal. The lawns are covered with the corpses of small birds. The gardener rakes them into little piles and carries them out to be burned. The hand of the man in the portrait is little more than a claw.

As we continue to read this novel we are led to the realization that the gardener has secretly been corrupting the children for many years. Nauseated, you set the book aside, but it begins, slowly, to creep across the room toward you, inching forward like a caterpillar. You rush outside into the autumn noon and the smell of burning leaves. From the casements of the tower the women scream in support of George Wallace. You lie in the gravel road and he drives the Imperial over your body again and again.

Marches and polkas fall from the trees. The rhythm of life. Soon there will be snow. Soon the river will be covered with ice. Soon, soon, silence.

You have become the Prince of Abolie.

Mate

Once more I ask you, Regina—is it fair? And if you tell me that it is, I say again that it is *not!* I have been here, outside your door, for a very long time now, waiting for a reply, and this in itself is an unfairness. Moreover, I am uncomfortable and sick, and though you may say that I am not *always* sick, this is a very small consolation. One is only more or less sick in any case, more or less uncomfortable, and it is only by comparing the lesser to the greater degree that the former may be made to seem desirable.

Already it is seven o'clock!

Perhaps it isn't a simple matter of black and white. And perhaps my case does not bulk very large among all those that come within the scope of your authority, but then the very fact of its insignificance is an additional source of misery, leading me to suspect that my complaint will never be attended to. Try to put yourself in my place.

At least, Regina, you could *listen* to me! Or look at me. I do exist. I am tangible. I even have teeth.

After all, we are not that very much different, you and I. Are we? You have your vulnerable side too, you know. You need affection, praise, recognition. Your pawn development is weak. Your bishop is exposed. You are drowning, Regina. Save me!

Listen. I love you. I shall bend down to the face in the pool and whisper that. I love. I shall die tomorrow. I shall strew flowers over the still water. I shall carve your drowned, unhappy face in marble. The floating hair. The staring eyes. Orb and scepter. You shall see yourself then as in a mirror.

These are only words. Regina, I am trying to express my emotions. I cannot discuss these things without a certain ambivalence, without some confusion. You must try to understand me.

What time is it now?

I too would prefer simplicity. A one-to-one ratio between this lily in my hand and what it is supposed to mean. You have allowed all things to have too many meanings, and the meanings contradict each other.

And at times, Regina, when you thought I was looking the other way, you have cheated.

You may say, of course, that you have never undertaken to guarantee these claims to justice, that others, speaking without authorization, made these promises in your name. And though I may grant the probability of this, yet reflect, madam, that this in itself is an additional grievance. Shall we not contemn the authority that has not sufficient power to restrain the abuse of its own name? Shall we then respect that authority more or less? Shall we not, in time, learn to ignore such impotent authority altogether?

Or do you feel, perhaps, that the need to address such complaints as these to *someone* is so forceful that no amount of inaction, injustice, incompetence, and vain pride on your part can imperil or challenge your position?

Alas, the very existence of this document would seem to confirm that that is exactly how you feel!

Ignore me then. Ignore my love. Ignore my pain. Ignore everything I've said. I concede the game. I have lost too many pieces. I wasn't really that interested in it when, at your invitation, I began. I forgive you. But I want you to understand this—unless I receive an immediate reply, I intend to publish an account of everything that passed between us.

Now, shall we play another game?

The Assumption

He said.

I decided I would study very hard and pay attention to everything that was said and see if I understood it and if I did to decide if I agreed with it and see if I understood why I disagreed with it if I didn't agree with it so that I could come to understand better *why*.

She said.

Another blue day, children! Another blue day has found us together again.

Above the blackboards on three sides of room 334 are the little acorns and walnut shells where the children live. Now they are all sitting behind their desks, like obedient little drifts of snow on a high brick wall. Some have bodies but no faces. A few of them are nothing more than zigzags. She knows all their names. She has met their parents. Chicken Little. Henny Penny. Ducky Lucky. Goosey Loosey. Turkey Lurky.

These are the flowers in her garden, the jewels in her casket. She enjoys, without a sense of shame, the luxury of each warm tear that trickles down her face. She is represented in the midst of children. Caritas.

Open your books.

Your mouths.

Your eyes.

Open them wider. She said. What have we learned today?

The skies are filled with their beseeching hands. How little they are! How small!

Tom. She said.

Any of us could die at any minute, Miss Locksy. If I died this minute I'd want to know that I was making the best use of it. He said.

We would all be very unhappy if you were to die. Tom. But I think that right now we should get on with our history lesson. She said.

What lesson does history have to teach us?

If these children were to look outside the windows of room 334 they would see a lovely fall day, rivers and mountains, poplars and oaks, a wilderness beneath an immense blue sky. They would see the sky falling and the scheming fox. But they would not see us, for we are invisible. The writer is invisible. The reader is invisible too.

Children, children. She said.

There are people—and Miss Locksy among them—who take pleasure in serving those who are less fortunate, or in some way smaller, than themselves, who are made unhappy by these photographs of children starving in Biafra, whose kiss is unpremeditated.

She rises into the air supported by their exquisite angelic forms. Cherubim and seraphim beyond numbering sing ballads and popular songs. The souls of children who have died of poetry. The exaltation of love. Some have no eyes. Some have used the black Crayolas to cover their faces, but their wings are white, though aerodynamically unsound. They whirr like the wings of hummingbirds. Higher and higher. Pink clouds. The world is far below.

What will we do with their lives?

And then they came to a river.

Jump on my back, Turkey Lurkey. Jump on my back, Goosey Loosey. Jump on my back, Ducky Lucky. Jump on my back, Henny Penny. Jump on my back, Chicken Little.

She said.

The sky is falling and we must tell the King.

✑ Slaves

The Baron slept in the living room, which was also the kitchen, on a Castro convertible. Danielle and Paul, since it was Paul's apartment, slept in the bedroom. The bedroom was no more than a hole in the wall. The bird, Nevermore, had spent the winter there with them, because it was warmer. Now her cage was back in the living room with the Baron.

"Why are you molting?" the Baron asked of Nevermore, twiddling a tail feather in her face. "Do I molt? Do I get my feathers all over everything?" Nevermore squawked.

If the Baron were to put his finger in the birdcage, Nevermore would bite it. Paul was the only person who could handle the parakeet. It belonged to him—a Christmas present from Danielle.

They were still in bed, Danielle and Paul, making love. Meanwhile the Baron prepared breakfast: bacon and eggs, unfrozen orange juice, coffee. He cleared the table of two dirty coffee cups, a paperback edition of *Candy* (the pirated version, since that was more exciting), Danielle's turquoise hairband, and a pile of wadded paper napkins that had been used as Kleenex.

The radio was going to bake a sunshine cake. It wasn't really so hard to make. The Baron changed stations. An announcer read stock market quotations to the Baron. AT&T was up.

Danielle, in a Matisse-ly floral muumuu, came out of the bedroom.

"Isn't there any more nice music?" she asked.

"*This* is music, for those who understand it," the Baron replied, ladling grease over the egg yolks. The Baron had once been a business administration major.

"Last night at the discotheque they played the new Tab commercial for fifteen minutes running. It was just like a French movie. I want to get a record of it for Paul to listen to."

"For my own part," the Baron said, his gaze intent upon the frying eggs, "*I'm* going to make a sunshine cake."

"Did you feed Nevermore?"

"It isn't really so hard to make. I use Betty Crocker's Sunshine Cake Mix."

"Because he's nervous this morning."

"Then add a smile and let it simmer." The Baron smiled winningly, but Danielle didn't see it. She was pouring orange juice into three glasses.

"Besides," he said, "it's a *she*, not a *he*. You can tell by the name, Nevermore. That's a girl's name."

"I don't see that it makes any difference with birds. After all, they only lay eggs. Anyone can do that." The toaster ejected two crisp slices of toast. Danielle replaced them with two mooshy slices of Tastee white bread. "Paul," she called, "breakfast."

"I'm getting dressed, beautiful."

Danielle, it is true, was beautiful, but she was worried about her weight. She was a dancer, and dancers always worry about their weight.

"We were fighting last night," she confided to the Baron, "and I lost another goddam contact lens. Now I can only see out of my right eye."

"You should take out your lenses before you start fighting."

She ignored his joke. "They cost so damn much *money*."

"So get insurance."

"That costs more. Anyhow, Paul is going to pay for it." Paul came out of the bedroom, bare-chested, swinging his arms with athletic grace. He had been a shot-putter in undergraduate days.

"Aren't you, my beloved?" Danielle asked.

"Sure," he said, "I love to pay for things."

He took one of the glasses of juice (the biggest) and drank it in one long gulp. He fiddled with the radio dial and came in on the tail end of "Sunshine Cake." He began to sing along with the radio. He had a resonant baritone, but he couldn't keep in one key. Danielle and the Baron began singing too. Then the song ended, and there was an advertisement for frozen clams.

The Baron put two eggs on each plate and three slices of bacon. Danielle portioned out the toast and poured the coffee. Paul went to the icebox to get the cream for his coffee.

"*Now*," said the Baron, "can't we listen to the stock market again?"

"I like this better," said Paul. What Paul liked better was Mantovani playing the theme from *Peyton Place*.

The Baron was in the foyer, reading the titles of the books in the bookcase. They were dull books that belonged to Paul. The Baron had never heard of their authors: Trelawney, Maitland, Hulme, Wedgwood.

Paul was studying English literature at Columbia Grad School. He was bright, but he'd dropped out of all the good colleges he'd gone to and finally had to take his BA from NYU. These books were from the time, years and years ago, when Paul had been majoring in history at Swarthmore.

The Baron was waiting around in the foyer because Danielle wouldn't come out of the bathroom, where she was combing out her long black hair. Like Nevermore's feathers, Danielle's hair seemed to get into everything: the bedsheets, the food, even the Baron's own laundry. It caused him more to wonder than to be annoyed. Innocently, he would tell Danielle when he found one of her hairs in some new, unlikely place, and she would suppose he was complaining. But the Baron almost never complained. He was seldom that sure of himself.

"Will you be very long?" the Baron asked again through the thick door.

"No."

"Because I am terribly in *need*."

She came out of the bathroom with her hair piled in an elaborate bouffant steadied by the turquoise band. She wore pink tights under a black leotard, and wornout Capezios. Yesterday's makeup was still smudged around her eyes.

"It's all yours."

He was in such a hurry he didn't even lock the door behind him. Once he was on the stool it was too late. While he sat there, he worried about whether he had a soul. The problem had been disturbing him for several days.

In the bedroom Danielle began stripping the bed in search of the contact lens she had lost. "Don't you want to help me, Paul?"

"Sorry. I'm busy writing my paper for Seventeenth Century."

"But you're *reading*."

"I'm reading the book that the paper has to be about. Here, listen to this—it's called *Casualties:*

> Good things, that come of course, far lesse do please,
> Than those, which come by sweet contingences.

Now, does that sound like anything I'd read for pleasure?"

"It doesn't make any sense. Why is it called *Casualties?*"

"Not deaths, dimwit. Casualties—things you do in a casual way, like getting laid."

"You always pick such dull things to write your papers about."

"They're only dull from a distance."

"Like the river," she said, forgetting in the instant to search for the lens. She squinted her left eye shut and looked at the river, shimmering grayly in the morning sun. The details of the Jersey cliffs, the little houses and particular trees, seemed peculiarly clear. She wondered what it would be like to live in Jersey. There was something vaguely frightening about the idea.

She opened the bedroom window, and a breeze stirred through the room, brushing with gentle insistence against the edges of fabrics and loose papers. Paul was saying something. For some reason she wanted to cry. "What did you say?" she asked Paul.

"I asked you if you'd get my shirts from the laundry. Today is Thursday."

"I will—but after class." At night Danielle worked in a bar, standing in a little glass cage and dancing, but in the daytime she studied ballet.

"The ticket's in my billfold," Paul said irritably.

She really couldn't see what *he* had to be irritated about! She looked through his billfold. "Jesus Christ!"

"What?"

"You still have the piece of paper in here with Dr. Minzer's address on it. Isn't that rather careless?"

"So? Who's going to see it? And if they do, I can say he's an analyst that a friend recommended."

"Except that right above his name you've printed Abortions."

He bent over the volume of Herrick with a look of studied unawareness. She dropped the subject. "Here's the laundry ticket. I'm taking a dollar to pay for it."

"Take a couple dollars. We need groceries.

"The Baron will get the groceries though, won't he?" Paul laughed. "What are you laughing at?" she asked.

"This." He read from the Herrick:

Here she lies, a pretty bud,
Lately made of flesh and blood:
Who, as soone, feel fast asleep,
As her little eyes did peep.

While he read, she watched a tugboat moving up the river drawing a coal barge behind it. "I think that's lovely," she said. Then she started packing her clothes for class.

"Can I help you look?" the Baron asked. He was still wearing his pajamas, faded and frayed.

"Would you? That would be nice. I have to go to class now."

Thursday was pointe class. She stuffed a new pair of toe shoes into the smelly bag. Last night she had darned the blunt toes with heavy pink thread.

The Baron pulled the unmade bed away from the wall, and, sprawling across it, he began to explore the cracks in the parquet flooring with his fingertips. Danielle pursed her lips. She didn't like him lying in her bed like that. But what could she say?

Without thinking of what he was doing, Paul idly caressed his muscly stomach with his fingertips. When touched, the brown down tickled a little. His other hand held a book, which he did not read. He was not aware enough of the melody in his head to realize that it had usurped his whole attention. Because he was looking at the book, he would have supposed that he was reading it.

In blue jeans, a T-shirt, and sneakers, Paul looked like a folk singer—not deliberately, but because it was the easiest thing to look like. He liked rough fabrics and the grainy feeling of his hair coming down over the nape of his neck. Mercier, who was Danielle's analyst (a *lay* analyst), had said that Paul was probably a phallic narcissist. Paul couldn't really see anything wrong with that.

The sofa on which he was lying was the Doctor Jekyll, daytime aspect of the Baron's bed. The prosaic furniture of the room was not Paul's, but the books were, except for one shelf that held the *OED*. That belonged to the Baron. Paul was trying to buy it from him, but his asking price was too much. The rent was $150 (because of the veranda and the view of the river), which Paul paid, or, more exactly, which Paul's father paid. Paul's father was an attorney in White Plains.

The Baron's father had been a dentist, but he had committed suicide when the Baron was twenty and a junior in business administration school. He left a note saying he had never wanted to be a dentist. The Baron had dropped out of school. Except for the note, the Baron didn't get anything. His stepmother, who had inherited what little there was, had remarried and was living now in California.

Of course, he was not actually a Baron. That was only the way his friends talked. His real name was Baron Edward Blum.

"I'd like a beer," the Baron said. It was obviously too early for beer.

Paul didn't look up from his book, so the Baron tried another tack. "Nevermore is molting, but she doesn't have any molting food." Nevermore, hearing her name mentioned, squawked and tried to pull the clapper out of the bell that hung in her cage.

Paul took his billfold out of his pocket and gave the Baron a five for groceries. At first Paul had been embarrassed to let the Baron do all the housework and cooking and shopping, but now he took it for granted. "I'm feeling like pimentoes," he said. "What can you put pimentoes in?"

"In olives."

"No, I meant what hot dish."

"In a tuna casserole. Or in tunafish salad. Or in stewed chicken." The Baron cooked something with tunafish in it at least once a week. Tunafish chow mein was his speciality.

"Let's have stewed chicken." Paul lit a cigarette and dropped the dead match on the floor. That was his worst habit, in the Baron's opinion. The smoke curling up his cheek set up a tremor in his left eyelid.

The Baron had given up smoking at the time of Edward R. Murrow's death, but his real reason was that he couldn't afford cigarettes anymore. They'd gone up to forty cents a pack. It was about that time that he'd moved into Paul's apartment.

They were old friends, Paul and the Baron. Ever since fourth grade in White Plains. Paul thought the Baron was crazy, but he liked him anyhow. Paul thought most people were crazy. He was in his fifth year of analysis. He went to a real analyst, an MD, certified—not one of those lay analysts like Mercier. He paid $35 an hour. Danielle only paid $20. But she went four times a week. It ate up all the money she made dancing five nights a week at the discotheque.

So it was obvious to Paul that Danielle was crazy too, but he was in love with her. Paul's analyst said that he would know that he was completely cured when he liked people who weren't crazy better than the people who were.

"What did you fight about last night?" the Baron asked.

"About her dancing. I told her she wasn't getting anywhere with all this ballet crap." But the Baron had heard their argument, and he knew that Paul was lying. What they had really argued about (again) was the abortion.

"Well," said the Baron, "if things don't work out career-wise for a girl, she can always get married."

"But *you*," Paul said, "what will become of you?"

"I don't think about it. It's Christlike not to plan ahead. Maybe I'll go back to business school. Maybe I'll become a beatnik. Maybe I'll be like my father . . . a dentist."

"It's none of my business. Forgive me."

"That's all right, Paul."

"I didn't mean to bug you."

The Baron had gone to stand by the fireplace, where a greatly enlarged photo of Danielle hung. Nude, her breasts were only slightly unfirm; there was a scarcely perceptible crease on the underside of each full globe of flesh. The jutting of her hip was exquisite and bold. Last New Year's, when she was very drunk and Paul had gone off with someone else, she had offered that same lovely body to the Baron, exquisitely and boldly. He had refused, out of a misguided sense of nobility.

—*If people have a soul,* he thought, *nobility makes sense. But otherwise?*

"Do you think I have a soul?" he asked Paul.

"It depends," said Paul. "How much do you want for it?"

"What's a good price?"

"I'd say fifty dollars. And that reminds me—I should look for that goddam contact lens. It'll cost me fifty dollars at least to get another. I just don't have that kind of money to throw away. I'll have to sell some books." Paul went into the bedroom and got down on his hands and knees.

The Baron fingered the little disc of plastic in his shirt pocket. To think that it could cost so much money!

"Why are you molting?" he asked Nevermore. "Just to make more work for me? Is that it? Is that your game?"

"It's in this room somewhere," Paul said, without conviction.

"Why don't you let Nevermore loose? It's spring, and she wants to be free."

"The pigeons in the park would peck her to death."

"She probably prefers her cage anyhow. Kafka wrote about a cage flying in search of a bird. That's about the size of it."

Paul came back into the living room. He had given up the search. "I read in the *Times* a while back that the dime-a-dance girls at Orpheum Danceland kept a pet pigeon in their room. Why do you suppose they did that? Pets are all just pregnancy surrogates, I guess. Anyhow, a pigeon would be better than a cat. Cats leave fur."

"I'll get the groceries now," said the Baron.

"Yes," said Paul, "yes, you'd better do that." He lay back down on the couch again and looked at the photograph of Danielle. When he heard the door being pulled shut and the Baron's footsteps going down the stairs, he began, ever so lightly, to stroke himself through the blue denim of his jeans.

Danielle, whose body was so ripely feminine that one teacher, a man, had told her she would never be a dancer, had nevertheless a stiff and rather defeminized walk. The Baron recognized her by this token from across the street in the Party Cake Bakery. She was coming up from the subway.

He went to the door. "Hi there!" he called loudly.

She waved her big dance bag in the air, and her green damask cape parted in front to show the pink tights and black leotard. Demurely, she waited for the light to change.

"Are you buying cook-kies?" When she spoke, it was like someone who is drugged, or like a sleepy child.

"I'm buying bread. We don't have money for cook-kies." Unconsciously, he mimicked her intonation.

"Poor us."

The saleslady handed the Baron a bag containing a loaf, sliced, of pumpernickel.

"I have to get Paul's shirts," she said, giving the Baron her hand to hold. "Poor dear Paul isn't happy. I wish I could make him happier. He can't see any future for himself except teaching English. It was better when he wanted to be an analyst."

"Or a writer."

"I didn't know him then. That must have been years ago. Why *can't* he be a writer? He has an incredible sensibility. Sometimes. Have you read his poems?"

"His poems aren't very good."

"But they show great sensitivity." Danielle stopped on the street to open her dance bag and take out her change purse. She opened the change purse and took out a dollar bill and the laundry ticket. While she was in the Chinese laundry, the Baron stood guard over her dance bag. When she returned, he felt sad, like someone at the birthday of a much poorer child.

"I've got to go to Woolworth's to get Nevermore her molting food," he explained, handing her her bag.

"I'll come with you. I love to go to Woolworth's. Someday I'd like to work there. Think of all the things you could steal if you *worked* there!"

"What would you steal first?"

"First a pop Bach record. Then some Revlon lipstick. Then a boy parakeet for Nevermore. What would you steal?"

"Money," he said.

"I hadn't thought of that."

"And then slaves."

She pursued her lips. "Oh, I think one might find better slaves in New Jersey." Her eyes sparkled with the pleasure of fantasizing.

In Woolworth's they passed, in order, a pizza and soft drink stand, a candy counter, a cosmetics counter, a display of plastic flowers (29¢—None Higher), and a toy counter. While the Baron paid for Nevermore's molting food (35¢), Danielle drifted to the toys. She picked up the largest cap pistol from the counter, a convincing replica of a Buntline Special, and pointed it at the Baron.

"Bang," she said, "you're dead."

"Gaigh," said the Baron.

The saleslady, who was really too attractive to work in Woolworth's, came up to Danielle, as a nurse approaches the bed of a troublesome patient. "Is there anything I can interest you in?"

Danielle turned, gun in hand, on the saleslady. "Do you have slaves?" she asked. "Men slaves is what I was looking for in particular."

The Baron took her gun away. "Retarded," he explained to the saleslady. "That's why I have to go everywhere with her." The saleslady went away in a huff. Obviously she had not believed him.

"Marbles," said Danielle, surveying the toy counter. "And look *here*, here are balloons. That's what we forgot to get—balloons!"

"They come at two prices," the Baron observed.

"Yes, One box of twenty-five *big* balloons costs fifty cents." The box of twenty-five big balloons dropped through her spread cape and into the open dance bag on the floor. "And one box of one hundred little balloons costs a quarter. That's very reasonable." The cheaper box dropped into her dance bag too.

The Baron had opened a box of one hundred small balloons, and into it (for it was only half full) he stuffed the contents of a fifty-cent package of big balloons. He brought the box to the saleslady.

"I have to buy her these balloons," he said sorrowfully, handing the woman a quarter."

"Two cents sales tax," the saleslady said. He gave her two pennies.

Outside the store, in Riverside Park, Danielle nibbled a slice of pumpernickel. The Baron was massaging her spongy nape with strong, rhythmic pinches. "Guess what?" he said.

"What?" Danielle was staring at the Jersey shore. Then a squirrel caught her attention, two squirrels.

"I found your lens."

"Oh, good." The squirrels began to chase each other, playing peek-a-boo in the still-bare branches of the trees. "Did you tell Paul already?"

"No. Not yet."

His hand caught up a mass of her hair and made a ponytail of it. "And, if you like, I *won't* tell him."

"Don't, thank you. For, truly, it might have been lost."

They began walking home. Daintily Danielle avoided stepping on the cracks. She was thinking how nice it would be to be a squirrel, except she was really thinking of something else.

"What will you do with the money?" the Baron asked. "How much will there be?"

"Fifty dollars."

"And what will you do with it, Danielle?"

She turned on the Baron angrily. "I will buy a present for Paul!"

The Baron smiled and took her hand in his. He hadn't been taken in, not at all. "Perhaps," he said playfully. "When you go to pick it out, will you let me come along and help? I *did* find the lens, after all."

"Perhaps," she said. Then, "Yes, let's." They laughed, and Danielle did a skipping step without stepping on any of the cracks.

"Then here," the Baron said, "is a present for you." He took the Buntline Special out of his coat pocket. The barrel was almost a foot long.

"Bang. Bang. Bang."

Danielle giggled.

It was Danielle who, when they got to the door of the building, had the last word to say on the subject. "We've turned the tables, haven't we? Paul is *our* slave now."

He kissed her right there on the front stoop for all of Riverside Drive to see.

Nevermore squawked when a bright red thing passed outside the bars, but she didn't jump off the perch of her seed dish. It had been three days since she had eaten, and nothing could frighten her away from the food she had now.

The red balloon floated down to the unswept floor and bounced. It came down the next time on a blue balloon, and the blue balloon, blown up to its limit and with sharp grains of dust clinging to its fragile shell, burst. Sympathetically, the red balloon burst too.

Danielle was lying on the sofa, covered with balloons, singing the Tab commercial. Paul and the Baron were still blowing up balloons. They had already blown up one hundred and eighty of them, and there were seventy left to go.

The tops of the bookshelves were covered with balloons. The bed was covered with balloons and the desk was too. The bathtub was filled with balloons, and the kitchen counter was piled high with them. There were balloons all over the floor. Everywhere you looked there were balloons.

"I wonder," the Baron meditated, "whether balloons have souls."

At the end of her anthem, Danielle threw out her arms and legs and the balloons swirled up into the air, bumping lazily against each other, and then settled down again, some on Danielle, some to the floor. The window was halfway open, and everywhere in the room the riverbreeze stirred the balloons. They skittered about the room, as though they were trying to hide.

"Let's go outdoors," Danielle said, stepping out the window. She released a blue, ellipsoidal balloon into the wind. The wind blew it back into the living room.

"Hand them all to me," she said. Her tone was imperious. Paul and the Baron went about the apartment gathering the balloons, which they emptied in great armfuls onto the verenda. Danielle would release them one by one, into the cool wind.

The wind moved the balloons sideways along the apartment building, then at the corner lifted them high into the air. At a certain altitude, the wind, which seemed to be blowing in from the river, carried the balloons out toward New Jersey.

There seemed to be no end to the balloons, but even so Danielle was provident. She released them only one at a time, at measured intervals. Everywhere the blue sky was filled with balloons.

Then the wind changed.

The balloons began to fall down to the pavement and into the street. Pedestrians and strollers in the park took notice of them. On the Drive, cars slowed. One boy started collecting them, but in only a short while he had gathered more than he could hold.

Everyone was watching the Baron and Danielle and Paul.

Paul was the tallest of them and the most handsome from a distance. Standing between the other two, his hand raised over his head, holding a yellow balloon, he looked like a Christ in a Last Judgment. Danielle's hair was blowing in front of her eyes, and she had a hand raised to hold it back. From the street the Baron's figure seemed the least imposing of the three, but it was still necessary in forming the composition.

Danielle turned to her two companions. "Perhaps," she said in a playful tone, "they're free on the other side."

"No," said Paul, more seriously, "I think they're slaves there too."

"What difference does it make," the Baron asked, "if they have no souls?"

The wind picked up again. "All of them, all at once!" Danielle shouted.

In armloads they released the last of their balloons, and they drifted across the street and over the park and high above the river, moving westward toward the Jersey shore.

There were red balloons and blue balloons and yellow balloons and pink balloons and green balloons and orange balloons.

☑ ⃞X⃞ *Yes*

Once in the booth, with the curtain drawn behind her, Mrs. Roman closed her eyes. White pinpricks of light, constellations of the interior dark, twinkled to the rhythms of her own breathing. If freedom does exist, if it is not just another word to fatten the national rhetoric, then one must experience the thing at exactly such moments as this. It declares itself in this sudden intense awareness of one's own body, its distinctness and isolation, its animal mastery of space, its absolute, solipsist authority. Nothing may then intervene—neither the workaday calculus of consequence nor the slow sure arithmetic of precedent—between desire and fulfillment of desire. For with freedom one is equally the master of time: the present abrogates the future with the past.

The beauty of such freedom is insupportable for very long: it is too equivocal. The sheer intensity, unrelieved by action, will soon register as terror. Mrs. Roman teetered at just this brink. The pencil was in her hand. The ballot was spread open on the narrow wooden ledge. A bead of sweat, a premonition, formed at the center parting of her hair. Without breathing, and unaware that she held her breath, she marked her X in the upper square.

Wiping away the trickle of sweat, she refolded the ballot and left the booth. She dropped the folded paper into the slot in the padlocked ballot box. She smiled at Miss Haigh, who, other days of the year, was only an assistant at the library, in charge of the children's room, humblest precinct of the civic temple. Miss Haigh signaled the next voter to enter the booth.

Leaving the courthouse lobby she discovered that the rain had started up again. It would go on raining, intermittently, all that day. No single cloud could be seen in a sky of uniform, ageless gray. Prematurely, the elms of the small park were shedding dry green leaves on the dry tawny grass. The flag hung from the top of its pole wet and unwaving. Nothing seemed to celebrate.

With the automatism of habit Mrs. Roman worked the combination of her bicycle lock, wheeled it down the sidewalk to the street, mounted, pedaled away—and with movements as small and precise as these the world of buildings, streets, and sky repossessed Mrs. Roman, steered her, took her home. The sensation of that moment in the booth, the small secret treachery of her X, was at the mercy now of memory, and memory twisted it into mere wistfulness, shaded it with regret. She ought not, of course, have voted Yes. Always, on previous Referendums, she had voted No, and she had intended to vote No again today, but something had come over her. It was too late now to undo it. The ballot was in the box, the box was locked. In any case, what did one vote matter among so many? A drop in the ocean.

It was something she had never understood before, how anyone *could* vote in favor of the Referendum: now she couldn't really understand why *she* had. Perhaps it was always like that, for all the people who voted that way, a moment of giddiness, something out of the blue.

She stopped at the automat on her way home. The other stores would be closed because of the holiday. While the automat hummed soft Muzak to itself, she took what she needed—cornflakes, salt, soya meal, soup mix, bread, *TV Guide*, fresh oranges and onions, a can of tuna, freeze-dried peas—from the shelves and brought them to the out counter. Paying her charge card into the register she had an obscure feeling that by this action she were redeeming her vote, tipping the balance back to some more quotidian Yes.

Yes, automat. Yes, bicycle. Yes, street. Yes, Xavier. Yes, children, dinner will be ready in just a minute now.

She parked the bicycle in the garage beside the DeSoto, Xavier's pride and the first altar of their marriage. Since fuel rationing the car had left the garage less often than she went out of the house, but Xavier seemed to love it all the more for being an invalid.

The wind had once again taken the plastic lid from the garbage can, and once again the lid, with a wonderful, invariant tropism, had found its way to Mrs. Youatt's rock garden, which had become, during the summer's long drought, a garden of rocks only. As she was retrieving it, Mrs. Youatt called to her from a kitchen window. "Bea! Have you been to the polls?"

Mrs. Roman waved the red disc of plastic at her neighbor deprecatingly. "Yes. And shopping too."

"Good! Good!" Mrs. Youatt, with only one child to keep her busy, had a large sense of civic duty. "Were there many there?"

"Not very many. I think the weather is keeping most people indoors."

Mrs. Youatt shook her head disapprovingly—at such weather, at human weakness. "May I ask—what will you be doing this afternoon, Bea?"

"Nothing much. Some mending. The kids will all be in school, and Xavier's at the union office. Do you need me to babysit?"

"Would you, please? Just long enough for me to get in to the courthouse and back. What time would be best?"

"Anytime. Just come and knock."

She returned to her own backyard, dodging under the clotheslines, and wedged the lid tightly over the top of the can with a scrap of cardboard. She carried the bag of groceries into the kitchen, remembering only as she put them away in the cupboard that they were almost out of coffee. She made a neat mental X beside "Coffee" on the shopping list in her mind. Time enough to pick that up tomorrow.

She had forgotten already that she had removed tomorrow from her calendar.

Because the vacuum cleaner wasn't working, Mrs. Roman had to go about on all fours, picking the lint from the rug by hand. The plastic-bristled broom was worse than useless, a limp flimsy thing. Xavier kept promising to repair it himself and save money.

The poor old rug was as patchy as her mother's sick spaniel, the one with ear trouble, but the linoleum underneath was even patchier, and beneath the linoleum the floorboards had rotted through in places.

At three o'clock she heated the formula Mrs. Youatt had left for Jolene. Formulas, diaper pails, nights of teething and colic— for her all of that was done with. The pill might fail (the twins had proved that), but not the loop; the loop was infallible, hurrah for the loop!

Baby refused its bottle, dribbling the white froth out over its bib. No strategy or diversion, no amount of coddling, rocking, cooing, love, or being left in its buggy to bawl ignored, could overcome its sincere aversion to this surrogate mother, this non-Youatt. Mrs. Roman felt one of her headaches coming on. She carried baby and buggy upstairs to the boys' bedroom, closed the door, and barricaded herself in the kitchen against the noise. With any luck it would have cried itself to sleep before Mrs. Youatt returned.

She put water on to boil, then recalled that she'd had the last of the coffee at lunch. She turned on the radio, which immediately inquired whether there was enough excitement in her life. There wasn't, and she couldn't remember the time there ever had been. Excitement is not the *point* of life, whatever radios may think. Something else is the point.

Then music. We all like to listen to music when we're doing simple chores about the house. She set to work on the pile of mending, pushing a stone up to the top of the hill and letting it roll down the other side. But she couldn't concentrate, the day had turned sour on her, she was off her stride. She found herself waiting anxiously for the occasional news flashes, though she knew that nothing could be learned from these. The whole operation was handled by machines, machines being so much more reliable than people, especially at doing figures. The post mortem would not be released for two days. The day *after* tomorrow.

Not that there was any doubt at all that the Referendum would be defeated. It was always defeated. The Referendum was a kind of ritual, like going to Mass or confession. Its only practical consequence was that anyone with a job got the day off, or a half-day. If it hadn't been for her own inexplicable defection that morning she would not be feeling the least concern now.

The bottle of formula was standing, still three-quarters full, on the drainboard. Mrs. Roman removed the nipple and emptied it into the sink. It made large white bubbles as it went down the pipe. Upstairs the baby had stopped crying at last.

Mrs. Youatt returned just before four. "How was she?" she asked.

"Jolene was a perfect darling," Mrs. Roman said. "She drank all her formula like a charm and then she popped right off to sleep. I took her upstairs because it's quieter there once the children come home. How was it at the polls—did you have to wait long?"

"There weren't many there, actually. The weather, I suppose."

"Yes, it's been a miserable day."

"But that shouldn't be an excuse."

"Yes," Mrs. Roman said, "*we* made the effort, didn't we?"

The children came flooding into the house in wet coats and muddy boots, all five at once, noisy with their news. The school had held a mock Referendum.

"And was it defeated?" Mrs. Youatt asked gravely.

"Oh no, it passed," Marily assured her.

Mrs. Youatt shook her head. "Well, I hope none of *you* helped it pass."

"Children are like that, you know," Mrs. Roman said composedly, for Mrs. Youatt could scarcely challenge her authority on the subject of what children were like. "They have their mock Referendum every year, and it always passes."

"If that's so, then the teachers haven't been doing their jobs. It should be their first duty to instill a sense of responsibility. These children are all going to be voters one day."

Mrs. Roman smiled, wondering what Mrs. Youatt would have said if she'd known that Mrs. Roman herself had voted in favor of the Referendum. No one ever did ask *you* how *you* voted. It was assumed, out of politeness, that *you* had voted against the Referendum. It was always other people that voted Yes—old people, if you were young; Negroes, if you were white; the intellectuals, if you mistrusted intellect; the unemployed, if you had a job. But the *average* man and the *average* woman could be counted on to defeat the Referendum.

It came over Mrs. Roman then, with the force of revelation, like sunlight bursting out of a clouded sky, that she was no longer an average woman! What she had become, instead she could not imagine, she would have to find out; but whatever it was there had to be something slightly dangerous about it, even sinister. She had discovered her secret identity, and yes. . . .

Yes, it pleased her.

A Note on the Type

This book was set on the Linotype in Electra, a type face designed by W. A. Dwiggins. The Electra face is a simple and readable type suitable for printing books by present-day processes. It is not based on any historical model, and hence does not echo any particular time or fashion.

Composed, printed, and bound by The Book Press, Brattleboro, Vermont.

Typography and binding design by Virginia Tan.